PANIC
NO
MORE

Shannon Ryan

Broken Typewriter Press
5001 1st Ave SE
Ste 105 #243
Cedar Rapids, IA 52402

Broken Typewriter Press
http://brokentypewriterpress.com

Version 1.1.1

Acknowledgments

I'd like to dedicate this book to everyone who has believed in me and helped me get this far. To my friends and family who read multiple drafts that still needed work. To the writers who have sacrificed their time to educate me. To the Noble Pen critique group. To the Paradise Icon workshop. And to the editors who have seen fit to publish the rantings of a disordered mind.

You are too good for me not to thank you, but too many to try to name you all.

CONTENTS

1	The Horrible Creature	1
2	A Call for Help	27
3	Fight!	47
4	Drinking Tea	63
5	Dedication	81
6	Jump for Jesus	99
7	Missed Messages	113
8	Chinese Secrets	127
9	The Path to God	141
10	Home Invasion	153
11	Fire Related Disasters	171
12	Alligator Head Games	187
13	Business Meetings	195
14	The Dog Inflation Index	205
15	Electric Chicken	221
16	Fashion Tips	229
17	Batting Practice	239
18	JenJen is an Evil Genius	245
19	The Board Meeting	251
20	Walkies	259
21	The Escape	263

1

THE HORRIBLE CREATURE

Last night, the nightmare had come back, so Nick had already been awake when the third shift plant manager called him at 5 AM. The biggest mold injector had broken down due to some kind of computer issue. Getting up in the middle of the night to fix machinery was not Nick's job, but because his family owned the company, and he knew computers, Nick was often asked to do things that were outside of his stated duties.

He had gone straight to the administrative complex after finishing with the mold injector, but fixing the computer had taken several hours, mostly downloading software updates. He was running late. He grasped the door handle to his office, readying himself to walk in and get the day started, but he was unable to enter.

He wrapped his hand around the lever and tried to open it. Nothing happened. It wasn't that there was something wrong with the door or the latch, and there didn't seem to be anything physically wrong with Nick. He hadn't damaged himself working in the factory—he could move his arm normally when it wasn't on the door handle. However, when he touched the cool metal, he felt an emptiness inside himself, paralyzing him at the edge of the fight-or-flight response. His vision narrowed and his eyes started to tear. Perspiration beaded on his forehead, and only by the last few grams of will left at his disposal was he able to stop from wetting himself.

He ripped his hand away from the handle and staggered backward. He shook his head, trying to clear it. He felt bile rising in his throat. He was losing control. "Not here," he said to himself. "Not again."

The nightmare was always the same, a lead up to Nick's first panic attack fourteen years ago, when he was only twelve. It was a sunny Sunday afternoon, after church and Baker Family Dinner. He had been hiding from his family on the third floor of Baker House. Never wired for electricity, the third story had been closed off since the 1950s. Nearly a half-century later, the chandeliers hung covered with dust, the French oak paneling went unpolished, and the lavishly appointed rooms were used to store the relics of the Baker dynasty. The sign that had hung above Nick's great-great grandfather Clayton Earl Baker's dentistry office in Pennsylvania sat in a battered Queen Anne chair. The mountaineering equipment worn by the great explorer Nicholas Baker, Nick's great uncle and namesake, lay in the bathtub of a decommissioned lavatory, a far cry from the summit of Everest.

That first panic attack happened the same year as the car accident that had taken his father, a fact the psychologists found significant. After the accident, Nick had gotten into habit of walking up to the third floor and sitting by the stacked cardboard boxes containing his father's things, uniform cubes with "James Baker" scrawled on the side in permanent magic marker. Often, he would sit on the floor and recline against the stack as he played his Gameboy.

On Sunday afternoons, Nick's mother, Esther, and Uncle Earl would sit downstairs in the parlor, his mother making small talk with Reverend Collins while Uncle Earl drank Scotch and tried to look interested. Uncle Earl had exiled Nick from the parlor for playing his Gameboy, believing *Tetris* to be part of a communist plot and refusing to allow it in his presence. Despite this, or perhaps because of it, Nick had become addicted to the game.

After playing *Tetris* for about an hour, Nick would enter a trance state induced by the game's hammering music and rotating, dropping blocks. All his worries would leave him and his only thought or worry would be the shape of the next block.

On that Sunday, a sound in the hallway pulled him from his trance, and he paused his game to listen. He heard footsteps and voices coming down the hall. Since people rarely visited the third floor, he set down his game and walked to the door to investigate.

In the hall, his adopted cousins, Larry and Carrey, the world's largest fifth graders, stood looking up the attic stairs. The staircase was hidden behind a heavy oak door, and the treads were made of simple oak planks, unlike the grander staircases in the house, which were covered in marble slabs and heavy rugs.

Larry and Carrey were a grade behind Nick even though they were older by a year. Before Uncle Earl and Aunt Sonia adopted them, they had been in an eastern European orphanage. Because of this, they had needed to catch up with the curriculum and improve their English.

Nick had heard Uncle Earl bragging that their guidance counselor lauded the boys for assimilating so well into the western school system. The counselor noted that usually foreign students, new to both school and culture, had to deal with bullying, yet the brothers seemed untouched by that particular complication. To Nick, this was no great surprise. Larry was already massive for his age, and both boys were strong and fearless.

"I do not think he go up there," Larry said, looking up at the attic.

Carrey shook his head. "I think you are wrong. He will go."

"Um," Nick said, "what are you guys talking about?"

Carrey looked up at the attic door. "Larry says you are afraid to go into attic."

Larry was right.

"Why does he say that?" Nick asked, his voice cracking. He didn't like the sound of that.

Larry shook his head and put his arm around Nick's shoulders. "Cousin, do not worry. You are... soft boy, not brave. Chicken. That is okay. Not to be ashamed of. Not much anyway." He smiled. Or at least, he showed his teeth.

"Please, Cousin Nick is a Baker." Carrey thumped his chest. "He would not let down his ancestors."

Nick might have been a video-game-playing geek, but he didn't want to be thought of as a chicken. He *was* a Baker, after all. "I'm not afraid," he said, failing to keep his voice from cracking.

Carrey pulled Nick away from his brother's embrace. "There, you see? Cousin Nick is not afraid." He gave Nick a gentle shove toward the stairs. "Climb stairs and show him."

Nick took a few tentative steps up the stairway, the wood of the rarely-used treads squeaking underfoot. As he climbed, he realized his breath was quavering from fear. He searched his mind for excuses to turn around, a way to stop and somehow not lose face. He could find no such scenario. He had said he wasn't afraid, and if he turned back now, his cousins would know he was a coward.

A stair behind him squeaked, and he jumped as Larry's beefy hand landed on his shoulder.

"Having trouble with stairs, Cousin?"

"No. No, I'm fine," Nick said. He willed his foot to rise to the next stair, then the next. Despite the cold, he could feel sweat on his brow. He hesitated to mop his wet forehead, afraid it would expose his weakness to his cousins, who he could hear following him up the creaky stairs. He tried to concentrate on breathing slowly and moving upward at an even pace, but still, his brain kept searching for a way out. None came, of course.

He arrived at the top of the stairs, and his hand reached out for the doorknob. His heart pounded like a bass drum. He could hear it in his ears as strongly as he felt it in his chest. The sweat on his brow had reached the ridge of his nose, and commenced searching for a route further south. He succumbed to the impulse to drag the back of his hand across his forehead.

"Go ahead, Cousin. Open door. I do not think it bites," Larry said playfully.

Biting his lip, Nick reached down, grabbed the doorknob and turned. He opened the door an inch, paused to steel himself, and opened it wider.

Larry pushed him into the room and slammed the door shut.

Nick spun around and pounded on the door. "Let me out! Let me out!" He grasped at the doorknob, trying to budge it with all his strength, but it refused to give.

From the other side of the door, he heard Carrey say, "Did you hear something, Brother? They must be calling us from downstairs." Nick heard their footfalls on the squeaky, wooden steps. Surely they were trying to trick him, pretending to leave while holding the door shut. They wouldn't just leave him. Would they?

Nick listened a long time at the door, hoping to hear them coming back up the stairs. He tried the doorknob again, and still it would not turn. That didn't make any sense. The door didn't have a lock on it. Had they done something to wedge it shut? Nick started pounding on the door, and didn't stop until his fists hurt. "Let me out!" he yelled. There was no answer.

After a few moments, huddled by the door, willing it to open, trying to turn the handle, he gave up. He was not going to get out of the attic anytime soon. There was no getting away. He turned and looked into the space he had feared for so long.

If the third floor was an archaeological dig of Baker history, the attic was the Baker Egyptian City of the Dead. Everything was covered in a thick layer of dust, which did little to mute the appearance of a mad doctor's laboratory. The first thing he saw was a large worktable, covered in evil-looking metal instruments and little jars of teeth. Along the wall was a large bookshelf that rose from floor to ceiling. On every shelf rested a collection of skulls.

"What the hell," he heard himself say aloud, almost immediately regretting his utterance, as if some part of his subconscious worried a monster might have overheard.

To the right of the skulls was what looked to be a chemistry set from the type of movies they played on late-night television. All the beakers and test tubes were still filled with murky sludge, as if the original contents had evaporated and mixed with the dust of ages. Small bottles lined the table. Nick crept forward to pick one up and read the label.

Baker Baby Blues, an opium medicine to soothe the crankiest baby, recommended for colic and teething.

He set down the bottle and turned to the left to find a six-foot-tall, angry-looking metal spider. He gasped. The creature wasn't moving, though, and after he squinted at it for a moment, the metal spider resolved itself into an instrument of torture—not a real improvement. The spider-like machine had a thick metal base and a crank on the side. The limbs of the "spider" were a collection of articulating metal arms covered in gears and chains. At the end of each arm was a blade, or a drill, or a pair of pliers. The device hung over an industrial-looking chair with a headrest, waiting for its next victim.

Then, Nick saw a metal plate on the front of the device reading, "BAKER," and items in the room seemed to change context. His great-great grandfather had been a part-time inventor of dental equipment; this must have been his workshop. The jars of teeth and skulls were for experimentation. The sharp and frightening instruments were his ancestor's inventions. The wicked looking torture chair was some prototype for a dentist's surgery. The mad scientist's chemical set was where he had invented his patent medicines.

Nick walked past the dentist's chair, leaving the work area behind him, and rounded a corner to find a comfortable-looking nook, tucked into a brightly lit gable. A large painting of a nude woman lying on a chaise lounge hung on the wall. Nick took a moment to examine the painting, impressed at how lifelike it was. Despite Reverend Collins' recent sermon on the evils of flesh, Nick enjoyed as healthy an interest in the female body as most twelve-year-old boys.

The nook also held an over-stuffed chair and a chaise lounge. Although the half of the chaise nearest the gable's window was faded from sunlight, it was still recognizable as the one in the painting. Was the woman in the painting a relative? Gross.

He sat down on the chaise, which poofed out a cloud of dust, and looked out the large gable window. His Uncle Earl's car was still parked across the street, so there might be a chance Larry and Carrey would come and let him out. If they didn't, however, how long might he live in the attic until someone thought to look for him? How long could he survive without food or water, or a bathroom?

He really wished he hadn't thought of the bathroom. He turned away from the window, looking for something to pee in. In the brightest part of the nook stood an easel covered in a white sheet, and beside it rested a vase of ancient flowers. He pulled the desiccated stems from their vase, throwing them in the corner, and relieved himself into the vase, facing the sheet covered easel. The experience was comfortingly like using a urinal set into a white wall.

When he finished his business, having stared at the covered painting for a few moments, he started to wonder what was hiding under the sheet. Maybe it was even another nude. Moving the vase of urine so he wouldn't accidentally tip it over, he pulled the sheet away and gazed at the canvas beneath.

At first, he thought the painting must be some kind of modern art. He couldn't make sense of it. His point of focus wandered around the canvas as his brain tried to make sense of the images he was seeing. He looked away from the center and realized the background was a simple forest landscape. He shifted his gaze inwards, following the leaves and branches of the trees back toward the focus of the painting, a clearing in the woods. In that clearing was the subject of the composition, but he still couldn't comprehend it. He squinted hard, and suddenly he knew what he was seeing.

He screamed.

The nightmare always ended with him screaming, and he had never been able to remember anything between that and waking up in the doctor's office, despite the efforts of his therapists.

With the back of his trembling hand, Nick removed a layer of sweat from his forehead and dried it on the leg of his pants. He took two deep breaths, trying to will his heart to beat at a normal rate.

He was at work. This was his office. He had to go into his office. No. He should run. He should turn and run. He turned and took a deep breath in preparation of sprinting down the hall.

Nick didn't run. He turned back and faced the door. Despite the recent return of the nightmare, he hadn't been having any trouble functioning, not until this morning at least. Other than waking up screaming in the middle of the night, he had been living his life as usual. And now, this morning, he was afraid to walk into his office? That was irrational.

His office door wasn't anything special, just a plain oak door in the Baker Administrative Complex, a wide, mass-produced door with a stainless steel handle, not some custom-made piece of early American craftsmanship like the doors in Baker House. The only thing frightening behind it was a mound of tedious work he had to get done. Yet his heart beat like he was running a marathon.

He refused to succumb to irrational thoughts. Telling himself he was the master of his mind, he took two steps forward and threw open the door. As soon as he did so, though, he reflexively dropped into a defensive crouch, like he knew kung-fu, which he did not. He glanced nervously around, looking for some kind of threat, and found none.

Crouching there at his doorway, he decided his current pose didn't make him look like a kung-fu master. It might, however, suggest to the casual observer that he had soiled his Dockers. After glancing around to make sure no one had seen, he straightened up and walked in, pulling the door shut behind him.

Nick's office was just as he'd left it. The desk was covered in equal parts computer equipment, soda cans, code specifications, and vending-sized Doritos bags. Motes of dust were busy burying a collection of obsolete computer books in the corner, some of them as much as four years old. And the closed floor-to-ceiling blinds along the far wall blocked his indecent view of the defiled courtyard.

He sat down at his computer and looked at the emails that had come in over the past ten hours. Most of it was spam, but there was a company-wide reminder from Uncle Earl about the Creative Director position, which would be closing today, and JenJen had sent a note about using his computer later. She wanted to use his faster graphics card for some rendering. He sent her an affirmative reply.

Trying to settle into his routine, he checked out his regular *Global Fight!* forums, but he couldn't concentrate on them. He couldn't stop glancing over his shoulder, like someone was sneaking up on him. The air felt heavy, making breathing a chore. He inhaled deeply, trying to get enough oxygen. He was going to suffocate if he didn't get out of his office. Standing up, he took two steps toward the door.

A soft knocking stopped Nick in his tracks.

The knock sounded like it came from behind him, like someone was tapping on the glass door of the courtyard. This was ridiculous. No one could be out there. It was too disgusting. The knock must have come from his office door. He was breathing in short, shallow gasps, and his vision was starting to darken. He forced himself to take even breaths and lurched forward to open the hallway door. He almost called for help, but the words froze in his throat.

What if he was going insane? But that couldn't be possible because he was worried he was going crazy, right? He remembered reading somewhere that crazy people never thought of themselves as crazy. Did that mean he was a hypochondriac? Maybe he was a crazy person, but incredibly insightful for a crazy person? Maybe he was only having some kind of nervous breakdown. Wasn't family history a good indicator of insanity? Supposedly, his great-grandfather Earl Prescott Baker, Sr. had gone insane. Bakers were nothing if not obsessed with tradition.

Nick glanced over at the door of his office bathroom. Maybe he would feel better if he splashed some cold water on his face. But that would mean going through another closed door, and he didn't know if he was really up to that. Then again, if there was something horrific in the bathroom, would it be responsible to leave it for janitorial?

No more messing around now. Nick straightened his tie. It was time to be a man. A twenty-six-year-old should not be afraid to open a bathroom door. A twenty-six-year-old was a man, not a boy afraid of monsters. He strode forward, method-acting confidence, gripped the handle, and pushed the door open. Inside was a handicapped-accessible bathroom, a remnant of the Baker Administrative Complex's history as the heart of Baker Village.

Baker Village had been Uncle Earl's grand attempt at expanding the Baker fortunes, an attempt to capitalize on aging baby boomers. Uncle Earl planned to build a luxury retirement community. To make room for this capitalist paradise, he had stripped the trees off a few hundred acres of virgin forest the family had owned for over a century. Honestly, the idea had been a good one from a business standpoint. They had just finished the first phase, the giant building that would have served as community center, shopping mall, and nursing unit, the intended heart of Baker Village, when the county had announced a new landfill less than a mile down the road.

Nick walked into the bathroom, only looking behind himself twice, and made the mistake of glancing in the mirror. His cheeks were flushed. His eyes were red. And his hair, usually neatly combed at this time of day, was unruly. It was not a good look. He splashed some cool water on his face, and then used his wet fingers to smooth his hair. Now at least, he *looked* like a sane person.

Maybe he should go home sick. He was already in the bathroom with his stomach churning viciously. A brief but vigorous vomit was probably within his grasp. He looked at himself in the mirror and retched a couple times, but his heart wasn't really in it.

No, he needed to get control. He firmly told himself that he was the master of his emotions. Out in the office, there was another soft knock. Was someone messing with him? Knocking on his door and then running away before he could open it?

Nick ran to the office door and threw it open. "Ah hah!"

There was no one in the hall.

Nick closed the door, went back to his desk, and sat down heavily, making the hydraulic cylinder sigh. He was letting his imagination run away with him. Maybe he had imagined the knocking, or maybe a stray piece of cardboard had blown against the window. Yes, that was it, just a random piece of trash on the wind.

There was another knock. This time, it followed a pattern, the classic "shave and a haircut."

He turned and looked at the hallway door. He didn't see anyone through the little security window. Swiveling in his chair, he examined the blinds that blocked his view of the courtyard. He wasn't going to find anything pleasant out there. Unlike the bathroom, there was a reason to avoid the courtyard beyond the imagination of a crazy person. Not a month after they opened the new landfill down the road, pieces of garbage had begun dropping on Baker Village. At first, the county tried to be accommodating. Engineers were brought in and calculations were done, but they claimed there was no way so much garbage could reach Baker Village. The first engineering firm was replaced by a pricier one which did computer models based on a number of different variables, and they also failed to find a way the trash could reach Baker Village, let alone a way to fix the problem. Uncle Earl had then tried suing the county, but he had lost. The county had computer models showing the lawsuit had no grounds. The judge had refused to accept the bag of garbage Earl had brought to the courthouse as evidence.

The garbage piled especially high in the courtyards of what had been the nursing unit, the part of the building where Nick worked. He found it disgusting enough to permanently keep the blinds closed, hiding the floor-to-ceiling glass wall. The sedimentary layers of garbage had piled up two feet deep against the big windows and glass door, and they weren't even the most disgusting feature of the trash heap. The smell emanating from the squelchy pile was really something to write home about—if you could see through your tears, and your paper didn't turn black. Nick had named it Smellvis.

Uncle Earl had tried, in his own way, to take care of the problem. He'd told the landscapers to clean up the garbage. They quit. Then he tried to get the cleaning company to deal with it. They threatened to triple their rates. Uncle Earl shifted his focus to the employees, putting out a memo stating the courtyards were their responsibility and threatening reprisals. They had called his bluff, and now there was an uneasy standoff between management and staff. Uncle Earl was determined to hold his ground. He recognized someone would eventually have to clean up the trash, but come hell or high water, he was not going to pay for it.

Sighing, Nick took hold of the cord and pulled the blinds open. On the other side of the glass, a whirlwind was in progress, floating a Twinkie box, a dirty diaper, and four plastic bags in lazy circles above the hip-deep garbage. There was also a little man dancing in the trash.

Or at least Nick thought it had been a man at first glance. It was... well... humanoid at least, a term Nick had never needed outside of discussing *Star Trek* episodes. The creature was shirtless, with sinewy muscles. It wore only a stocking cap and blue jeans. If it was wearing shoes, they were buried deep in the garbage. Although it wore clothes, there was something non-human about the creature. It was under four feet tall, possibly quite less depending on how deep it had sunk into the trash layers.

What struck him most about the thing's appearance was the facial hair. To call it a goatee would have been an understatement. Bright red, it started under the creature's chin and shot forward about a foot, like a unicorn's horn but furry.

Again, Nick felt fear rise inside him, like a filling cup threatening to run over. Now, however, there was a physical thing for him to be afraid of. This somehow made him feel more at ease, or at least it would have if not for the paralyzing terror.

The diminutive creature pirouetted in rotten refuse, spinning and leaping after the floating diaper, a maniacal smile on its face, its red goatee bobbing and weaving like a lightsaber. There was something hypnotic about the dance, as the creature moved at the same pace as the whirlwind, making the floating trash appear to dance with, or possibly in command of the creature. Suddenly, as if noticing Nick, the creature stopped—although the garbage kept on moving. It turned then and pointed at Nick with a tiny finger. Its red beard quivered, pointing at Nick as well.

Then the little creature did something so strange Nick forgot to be debilitated by absolute terror. The thing slid its hand under its waistband, pulled out a surprisingly large penis for such a small creature, and started vigorously stroking itself, or rather *himself*. He winked at Nick and grinned, and then took a step toward the glass door.

Nick's mother had taken him to church every Sunday since the day he was born. Every week, for as long as he could remember, he had listened to Reverend Collins warning the congregation to be vigilant, for if they let their guard down, if they let their faith waver, there would be something coming to call on them, something demonic.

Nick had always thought he was full of crap.

Even if Reverend Collins was right, what demon-warranting infraction had Nick committed? Still, it was very small for a demon. Nick didn't have the *Jane's Demon Recognition Guide* on hand, but he assumed that, for a demon, he had caught a minnow.

So maybe it wasn't huge, but Nick was pretty sure that when it came to the demonic, a little went a long way. He wondered what the creature wanted, and since Uncle Earl had taught him to make the first demand at any negotiation, Nick shouted at the glass, "*What do you want of me, demon?*"

With his free hand, the creature cupped his ear. He pointed at the sliding glass door separating them, shrugged, and then started stroking his beard, which oddly paralleled the activity of the other hand.

Without missing a beat, Nick reached out and verified the door was locked. There was still only a double-pane of glass separating him from the masturbating demon, but now he couldn't just walk in.

The creature scowled.

Nick hadn't even locked the door so quickly in fear of the demon. His actions had been in anticipation of Smellvis. The layers of compressed garbage, baked in the midday sun, watered by the rain, ripened to produce a smell capable of turning away even the most seasoned sanitation worker.

Without looking away from the creature, Nick reached over and yanked the blinds closed. With the courtyard gone from his vision, he heaved a huge sigh of relief. Intellectually, he knew the little demon was still there, but at least he didn't have to watch the thing stroke his wang.

On the other side of the blinds, the thing knocked lightly on the window.

Nick backed away until he was up against the far wall. Maybe it was time to go for a walk. It couldn't hurt to put a little distance between him and the little demon. Maybe if he left it alone, it would go away.

The area designed to be the nursing unit of Baker Village had become the Information Technology department for the Baker Administrative Complex. Nick worked for Edutacular, a subsidiary that his uncle Earl had purchased. It had been founded when *edutainment*, the merging of computer games with educational information, was the latest buzzword.

The center of the nursing unit belonged to their core systems people—the friendly techs who went out and fixed computers, along with George, the scary, bearded systems administrator who rarely emerged from the recesses of the server room. Nick pictured him as one of the dwarves from *Lord of the Rings*, forever toiling in the cold darkness, with the exception that his tunnels utilized fiber optics and encryption.

Next to the systems people was the application development team. They wrote internal programs to track inventory and make sure production lines kept moving in the main plant, as well as maintaining the company websites in conjunction with the PR department.

The last stop for the old nursing area was the break room that mainly served the computer people. It was empty, so Nick kept walking. He passed through the area that had been the community center, now a common room for large meetings, and through the shopping mall area, now converted into offices for Legal, Human Resources, and Accounting. He reached the other end of the building; originally planned to be the executive offices for Baker Village, they now housed the reception area and his uncle Earl.

Once he reached reception, he started feeling more normal. Was it his distance from the demon which calmed his nerves? Then again, if he had hallucinated the demon, maybe it was just the distance from his office and the awful project he was working on.

Nick smiled when he saw Delores, Uncle Earl's personal assistant, working the reception desk. She had been with the family for over twenty years. When he was little, his father would bring him to work at the old plant. Delores would play with him and make him hot cocoa. She was one of those few long-serving employees Nick thought of as family. The desk in front of Delores was covered in stacks of paper, many of them covered in dollar signs and legalese. She was loading them into binders.

Nick leaned up against the reception desk. "My uncle has you working reception *and* sorting papers?"

She looked up from a stack of thick documents and smiled. "Hi, Nicky. I'm covering the desk while Bonnie's out sick. And these are no simple papers. They are for the annual report, important documents that have to be ready for the shareholder meeting." She gave the current pile a scrutinizing look, shook her head, and dropped the whole stack into the trash. "Are you going this year?"

Nick made a face. "There's no use giving me a binder full of accounting stuff. Let Uncle Earl handle that, and leave me alone with the computers."

"Your uncle isn't going to be around forever, you know. You need to take a more active role in the company. You may need to take charge some day. Earl may even want to retire."

"Can't Larry or Carrey run the company? I bet they'd be good at it." Despite the torment they had given him as a child, Nick loved his cousins, they were family after all, and according to his mother, you have to love family. Over the years, he had also noticed that the less he saw them, the more lovable they became. He would really love them if they moved to California.

Delores shrugged. "They might be, but they're adopted. As far as Earl is concerned, they aren't Bakers by birth. You know your uncle is all about family legacy. When I'm done putting together the document, I'm going to scan the whole report and send it to you in an email. Promise me you'll at least look at it."

Nick sighed. "Can we talk about something else?"

Her face took on a look of concern. "Something's bothering you, isn't it?"

"It's just been a rough morning." He really didn't want to discuss insanity and demons with Delores. The woman spent every day working with Uncle Earl. She had her own problems.

He nodded toward the large oak door behind which, presumably, sat the family patriarch. "Is he in?"

Delores tried to hold back a smirk and failed. "Mr. Baker has given directions not to be disturbed. However, he isn't on his phone..." She pointed at the large telephone which lived on the reception desk with its hundreds of buttons and lights as if Nick could somehow glean its current state of affairs. "...I would guess that he's playing games on his computer or practicing his putt. I am sure he has time to talk to you."

Uncle Earl's door held three fancy brass plaques. The first read, "Earl Prescott Baker III," and the second one read, "Chairman of the Board." The third read, "Chief Executive Officer." Nick knocked and waited.

From inside the office, Uncle Earl yelled, "Come in."

Originally built to lure a director for Baker Village, Uncle Earl's office was all oak and leather with thick, soft carpet. The room smelt of old leather, cigar smoke, and Scotch whiskey, much like Uncle Earl.

Uncle Earl was dressed for a golf outing. He reclined in his leather office chair with his hand resting lightly on his computer mouse, probably playing video poker. His legs were crossed, showing off his checkered high-water pants and Argyle socks. These were joined by a plaid sweater-vest and a matching cap, strategically covering his bald spot. The *piece de resistance* of the ensemble was his good luck charm, an over-sized red bow tie. To the casual observer, he might look corny, but Nick secretly believed his uncle wore the outdated ensemble to show the other members of his club that he had more money than they did and could wear whatever he wanted. The clashing patterns played with Nick's head, like one of those optical illusions he could never quite get to turn into a three-dimensional shape no matter how much he squinted at it.

He paused his computer game and motioned with his cigar for Nick to sit down. "Nick, my boy, what's on your mind? You look a little off. Do you want a cigar? I have real Cuban Montecristos. I don't want you to know what I had to go through to get these things, but let's just say that Venezuela will not want for dental floss anytime in the next decade."

Nick opened his mouth to speak, but before any words came out, he reconsidered how much detail he should give his uncle. He was sure the creature had been a demon. He was just as sure that Uncle Earl wouldn't believe him, or in a worst-case scenario, might have Nick committed. Instead, he tried to think of a more-believable creature that Uncle Earl would consider as vile and undesirable as the demonic. "I saw a hippie in my courtyard."

Uncle Earl leaned forward, a shocked look on his face. "I can see how you'd be worried," he said gravely. He paused for a moment as if to consider his position. "I know I wouldn't like to see some dirty hippie hanging around outside my window first thing in the morning. What a horrible shock. Was he out there in the trash? Why would anyone stand in the trash?"

"He wasn't standing. He was dancing. And he was... touching himself." Nick didn't want to offend Uncle Earl with vulgar language.

"Touching himself, where?"

"Well, on his..." Nick's mother had taught him never to use the word penis. "He was masturbating."

"Masturbating! Are you sure?"

Nick nodded. "He was really going for it."

Uncle Earl slammed his fist down on his giant, oak desk. "Nobody masturbates at my company. Call security. We'll have him rousted." After a moment, he said, "Well, why aren't you moving?"

"You laid off the security people."

Uncle Earl pounded on the desk again. "Damn this economy." He pursed his lips. "Well, I guess if he's still there when you get back to your office, call the police. It can be your first duty as vice president. See if you can get the cops to rough him up a little. Give them some money from petty cash if it helps."

Ever since he had seen the job posting, Nick had the sneaking suspicion his uncle had designed the new vice president job specifically for him. He hadn't even applied. "I'm not really interested being a vice president. I'm happy where I am."

"Nonsense. You might like what you're doing now, but it's time for you to get out of the bush leagues. You're a Baker, and you're destined for great things. And you know, you are getting to the age when you're going to want to marry and settle down. You want to be a good provider, don't you?"

"Marry? I don't even have a girlfriend. Besides, I make enough money here. I haven't even touched my trust fund."

Uncle Earl looked like he had swallowed something rotten. "Enough money? Who has been putting these concepts in your head? I told your father he should never have sent you to a public school." Then the old man changed gears. His look of disgust at the idea of public education was replaced by a mischievous grin. "Besides, you never know what the future will bring. You're a wealthy, eligible, young bachelor. Someday you're going to find yourself with a wife. That penny-ante trust fund isn't going to seem like much when you have a family to support."

"That penny-ante trust fund makes more than you pay most of your employees."

"Don't give me any of that downtrodden workers talk, comrade," Uncle Earl said, rolling his eyes. "That's just capitalism, the best system on Earth, and if you don't believe it, you can move to Moscow."

Nick didn't even bother to point out Russian communism had ended twenty years ago. He'd tried before, but Uncle Earl would just rebut, "Once a commie, always a commie."

"I know you bought Edutacular so I could run the division—"

Uncle Earl waved in protest. "Nonsense, we were cash rich and had to diversify." There might have been some truth to this. Uncle Earl had bought Edutacular before the failure of Baker Village. Still, Nick was sure his acceptance of their job offer had been the deciding factor.

"So you bought the software company that had just hired me?"

Uncle Earl shook his head. "Nick, Nick, Nick, you always think I'm up to something. Because you were going to work there, I took a close look at the company. Edutacular was a solid investment. Plus, we've seen a real synergy effect. *Plaque Blasters* has gotten our foot in the door of several dentists' offices."

"So, after running the division so successfully, now you need a vice president to oversee it?"

"It's more than that, Nick. We need a creative director for the whole company."

"Why do we need a creative director?"

Spreading his hands, Uncle Earl said, "I need someone to liaise with all the creative types we have working for us now, graphic designers, PR people, and Internetting people. I don't get along with those pinkos."

"Pinkos? You do realize that the Cold War is over, right?" Okay, he'd let the first reference to communism go, but this was just ridiculous.

Uncle Earl pointed at Nick. "Don't you believe a word of it. That's just what they want you to think. You think Vladamir Putin isn't KGB? Trust me, he wears red underwear."

Before Nick could ask when Uncle Earl had seen Vladamir Putin's underwear, there was a gentle knock at the door.

Nick jumped up out of his chair. His eyes went wide. All he could think about was the gentle knock at the courtyard door of his office. Had the creature followed him? "Don't open the door," Nick begged. "It might be that thing."

Uncle Earl quirked an eyebrow. "Wow, that hippie really did get you riled up." More loudly, he yelled, "Come in."

The door opened and JenJen stepped into the office. Nick did a double take. JenJen usually wore jeans and a sweatshirt in the office, but today, she was wearing a skirt and high heels. Her long, copper hair was ironed straight, and she was wearing more makeup. Her jacket looked crisp and professional, while simultaneously trying to drag Nick's gaze deep into her cleavage.

Nick tried to look casual, like any old friend had walked into the room, like a *man* friend had walked into the room. He told himself that JenJen was a work colleague, someone he admired for her talent and intelligence, someone with a boyfriend who played minor league baseball, a man capable of swinging a wooden club and knocking a hard, leather ball over four hundred feet.

"I'm not interrupting, am I, Mr. Baker?" JenJen said tentatively. As she talked, the movement of her head would plunge strands of her hair into her cleavage, drawing Nick's eye. He pulled his gaze away, simultaneously embarrassed he had looked and regretful he didn't have enough time to memorize the view. Why couldn't he rid himself of these lustful thoughts? Maybe he did deserve a little demon.

Uncle Earl shook his head. "No, of course not. We were just discussing hippies."

"Oh, I um..." JenJen seemed nervous. She took a couple steps into the office, unstable on her heels in the thick carpet, like a baby fawn taking its first steps. "My parents met at Woodstock."

Uncle Earl's eyes narrowed. "What do you want, young lady? State your business. I have a noon tee time at my club."

"Yes, Mr. Baker, I saw on the company website that you're looking for a creative director and vice president. Well, I've been the head designer for Edutacular since the move from Cincinnati, and I think you'll find me a good match for the job." JenJen passed Uncle Earl a binder. "Here is my resumé and a sample portfolio of my work."

He opened the binder and scanned over the cover sheet, not even bothering to look at the art samples. "Thank you for your interest, Miss... Jenkins. I can see you are qualified for the position. We will contact you if we need any more information." His tone should have been enough to dismiss her.

JenJen didn't seem to get the hint. She nodded a little too much. "Yes, sir. Thank you." She smiled and waited.

Uncle Earl made a shooing motion, like he was swatting at a mosquito. "Thank you for stopping by, Miss... You should hear from us shortly." He watched as she wobbled out of the office.

"Nice tits, if a little plain," he said, as soon as the door shut. "But she's not too bright if she thinks I'm going to give her your promotion. See all the trouble you cause by not just accepting the job? You've made that poor girl think she actually has a chance." He casually tossed her portfolio into the trash. "So, what's on your dance card this afternoon? Want to go to the club, have a few drinks, hit the links?"

"Not really." Even if Nick hadn't been pissed off at his uncle for the way he had just treated JenJen, he hated golf. Uncle Earl insisted he play, claiming all businessmen were golfers, a piece of knowledge passed down from Earl Prescott Baker Sr., allegedly before he went insane. "I have a lot of work to do for the product demo next week." This was true. Spending the morning hiding from the thing in his office hadn't done any favors for his project timeline.

Uncle Earl stood. "Walk me to my car, Nick. Grab my clubs while you're at it." He grabbed his umbrella and stepped through the door without looking to see if Nick was following.

Nick picked up Uncle Earl's Louis Vuitton golf bag loaded with custom-made clubs. The bag and its contents cost more than a new, mid-sized sedan. He followed Uncle Earl through the lobby.

As they walked through reception, Delores asked, "Are you boys out for the day?"

"I am," Uncle Earl said. "Nick's going to be minding the store," he added, as if Nick would have any idea what to do in a crisis.

Nick turned to look at Delores and shrugged. If any real decisions needed to be made, Delores could handle them.

Delores just smiled and returned Nick's shrug.

Uncle Earl strode through the front door, raising his umbrella just in time for it to catch a glancing blow from an empty milk carton. He led the way through the parking lot, following a winding path designed to avoid piles of fallen garbage.

"You know," Nick said, ducking a circular piece of cardboard spinning at him like a buzz saw, "if you really need a creative director, Jennifer Jenkins is perfect for the job."

Uncle Earl looked back at him. "Really? Who's that?"

"Jennifer Jenkins, the woman whose portfolio you just threw away."

"What? That mousy little thing? We don't need some slip of a girl as a vice president. We need a real man, with a firm handshake and the voice of command." Uncle Earl dropped his voice half an octave and raised the volume a few decibels. "We need a Baker."

"This is the twenty-first century. Women work in business. My mother sits on eight boards of directors."

"Your mother," said Uncle Earl, "is no ordinary woman. She was a woman capable of marrying a Baker man, a man of vision, achievement, industry. No, Nick, when they made your mother, they broke the mold."

Nick neglected to mention that Uncle Earl, a Baker, a man of vision, achievement, and industry, was putting in three solid hours before spending the afternoon working on his golf game. He also neglected to wonder out loud if JenJen did have what it took to be a Baker woman.

As they arrived at Uncle Earl's Lexus, a piece of cantaloupe rind bounced off his umbrella, landed on the side of the car with a wet slurping sound, and stuck. Uncle Earl shook off his umbrella. "Explain to me how a melon rind can get picked up by the wind and carried almost a mile. It just doesn't make sense. Some days, I feel like someone has it in for me."

Folding his umbrella, Earl tossed it into his trunk and motioned for Nick to put the clubs in after it. "We have to start moving you up the ladder. Like I said, your priorities are going to change someday, and I'll wager someday soon." He opened the Lexus door. "You sure you don't want to come with me? I promise not to tell the boss." He gave Nick an exaggerated wink.

Nick shook his head. "No, thanks. I'm under a deadline. Edutacular's contract has a penalty clause if we don't finish the mini-game on time." Better to make an excuse than try to explain—again—that he didn't enjoy golf. Uncle Earl wouldn't listen anyway.

Uncle Earl sighed. "Seriously, my boy, you need to think about your future."

"I know. I know," Nick said, exhausted at their circular argument. "You want me to take the job."

"Well, that too, but I just mean you should take advantage of these nice spring days and get out on the golf course. I hear it's going to be a hot summer."

Nick nodded. "Okay. Maybe next week."

Uncle Earl got into the car. "I'm going to hold you to that." He pulled the door closed, signaling the end of their conversation.

As Uncle Earl drove away, Nick hurried back to the lobby, dodging the occasional piece of falling garbage, a skill all the administrative complex employees learned quickly. Inside, Delores was just finishing up a phone call. "No, Mr. Stafford Jennings, Mr. Baker is in meetings all afternoon. Yes, you have a good day too," she said, hanging up the phone.

Nick stood outside his office door, just like he had earlier. Should he take the job? JenJen actually wanted it, and she was the better choice. Nick was a programmer, not an artist. Would it be wrong for him to take the job if she didn't really have a chance? Would it get Uncle Earl off his back, at least temporarily?

Under his arm, he held her portfolio. Even if she wasn't going to get the job, he couldn't bear to see her art thrown in the trash. And he was sure putting together a professional portfolio was expensive. He'd just have to hide it for now. Yep, he'd have to go into his office and hide it somewhere. Just walk right through the door like any non-crazy person.

He was going to have to go back into the office sooner or later. Maybe the thing would be gone. If it was, did it mean his hallucination had ended? And what if the creature was there? Should he do as Uncle Earl had suggested and call the police? Or for a demon should he call the church? Animal Control?

He pushed the door open and walked into his office, putting one foot in front of the other and breathing normally. After burying Jen-Jen's portfolio in the back of a desk drawer, he crossed the room and pulled open the blinds. No demon in the courtyard, but something seemed off. It took him a moment to figure it out. The garbage sat nearly a foot lower against the glass wall. When he knew what to look for, it was obvious. The garbage had left a layer of crud on the glass, sort of a high-water mark for the refuse. The demon had stolen his garbage. He felt ambivalent about this latest development. If he hadn't seen the demon, he'd think he had been visited by magical garbage elves.

Did sane people think about magical garbage elves? Then again, did sane people spend their day unit-testing simulations of sheep behavior?

Nick's latest project was a mini-game conceived as a companion piece to a documentary on ancient Greece. The producers of the show were paying Edutacular a boatload of money to design and code a sheepherding simulator as a way of showing what life was like in ancient Greece. The main character was a nameless shepherd, which the development team had named Adrian, after Marine Corporal Adrian Shephard from *Half-Life Opposing Force*. Unlike Corporal Shephard, who got to kill aliens, Adrian the shepherd could only guard his flock—end of story. A boring game based on herding sheep.

He had loaded the newest code from the repository and was busy tweaking the bumping algorithm—the subroutine that prevented two sheep from occupying the same space at the same time, which in real life would cause a sheepsplosion—when he started to feel like someone was watching him. He swiveled around to look at the door to the hallway. He couldn't see anyone in the little window. He swiveled back. Then he turned again. There! Had something just ducked out of the window? Or had he imagined the movement?

Standing up, he crept forward, never taking his eyes off the little window in the door. He grasped the door handle and threw it open. Someone or something touched his nose, and said, "Boop."

Nick screamed and fell back into his office.

JenJen stepped back quickly from his freak-out. She raised an eyebrow and started to say something, but then, apparently, decided to ignore it. "Hey, sheep-boy, I hope you didn't finally decide to do some work. I need to use your computer."

"You touched my nose," Nick accused from the carpet.

"Sorry," JenJen said, "I didn't know you had a nose thing."

Nick shook his head and stood up. "I don't have a 'nose thing.' You just surprised me is all."

"Um, yeah. So about the shepherd program..."

Nick reached for his most sarcastic voice, "Oh wow. I'm so excited about this project. I never realized how fun and interesting sheep could be."

"Are you serious?"

Apparently, Nick was incapable of producing enough sarcasm to convey his true feelings.

"No. It's really a crap idea from the start, right? Let's take a job, historically known for a lack of anything much going on, and make it into a computer game. Ninety percent of the kids who play this will quit playing as soon as they realize you can't shoot anything."

JenJen shrugged. "I don't think there was a whole lot of shooting in ancient Greece. Besides, if no one's going to play it anyway, why sweat it?"

"But a lot of cool stuff did happen in ancient Greece..." Nick paused for a moment. "Wait one minute. Did Jennifer Jenkins just tell me to half-ass something?"

The corners of JenJen's mouth turned up a barely perceptible notch. "Well, maybe just this once."

"Do you mean," said Nick, trying to keep a serious tone to his voice, "*the* Jennifer Jenkins, perhaps the most perfect employee in the Edutacular division of Baker Dental Distributing, is telling me to slack off? To put in the minimal possible effort and do something like surf the Internet on work time?"

Now she blushed. It was adorable. "I suppose you could use the extra time as an excuse to brush up on your skills. Maybe you study lightweight database systems. Even smaller games are starting to use database indexing for accessing assets." She paused for a moment and then added, "Besides, I need to use your machine later for some rendering."

"Ah ha," Nick said. "Finally we get to the ulterior motive. You're after my hardware."

She pretended to look embarrassed. "Maybe just a little."

Nick sighed. "When did studying database implementation become more fun than writing computer games?"

"Probably about the time your uncle bought the game studio and moved it here."

Nick nodded in resignation. "I believe you are on to something."

JenJen walked over to the office door and closed it, careful not to make a noise. "So, speaking of your uncle, did he say anything about my portfolio?"

"Um. He did mention it, yes."

"What did he say?"

"He thought you were a little on the shy side."

She slumped a little. "Oh."

Wanting to cheer her up, Nick decided to put it in the best light. "I told him you were very well-qualified for the position, and you would be an excellent choice."

"That's great. Thank you, Nick." She reached out and pulled him against her in a tight hug. Her hair smelled like strawberries, and her breasts pushed firm against his chest. Nick was stunned by this outpouring of emotion. Like most people in the tech industry, JenJen was not touchy, and twice today, she had made physical contact with him. Too late, he tried to silence his brain and just enjoy the feel of her body against him, but before he had fully recovered, JenJen had let go and left his office.

Had he done the right thing? She might be happier for the moment, but had he raised her hopes just so they could be dashed when she found out she hadn't gotten the job? She would probably be pissed off. Then again, there was a possibility Uncle Earl would realize JenJen was the right candidate and promote her. There was also a possibility a squirrel would invent time travel.

2

A Call for Help

About an hour later, JenJen returned, and Nick sat in his office pretending not to check her out as she worked at his computer. Today, she was rendering on a new cut scene as well as pre-rendering the 3D model of the five different types of sheep that would make up Adrian's herd in fifteen different poses. After a while, though, he began to fear that he was obviously leering at her, and decided to take another walk around the office. He returned to reception and chatted with Delores to relieve the monotony. It was just over a quarter mile from his office to reception, a nice stretch of the legs. By the time he returned, she was just finishing up.

He sat down at his desk, cracked his knuckles, and logged into his computer. Opening the sheep class and scanning through a thousand lines or so, he found the method he had been working on, tapped the enter key, and prepared to insert a new line. He cleared his mind of non-programming thoughts and started to type.

The phone rang.

Nick picked up the receiver. It was Rudy. "Hey, Toxic. What are you doing?" Rudy said, using Nick's college nickname.

"Well, this morning, I had a staring contest with a demon, which has led me to believe I may be going insane. My Uncle Earl is trying to promote me. And, just now, I was trying to get some code written," Nick said, listing his troubles in order of severity. Rudy was not only his oldest friend, but he also had the ability to process statements like, "I had a staring contest with a demon and might be going insane," at an objective face value bordering on sociopathy.

"What kind of code are you writing?" Rudy asked, apparently uninterested in demonic hijinks or just not listening that carefully.

"You remember those educational games we played in school that were crappy, but more fun than cracking an actual book?"

"Yeah."

"Something for a documentary film. I'm coding a mini-game about the lives of ancient shepherds in the Greek mountains."

Rudy considered this for a moment. "You know what's crazy about that? I used to think working as a video game programmer would be really cool, but that has got to be the lamest thing ever."

Nick realized he was nodding at the telephone receiver, and said, "Lately, it seems that way."

"How do you do something like that?" Rudy, a professional student who lived off his parents, was fascinated by the things people did in offices.

"Well, I've spent most of the week trying to research the behavior of sheep herds. Originally, I was trying to come up with a set of behaviors for each individual sheep, but after talking to JenJen this afternoon, I've decided to half-ass it. We did a fishing game a couple years ago, and I think I can use the fish-school algorithms for the herd movement."

"So, you're still working with JenJen. You see her naked yet?"

Nick blushed. "No, Rudy. JenJen is a friend, and she has a boyfriend. Even if she weren't dating Steve, we would still be just friends. Besides, a gentleman isn't supposed to ask things like that."

"Fuck that noise. Don't sell yourself short. I know you totally want to tap that. She's totally in your league. If it weren't for those sweater kittens, she's like a five, maybe a six. If I were you, I'd lay her across my desk and wrap my hands around those big, round titties—"

"You are aware I work in a real office, not an office in a porno. There is a difference." Nick was often amazed by Rudy's ability to sexualize anything.

"Don't just dismiss the idea. I'm sure things like that happen in real life. I have to believe. Of course all the girls in those movies are way hotter—"

"Rudy, just drop it." Rudy might be Nick's oldest friend, but Nick didn't have to listen to him insulting JenJen. He probably just hadn't seen her at her best. He hadn't seen the way those little locks of hair played peek-a-boo in her cleavage, and as far as Nick was concerned, that was just fine.

"You sound preoccupied. I can go if you're busy," Rudy said.

"No, I'm just feeling a little agitated. Remember when I was twelve and I had that panic attack? I'm having those dreams again. It's freaking me out. Also... I think I'm hallucinating or something."

"Are you on drugs?" Rudy asked. "I don't usually hallucinate unless I'm on drugs."

"No, I'm not."

"Would you like to be? I've always wanted to expand on some of Ronald Sandison's experiments with lysergic acid diethylamide. I bet I could design a regimen of enhanced therapy which would get rid of those hallucinations in three weeks." Amongst Rudy's collection of PhDs were concentrations in pharmacology, chemistry, and psychology.

"No, Rudy... Wait, isn't that LSD?"

"Hey, I'm just offering you some therapy. It's your choice. Are we still on for murder and mayhem tomorrow?"

"Definitely." Hanging out with Rudy would be a welcome change from dealing with Uncle Earl and demons. "I picked up Doritos and liquor. I figured we could order a pizza later if we get hungry."

"Awesome, I'm looking forward to having Nick Toxic mix me a drink. When should I come over?"

"Well, I was thinking six, but if you want to come over earlier, I won't be doing anything."

"Okay. See you tomorrow."

Nick spent what was left of the day mapping JenJen's new sheep renders to the fish school AI. When he was done, he tested the two together. Other than the weird way the sheep wagged their tails, things were looking good, or at least good enough.

Nick let his guilt over getting a late start win out over his fear the demon would return, so the lights were on in the parking lot by the time he left his office. He did hurry through the trash littering the parking lot, just in case the creature was lurking outside for him. Taking a small broom from his back seat, he wiped the trash off his car, so debris wouldn't splatter anyone on the road behind him.

Despite the age of his Corolla, Nick had done his best to maintain it, and it purred to life on the first turn of the key. Leaving late meant less traffic, so he could give the car a little gas on Highway 965. He might have scraped off the worst of the garbage, but he wouldn't mind losing a bit more here and there as long as he was the only one on the road.

Nick was so familiarized with his route home that instead of keeping his attention on the road, he found his eyes drifting to the apple blossoms which had just started bursting from the trees along his drive, a sure sign that spring was finally here, a lovely white and pink bouquet. Anticipating his turn approaching, he looked away from the apple blossoms. A small creature was standing in the middle of his lane, pointing its long, red beard at him.

"Shit!" Nick yelled, stomping on his brakes, and pulling on the steering wheel. He over adjusted, and the Corolla started to slide sideways. He panicked, jerking the wheel the other way, pulling the car onto the loose gravel shoulder. The front tire of the Corolla caught a pothole in the gravel, and suddenly the car was rotating lazily over the loose gravel. Nick took a deep breath and watched helplessly as the landscape went by in panoramic view. Ditch. Road. Trees. Ditch... It wasn't the best view.

With a squeal, the car hit the blacktop of the Downcastle turnoff. The Corolla went up on two wheels, and for a moment Nick thought it was going to flip over. It hovered like that for what seemed like a minute, but in retrospect was probably less than a second and then settled down with a thump.

Nick opened his eyes. He didn't even remember closing them. His Corolla was sitting askew on the road, practically nose to nose with Downcastle's only patrol car. Gravel dust slowly settled over both cars.

Kevin Coltrane, the Downcastle police officer, had been hiding behind the large sign that welcomed people to Downcastle, as if anyone would go there on purpose. Most visitors ended up there after getting lost on their way to the airport. Just in case Nick didn't know he was in trouble, Kevin turned on his lights.

After taking a moment to partially regain his composure, Nick pulled his car onto the shoulder and turned off the engine. He watched as Kevin got slowly out of his cruiser and walked up to Nick's driver's-side window. He figured the officer would want his driver's license. His palms were sweaty, and with his hands shaking, his fingers couldn't get purchase on his wallet. He unbuckled his seatbelt to try for a better grip.

Kevin knocked on his window with the butt of his flashlight. When Nick rolled it down, he said, "License, registration, and proof of insurance, please. How much have you had to drink tonight?"

"Oh hi..." Nick paused, wondering whether it would be better to address Kevin as Officer Coltrane. Downcastle was a small town, and Kevin's mother lived in same condo building as Nick. He realized he had paused for too long. "...Officer Kevin. I haven't been drinking. I'm going home after a long work day." Again, he reached for the wallet, but it was wedged in his tight pants pocket, and his fingers couldn't get a grip on the leather.

Kevin tapped his flashlight against Nick's unfastened seatbelt. "You know there's a five-hundred-dollar fine in this state for driving with your seatbelt unbuckled."

"But I just unbuckled it so I could get my wallet out. I knew you would want to see my driver's license."

Kevin shined his flashlight directly in Nick's eyes. "Then why haven't I seen it yet?" The policeman seemed agitated.

"Just a second," Nick said, digging in his pocket. "I've just about got it. Besides, you know me, Kevin. Your mom owns the condo next to mine. I fixed her laptop a couple weeks ago."

Kevin took two steps back and pulled something dark and shiny from his belt that looked like a toy in his beefy hand. He pointed it at Nick. "Get your hands where I can see them. Get out of the car. Now!"

Nick immediately raised his hands, then he slowly reached for the door handle.

"Keep your hands where I can see them," Kevin yelled. The police officer's face had gone red.

Nick returned his hand to the raised position. "Can I open the door?"

"All right," Kevin said, "but do it slowly."

Nick thought about saying that he had been doing it slowly, but not wanting to argue with a man holding a weapon, he did it even more slowly. "I'm reaching for the door handle," he announced before fumbling for the door handle. "Slowly," he added. There was no reason to make Kevin any more nervous. As soon as the door latch opened, Nick slowly raised his hand again. Resting both hands on his head, so there would be no misinterpretation of his actions, he pushed the door open the rest of the way with his foot.

"Get out of the car and put your hands on the hood," Kevin commanded.

Nick placed his hands on the hood. "I'm still a little in shock, you know. It's not like I was trying run myself off the road." A giant hand gripped the back of Nick's collar and shoved him down on the hood, pressing him against the warm metal. It smelled like warm engine oil.

"Am I being arrested?" Nick demanded.

"Have you had any drugs or alcohol tonight?" Kevin asked.

"Why? Do you have any?" It was probably the wrong thing to say, but Nick's nerves were fried and his filters weren't working right.

"Are you a member of Al Qaeda?"

"I go to the Church of Great Savings."

Kevin slammed his fist down on the hood next to Nick's head. "Just stay down on that hood, and there won't be any trouble."

Nick heard Kevin's retreating footsteps crunch on the gravel shoulder. From his vantage point on the hood, he could just barely see Kevin. The policeman reached into the car and pulled out a radio.

"Downcastle PD One calling Johnson County Sheriff."

More static brought a new voice. *"Go ahead, Downcastle."*

"Requesting assistance for suspect identified as Nick Baker. Suspect refuses to show identification. Check for outstanding warrants."

Exasperated, Nick stood up from the hood and turned toward Kevin. "It's me. Nick Baker. I live next door to your mother." He took a step toward Kevin.

"Suspect on the move," Kevin yelled before dropping the radio. Again, he drew the little black thing from his belt. He took three running steps forward, displaying surprising spryness for such a big man, and dropped to one knee.

Nick stood frozen as Officer Kevin pulled the trigger. Darts with wires attached shot out of the device, missing him entirely. The first dart embedded itself in his car door. The other hit a rust spot, and embedded itself somewhere inside the engine compartment. Before Nick even had time to react, there was a quick *clap, clap, clap, clap, clap* noise, and smoke rolled out from under the hood.

"Holy shit!" Nick said. "Was that a taser? Did you just taze my car?"

"Stand back!" Kevin yelled. He pulled the baton from his belt. "Down on the ground!"

Nick looked at the ground. Under a covering of rough gravel was a layer of wet mud. "Is that really necessary?"

Kevin smiled. "Looks like we're going to have to do this the hard way." In one fluid movement, Kevin twisted Nick around, and used his baton to lock Nick's arm. He pushed Nick to the ground, knocking the wind out of him.

By the time Nick had caught his breath, the wet was already soaking into his dress shirt, and he figured it was only a matter of time before it made it into his Dockers. He felt Kevin's weight lift off him, and he lifted his face and turned his head to see the officer.

"And stay down," Kevin said. He quickly handcuffed Nick, and for additional displeasure used plastic cuffs to secure his ankles.

But Nick wasn't looking at Kevin anymore. He was looking at the small figure walking across the roof of the patrol car. He craned his neck around to get a better look. The creature walked easily down the sloped windshield, and Nick got his first look at the thing's feet. Only they weren't feet, they were hooves.

Perhaps hearing the tap-tap-tap of little hooves on the hood of his car, Kevin turned around. He froze. "What the shit is that?"

"You can see him too?" Nick asked. This changed everything. He wasn't insane. He was damned, but he wasn't insane.

Kevin yanked a weapon from his belt—not the taser this time, but his revolver. He fired at the creature. He was not standing that far from Nick and the sound of the handgun was painful. Nick's ears started to ring.

The bullet missed the demon, and the windshield of the patrol car exploded into a spider web of cracks. The creature looked at Kevin and shook its head in disapproval. He looked down at Nick and shrugged.

Kevin aimed the gun carefully, and the creature started running. He started firing wildly, blowing holes in the cruiser's windshield, hood, and emergency light bar. He never hit the creature—which Nick might have taken as a sign of its supernatural nature if Kevin hadn't missed him with the taser at point-blank range. It scampered into the woods, and Kevin fired twice more in its direction.

The next twenty minutes or so passed without incident. The sun set. Nick lay on the ground, listening to the ringing in his ears and letting the mud further saturate his clothing. Kevin paced back and forth, trying to shove bullets into his revolver with shaky hands, dropping a few. Occasionally he would aim his gun into the woods and squint at the darkness, then mutter to himself that the creature was somehow involved with al Qaeda.

"Terrorist bastards come over here and shoot up our police cars," he said amidst his pacing. He stopped and squatted down to look Nick in the face. "Do you have anything to do with them? Who do you work for?"

"I work for Baker Dental Supply," Nick answered.

"Don't get smart with me," Kevin said. "I bet you have a copy of the Koran."

Actually, Nick did have a copy of the Koran, it was at home between the Talmud and the Book of Mormon. He had bought them for a comparative religion class in college.

As he lay there, he realized that somewhere, in the dark recesses of his mind, part of his brainpower was dedicating itself to readying him for death, and making that realization, he suddenly became very afraid. It made sense after all. He was handcuffed, prone and helpless. Someone was randomly pointing and firing a gun only feet from where he lay. And not far away, out in the woods somewhere was a creature of hellfire and nightmare, probably rubbing one out.

Nick listened to the sound of a car approaching. Headlights reflected off the shattered windshield of the police cruiser, and tires crunched on gravel as the car pulled over to the shoulder and stopped. Nick realized it must be the sound of Kevin's backup. From the first word, Nick knew who that backup was.

"Goddammit, Kevin, what the hell have you done?" The "god" part of goddammit was stretched out for almost five seconds. It was a trademark explicative of Troy Heron, who was serving a life sentence as Downcastle's mayor. "Have you been shooting your gun off out here?"

"Please step back, Mayor Heron. I have apprehended a dangerous criminal. I think he's a terrorist. I think he has allies out in the woods. They travel in cells, you know."

"You idiot. That's no terrorist. That's Nick Baker."

"That's who he says he is," Kevin said, an edge of uncertainty creeping into his voice. "But I definitely saw someone out in the woods."

"Nick Baker is the son of Esther Baker, the nice lady who bought all those computers for the library." Personally, Nick didn't think of his mother as nice, but hoping for some relief from mud-soaked pants, he decided not to argue with the mayor.

"So what? The law is the law." Kevin belted this out like it was his personal mantra.

"And Kevin," the mayor said conciliatory, "can you tell me exactly which laws have been broken?"

"Well, reckless driving, failure to control vehicle, failure to wear a seatbelt, interference with official acts—I told him to stay face down on the hood of his car, and he didn't listen. Also, I'm considering taking him in for a drug test. We should probably get a warrant and search his house for a copy of the Koran."

"Do you think maybe, just maybe, you've been having a bit of a hard time lately? And maybe this nice, young man had a bit of trouble on the road, and just maybe you overreacted a bit?" The question was followed by a marked period of silence.

"Maybe." Now Kevin's voice became meek. "I'm really sorry, Mayor Heron. I guess I just panicked. You know I've been going to all those Homeland Security classes, and they tell us that whenever something looks suspicious—"

"Why don't you help him up then and take off those handcuffs?"

Kevin didn't seem to know when to quit. "But he didn't show me any identification. He might have been a serious threat."

Heron cleared his throat. "Now, Kevin, that's Nick Baker. You know it, and I know it. Hell, he lives next door to your mama, doesn't he? What do you think she's going to say when she finds out about this?"

"I don't know," Kevin said, hanging his head in resignation.

Nick felt hands undoing the cuffs on his wrists and ankles, and the two men grasped his shoulders, picking him up out of the mud. Mayor and police officer helped steady him as he got his footing back.

After seeing the mud covering Nick, Mayor Heron turned to Kevin and gave him a disgusted look. "Now, what do we say, Kevin?"

"Sorry," Kevin said, refusing to make eye contact. He held out his hand to shake.

Nick reluctantly took the policeman's hand and shook it out of a desire to defuse the situation and the need to get home and into a warm shower as quickly as possible.

The mayor stepped over to Kevin and put a hand on his shoulder. "Why don't you take the rest of the night off? I'm sure Downcastle will be safe from the forces of evil."

"Okay, if you say so. But I tell you..." Kevin lowered his voice, but Nick could still hear him. "I think he's in league with the devil."

Mayor Heron gave Kevin a curious look. "So is he a Muslim or a Satanist? I think the two are mutually exclusive." He raised his voice just a little. "Go home, Kevin."

The policeman nodded and walked back to his car. Mayor Heron and Nick watched as he started brushing safety glass from his wounded windshield out of his front seat.

Heron shook his head. "I never should have sent him to those Homeland Security classes." He produced a white handkerchief and handed it to Nick. "Goddammit, that boy's dumb. He really does mean well. He's just an idiot. You can't help that. He was born that way. Do you think you can accept my apology, on behalf of both myself and the entire Downcastle community?"

Nick shrugged. "Of course, Mayor Heron."

"Are you all right to get home, Mr. Baker?"

"I'm fine," Nick said. To make a point, he walked over to his car and slid behind the driver's seat.

Heron had followed behind him. "I could give you a ride home, no problem."

"I'll be fine," Nick said. It took him a moment to remember how to use car keys, and he realized he must still be suffering from mild shock. He turned the ignition.

The car made a weird noise. The dashboard lit up dimly and then brightly. Several warning lights popped on. His clock reset itself to midnight and started jumping around to random times. Then everything went dark, and he swore the car made the Pac-Man death sound.

Nick looked up at Mayor Heron and smiled. "I guess I need a ride after all. Kevin tazed my car." As soon as he admitted his helplessness, the energy drained from Nick.

"Goddammit. I tell you what, Mr. Baker. I'll drive you home tonight, and the city will tow in your car and pay to have it fixed. It's the least we can do after this incident. We should probably handle your dry cleaning too."

Nick nodded. Tomorrow was Saturday, so he wouldn't need his car for work. It probably couldn't be fixed by Monday, but he could borrow a car from his cousins. "You don't need to do my laundry, but I would appreciate if you took care of my car."

The mayor grabbed his hand and shook it profusely. "Thank you, Mr. Baker. I'm glad to help. We'll set this right, whatever it takes, just..." his tone turned apologetic. "Just, don't sue the city, okay?"

That night, Nick hovered between sleep and wakefulness. His day had been too chaotic, and whenever he closed his eyes, he saw small dancing creatures with pointing red beards and red-faced policemen. Sometimes, they were dancing naked with each other. When the first beams of sunlight squeezed between the cracks in his venetian blinds, he greeted the new day with relief.

Still, he had gotten very little sleep, and he rolled over to rest his eyes for a few more minutes. His hand closed on some kind of paper. He thought he might be dreaming it, but a few minutes later he opened his eyes and the paper was still there.

He held the paper up to the light and examined it. It was made of a fine parchment, reminding him of some of the older Baker family documents or the invitations his mother sent when she had a party. Just like his mother's invitations, delicate calligraphy graced the page.

The Bakers must live up to their obligations.

There was no signature.

Nick considered this message for a moment, then flipped over the page to see if anything was written on the back. There wasn't. What did it mean by obligations? Was it about the mini-game? Did the producers decide to harass him at home? How did they even know he was planning to half-ass it? Was it something to do with the shareholder meeting?

He looked at the clock. It was only 7:30, too early in the morning to deal with mysterious notes. Maybe a nice shower would clear his head.

A few minutes later, he was in the shower, turning the problem over in his head. Maybe JenJen was the answer to this riddle. She was one of the two people he'd talked to about half-assing the mini-game, and he didn't think Rudy had been listening. Maybe she was playing some kind of prank on him. She did have an odd sense of humor.

As he was drying himself off, he mentally rehearsed what he was going to say to JenJen. How did you accuse a female friend of sneaking into your home when you were asleep? In many ways it was kind of a violation of trust. It was probably a good thing that he didn't sleep in the nude. Then again, that would never be a problem—Bakers didn't do anything in the nude.

After slipping into a clean pair of underpants, Nick phoned Jen-Jen's home number. "Hello," said a recorded male voice. "You've reached Steve and Jennifer. We're not in right now. Leave a message if you want to."

Nick adopted the most friendly and neutral voice he could. "Um, hi. This is Nick Baker. I'm sorry to call so early on a Saturday—"

There was a click and then Nick heard JenJen yawning. "Nick, what's up? Are you at work?"

"Sorry to call so early," he said again, "but did you break into my condo and leave a note about the mini-game on my pillow?" As soon as the words were out of his mouth, he realized he was being an idiot. JenJen might be a little odd in a geek-girl sort of way, but she wasn't the kind of person to break into people's houses on a whim. "Nevermind. I'm being stupid. Go back to bed."

JenJen paused as if taking a moment to process his statement. "Nick, has someone been in your apartment?"

"I don't know. I think so. There was a weird note on my pillow this morning."

Again she paused. "Okay, don't freak out, but whoever broke in could still be there. I think you should call the cops."

"No!" If he called the cops, Kevin would come over, and maybe this time he would shoot up Nick's condo. Still, she had a point. Someone might still be inside his apartment. "Maybe if I'm really quiet, they'll go away?"

"You have to do something," JenJen insisted. "There's somebody in your house. Nick, you might be in serious danger. If you don't want to call the cops, I'll call them for you."

"Wait," he said. He tried to think of a compromise that would not reprise the previous night's adventure with Officer Kevin. "Look, I don't get along well with the local cop. Just stay on the phone while I have a look around. Then if anything happens, you can call the police. It's probably nothing, really."

Even after he said it, Nick wondered if strange notes left on his pillow could be counted as nothing, especially considering yesterday's events. In retrospect, he wondered if he had really seen the little creature. Then again, Kevin had seen it too. If anything, Kevin's reaction had been more virulent than Nick's.

"All right," JenJen answered, "but be careful."

"I will," Nick said as he moved the phone to his left hand and slid the nine iron from his Louis Vuitton golf bag, a perfect match to Uncle Earl's—a birthday present. He held the club extended, ready to strike. "I'm moving into the hall now."

He checked the hall and found nothing, quickly making his way around the condo and reporting back to JenJen every step of the way. His hands were shaking, and the sweat from his hands made the nine iron slippery. Because the condo was less than a thousand square feet, checking every room only took a moment, even in his addled state. "I guess I'm alone," he said when he was done searching. "I'm sorry I freaked you out." He tried to sound nonchalant, but he was still a little shaken himself.

"Are you sure?" she asked. "You've checked everywhere?"

"Yes, I think I'm okay," Nick said, more for himself. "I have a really small place, so there aren't really any places to hide. If anyone was here, they must be long gone."

"I still think you should call the police." She sounded worried.

"I'll think about that," Nick said, knowing he wasn't going to do anything to bring him into contact with Officer Kevin. "Thanks for everything. I'll see you at work on Monday."

"If you're still afraid, I could come over if you want."

Nick blushed, feeling like he was twelve again, being called chicken by Larry and Carrey. "No. I'm fine. I just had a bit of a shock. It's just a piece of paper."

"Okay, Nick. I'm going to hang up now, but promise me you'll be careful, and you won't take any unnecessary risks." She hung up.

Indifferent to the cost of the custom golf club, Nick tossed it on the couch. He set the phone down on the coffee table and went in search of coffee. He had just filled the coffee maker with water when he heard a noise. If he were to guess, he would have to say it sounded rather like a small hoof stepping on the lid of his washing machine. He hadn't checked the laundry nook.

Nick's laundry facility was a large closet at the end of his dining area with double folding doors. This allowed his dining table to double as a folding area. The closet itself was just big enough to fit a washer and dryer, and possibly a small demon.

Nick slid the coffee pot back into the maker, and it chattered with the shaking of his hand. He calmly walked into the living room and took a deep breath. His mind screamed to call the police, to call Jen-Jen, to just walk out the door and never come back, but this was his home. After all, he was a Baker, and Bakers did not go gentle into that good night. He picked up the nine iron from the couch.

Nick made his way over to the laundry doors. As he approached, he smelled something loamy like fertilizer. He realized that throwing open the double doors would mean using both hands, meaning he would have to let go of his club. Could a golf club even kill a demon? He guessed he'd know in a minute. Maybe he should have grabbed the driver.

The smell was really strong by the door. It crept up his nostrils and made him want to sneeze. There was a tinge of something else in the odor, an animal musk, which seemed to trigger things in the primal recesses of his mind. Suddenly, holding the golf club didn't seem nearly so silly.

He set the nine iron on the table. This would have to do. There was no fast way to open the double doors short of pulling them down from their track. He grasped the handles, opened them as fast as possible, and jumped back. Before he even had a chance to register what was in the closet, he swung the golf club backward, preparing to strike, and accidentally embedded it in the plasterboard ceiling.

As he yanked at the club, trying to free it, he saw the creature. He stood on the lid of Nick's top-loading washing machine. He watched Nick and shook his head as if he were disappointed. He raised his hand as if he were about to say something.

Failing to free the club from the ceiling, Nick tried to intimidate the creature. "Hah!" he cried, jumping forward.

Nick's feint did not cause the creature to cower in fear. Instead, he grinned and jumped at Nick. His head snapped forward and his twin horns smashed into Nick's forehead.

Nick saw a flash of light. He felt himself falling backward, and distantly he understood some reflex should kick in so he could try to catch himself. No such reflex did kick in, and he dropped like a tree in the forest. He landed on the thickly padded carpet and lay dazed, the creature still on top of him.

The creature rolled off Nick and stood up. Again, it shook its head, and then, it spoke in an exasperated voice. "I'm just trying to help you out, Baker. Your family is flirting with disaster, and you seem to be the only reasonable one of the bunch. Don't allow your family to break its obligation to the Great Shepherd."

If Nick hadn't been so dazed, he would have asked some follow up questions, but before he had recovered enough to respond to the creature, it had walked out the door. He hoped it didn't run into Kevin's mother in the stairwell.

Despite his mother's evangelical tendencies, Nick had never considered himself a religious person. However, he had attended church on a regular basis, and he remembered the warnings of Reverend Collins about demons harassing those who slipped in their faith. As Nick lay on the floor, battered and bruised by the little demon he wondered if he should have paid more heed.

Letting out a little moan, Nick rolled onto his side. The room spun slowly for a moment, and he waited for it to subside. With the help of one of his dining room chairs he pulled himself to his feet. He leaned over it for a moment until he regained his equilibrium. His forehead felt wet, and when he touched it, his hand came away bloody.

He took a deep breath and walked down the hallway, occasionally steadying himself against a wall, and rounded the corner into the bathroom. He looked in the mirror and saw two puncture wounds in his forehead, leaking blood. He washed his bloody hand and then set about cleaning his forehead.

Thankfully, neither of the wounds were deep. Nick vaguely remembered something about a four-inch depression in the skull being enough to cause fatal cerebral damage. When he was done washing them, he put two adhesive bandages over the holes. Given that his attacker was supernatural in origin, he decided to talk to his doctor about a tetanus booster.

He returned to his bedroom and turned the fine parchment of the creature's note over and over in his hands. He finally had physical evidence that the creature was... what? It had masturbated in his courtyard. It had kind of run him off the road, but Nick really should have been watching where he was going. It had only attacked him after he wielded a golf club in its general direction. Then it said it was trying to help him.

Still, the creature was real, and if Nick had learned anything from twenty years of sermons from Reverend Collins, it was that anything supernatural could be considered a creature straight from hell, unless they were obviously angelic. Given his situation, there was only one thing to do.

He called his mother.

"Good morning, Mother. I was wondering if you could give me the direct phone number for Reverend Collins."

"Of course, dear. I have it right here. Are you ready to take it down?"

When she was done giving him the number, his mother said, "You shouldn't call him this early, you know."

"I'll wait past nine-thirty."

"Yes, but he's a minister. He has to worry about all kinds of ecclesiastical issues."

Nick sighed. "I'm sure he gets up early to do that sort of thing."

"He may have stayed up late."

Nick mentally kicked himself for trying to argue with his mother. She was incapable of letting anyone else get the last word. It would only make Nick frustrated and his mother angry. "I'm sure you're right. I'll wait until the afternoon."

"That's a good boy, Nick. I'll see you in church tomorrow."

"Okay, Mother. Bye now, and thank you for the number." He waited to see if she would have a parting thought. She often did, and if he hung up the phone early, she'd just call him back.

After a thirty second pause, she said, "Oh, honey, one more thing. Have you seen the morning paper? You might want to take a look."

"I'll do that, Mother. Bye now." The line went dead, and Nick finally hung up his phone.

He stared at the phone number. Did he really want to call in Reverend Collins? Over the years, Nick had alternated between thinking of the man as either a kook, a crook, or a charlatan. Now it looked like all the hellfire and damnation he had been spouting might have some merit after all. And demons were probably like bedbugs. Once you got them, you pretty much had to get in a professional to get rid of them.

Reverend Collins answered on the third ring. "The Church of Great Savings, the Reverend Collins speaking."

"Hi Reverend, this is Nick Baker. Sorry for calling so early."

"Nick! What an unexpected pleasure. I'm always happy to talk to a member of the church no matter what the time of day. What can I help you with?"

Nick tried to think of a subtle way to ease the topic of demons into the conversation. There didn't seem to be one. "Reverend, I'm being attacked by a demon."

"Say no more, Nick. Your mother is one of my oldest and dearest friends. If her son is suffering, I'm going to drop everything to help you. I have to visit the hospital this morning. Can you wait until one o'clock?"

"That would be great. Thank you, Reverend."

With nothing to do for a few hours, Nick decided to have coffee and read the paper. He would have to pick up a little before Reverend Collins came over. He wasn't much of a housekeeper, but his mother had taught him to always clean before company arrived, especially if that company was a minister.

On the front page of the paper, there was an artist's rendition of some kind of gigantic structure. At first, Nick wondered if the Iowa Hawkeyes were building a new sports arena. Then he did, what they eloquently call on television, a spit-take.

On television, no one has to clean up after a spit take. In reality, Nick had to get some paper towels, a few rags and a bottle of carpet cleaner to mitigate the damage. Once his coffee table and carpet were coffee free, he returned to the paper.

The headline read, "Controversial Minister Plans First Corridor Megachurch." The article started with the demographics of the Cedar Rapids/Iowa City corridor before smoothly transitioning into the size of the Church of Great Savings' congregation and the estimated cost of the facility, $300 million. It went on to reference the church's problems with the IRS as well as the Baker family donation of the land before concluding with quotes from a local environmental group about the consequences of knocking down another hundred acres of virgin forest.

Apparently, the land was part of 3,000 acres of prime woodland bought by his great grandfather, 250 acres of that forest had already been clear-cut to build Baker Village and 1,200 acres had been condemned and flooded when the reservoir was dammed up. Nick would probably have known this if he attended stockholders meetings.

Further down in the article were photos of Reverend Collins and Nick's mother, who, according to the article, was chairwoman of the construction committee. This was news to Nick, but it made sense since their family was donating the land, and who knew how much money. Maybe Delores was right. Maybe he should start going to some of those meetings.

3

FIGHT!

From its invention in 1831 by Joseph Henry, first secretary of the Smithsonian Institution, the electric doorbell has been used by rich man and pauper alike. Joseph Henry's work would later inspire Alexander Graham Bell to invent the telephone. Despite the device's rich history, Reverend Collins knocked on Nick's sliding patio door.

Nick looked up and saw the old cleric waiting on his patio; he set down the most recent *Global Fight!* strategy guide, got up off the couch, and hurried across the living room. Collins was grayer than Nick's childhood memory of him, and his belly was rounder, but otherwise, he had changed very little. Today, he was sporting his country-boy look: blue jeans and a flannel shirt. On the patio next to him sat a ten-speed bike.

Nick slid open the door and held out his hand. "Good to see you, Reverend Collins. Please come in."

Collins took Nick's hand in both of his and held it, forcing Nick to sort of tow him into the living room. "It's so good to see you, Nick. I'm so glad you called on me in your time of need." He pushed his way into the apartment without letting go, forcing Nick to back up. If he noticed the bandages on Nick's forehead, he was polite enough not to draw attention to them.

Nick pointed to the ten-speed. "Did you bike here, Reverend? Some kind of 'get healthy for Jesus' thing?"

Collins turned and looked at the bike. "No. It was just sitting out there. I thought it was yours. I brought the Holy Roller." He pointed to the large white Cadillac parked outside. "Come to think of it though, 'get healthy for Jesus' sounds like a great idea. We could do a whole range of health foods. There would be room in the new church for a health center, at least a few treadmills and weight machines. I don't think we can afford a swimming pool though. We'd have room though if the program takes off."

"Reverend Collins," Nick said, "can I get you something to drink?" Nick's mother had raised him to always offer visitors a beverage and a little snack. "I have some coffee on, and I have some cheese. I think it's cheddar."

"Please, Nick, we're not in church. We're all friends here, you can call me Willy." He paused for a moment, and in a conspiratorial tone, he said, "And being that we're not in church, do you have anything stronger?"

"Like Limburger?"

"Do you think you can scrounge up a small sherry or perhaps a port?"

"Why don't you have a seat? I'll see what I can do." Nick was pretty sure he didn't have anything like that. However, when he was in college, he discovered a talent, some called it a gift from God. Nick was a natural mixologist, born for changing a mixture of seemingly unrelated materials into a pleasing liquid. Events relating to this talent had earned him his college nickname, Toxic.

He walked into the kitchen and opened the refrigerator in search of alcoholic beverages. Way in the back, he found an old bottle with a trickle of spoiled wine. He grabbed it and pulled the cork. It smelled rotten, but it was a starting point. He also grabbed a mostly-empty two liter bottle of flat Dr. Onion, a celebrity impostor beverage he'd bought on a whim. Utilizing a funnel, he mixed the spoiled wine with the flat impostor beverage in the two liter bottle. Then he added some brown sugar, brine from a pickle jar, and a pinch of cinnamon. After shaking thoroughly, he strained it through a coffee filter.

The color and consistency looked right, so he poured a little into a cordial glass and took a tentative sip. It didn't taste half bad. Nick's right eye closed, and his head jerked violently to the left. He topped up the glass and poured another for the reverend.

He returned from the kitchen and found Reverend Collins making himself comfortable on the couch. He proffered the ad hoc beverage. "Here you go, Willy. I did have some port."

Reverend Collins took the improvised cordial and took a tentative sip. His right eye closed, and his head jerked to the left. "An interesting little vintage," he said when he had recovered, "with hints of caramel, dill, and cinnamon. Did you buy it from us?"

After looking suitably embarrassed for procuring groceries outside the fold, Nick said, "No, it was a gift." He took a sip from his glass. His right eye closed, and his head jerked violently to the left.

"Well, that's fine then. But don't forget, when you buy from the Church of Great Savings, you don't just save money, you save souls. The new church is even going to have its own gas station. It will be right on your way to work."

"That's great, Reverend. I'd never think of going anywhere else."

Collins raised his glass again, but paused as if thinking the better of it and set down the drink. "Now, Nick, let's get down to the business at hand. Tell me what's bothering you."

"Well, I called you because of a demon."

"Yes, I know, but what kind of demon? Are you riding the dragon?"

"Am I what?"

"You know, the H, the horse, the smack, Aunt Hazel, brown sugar, the H bomb, heroin?"

Nick was shocked by the suggestion. "No! I don't do drugs."

"If it's not drugs, what kind of demon are we talking about? Alcohol? Women? Men? Boys? Animals? You don't have to be coy with me, son. I'll be discrete. What kind of demon are we dealing with?"

Nick shook his head. "No, I'm not dealing with inner demons. There was an actual demon in my house, a little creature with horns. He was hiding in my laundry area."

"Interesting," Collins said, without missing a beat. "I wonder why. Do you have any idea why a demon would visit your house?

Have you been dabbling in the occult, fornicating, listening to Lady Gaga?"

Nick bit his lip. "Well, I do have a bit of a crush on this girl at the office and sometimes in the shower... I um—"

Collins waved off his admission. "Nick, stronger men than you have succumbed to that weakness. And no matter how often you rub those things, I've never heard of one producing a demon like a genie out of a bottle."

The reverend had a point. If occasional self-abuse could produce demons, Rudy would have to buy a bigger house. And Nick really wished he hadn't conjured that visual.

"Anything else you can think of?" Collins asked.

"Well, he did leave a note about the Bakers living up to their obligations. And on his way out, he said something about trying to help."

"He left a note?"

"Well, I assume it was him. There hasn't been anyone else in the condo, so um..." Nick couldn't believe the words about to come out of his mouth. "Could you perform an exorcism?"

The reverend looked at Nick for a long moment. "Are you entirely sure that alcohol or drugs had no role to play in this? I am a trained counselor." He held up his hand. "And I totally understand if you're not comfortable talking to me, being that I'm a friend of your mother. I can simply give you a referral."

"I know what I saw," Nick stated firmly. He worked a fingernail under one of his bandages and pulled it off. "The demon headbutted me and gave me these." He pulled away the other bandage.

Collins leaned forward and squinted at the holes in Nick's forehead. "I see. A demon did this?"

"Yes," Nick said. "I was trying to hit him with a golf club at the time."

Collins nodded. "Good for you." After a couple tries, the stout but elderly cleric pushed himself up from the couch. "Well, I guess you better show me this washing machine."

Nick walked him over to the laundry area and opened the double doors. To his embarrassment, the first thing Collins did was lean in and take a big whiff, dangerously close to Nick's dirty laundry hamper.

Reverend Collins suffered a short coughing fit. "Certainly is pungent in there, isn't it? I don't smell brimstone, though."

"Brimstone?" Nick asked. He'd heard the word before, but he thought it was just a word they used in fantasy games.

"Sulfur, the smell of rotten eggs. A calling card for the demonic." The reverend made a face as he took another sniff. "This smells more like the organic fertilizer in our garden center at the church. Have you been keeping fertilizer in here?"

"No, the condo association does all the gardening."

"Do you know their supplier? I guarantee I can cut them a deal."

"I'm not sure. I suppose I should ask," Nick said stiffly. He appreciated the fact that Collins was a motivated salesperson, but he wished he could focus on the matter at hand.

"Well, you should look into it. Your association will have more money and we will have more construction money for the church." He turned back to the closet. "So, it was just standing in here, and you say it was three and a half, maybe four feet tall?"

"Yes, but that's not the only place I've seen him. Yesterday morning, I saw him in my office courtyard, standing in a pile of garbage."

"A pile of garbage, you say?" Collins looked thoughtful. "Did he bring it with him?"

"No, the garbage was there because—that whole thing with the landfill."

"Oh, of course, how could I forget?" Collins opened the lid of the washing machine and peered inside. He sniffed again.

"The weird thing was that when he left, some of the garbage had disappeared."

"He stole garbage, you say?" He was sounding more skeptical by the minute.

Nick realized with a sinking feeling that he was losing the reverend's confidence. "You don't believe me, do you?"

Reverend Collins straightened and closed the washer "Well, son, I believe you saw something and, given my long relationship with your mother, I would be remiss in my responsibilities were I not to take you seriously." He put his hand on Nick's shoulder and guided him back to the living room area. "You sit down and relax. I'll bless your condo, and then I'll perform a cleansing ritual on you. That should drive away any evil spirits."

Nick smiled. "Thank you, Reverend Collins. You're a life saver." If a week ago, someone had told him that he'd be thanking Reverend Collins for performing an exorcism in his condo, he'd have laughed in their face. Of course, he would have had the same reaction to anyone telling him to check his washing machine for demons.

"I like to think I'm more than that, Nick. Now, don't you worry one bit. Let me just grab an exorcism kit out of the car."

Reverend Collins left and came back with a little box. On the box was written, "Church of Great Savings, Disposable Exorcism Kit. Fun for the whole family!" He tore off the shrink wrap and opened the box, which contained a small tray made of heavy foil, a few packets of salt, a tiny squirt bottle of water, and a cone of incense. "Usually, I charge twenty dollars for the kit and ask for a donation in exchange for my services. However, given the support your family has given the church, I'm letting you have this at no charge."

While he was working, Nick called Jim, the town mechanic, and confirmed his Corolla had been towed. Jim said that Mayor Heron had offered to reimburse him for a rental car and offered to drive him to the airport to pick one up. Nick declined. There was no reason to waste the town's money when he could borrow a vehicle from his family.

Collins poured the salt and squirted the little bottle of water into the foil tray. He said the Lord's Prayer while stirring it with his finger, then he poured it back into the bottle.

Seeing Reverend Collins was still busy, Nick dialed his Uncle Earl. Uncle Earl and Nick's adopted cousins, Larry and Carrey, had quite a large collection of vehicles which they shared. The last time he counted, they had five, and Larry and Carrey went everywhere together, so they wouldn't miss one for a few days.

"Nick, my boy, what can I do for you this morning? Did you decide to take that job after all?" One track mind, classic Uncle Earl.

"Actually, I wanted to ask if I could borrow a car for a few days."

"Your old junker finally fall apart?"

Nick held his breath for a moment to prevent sighing into the phone. "My car was doing just fine until the local cop tazed it last night."

"Why would anyone taze a rusty, old Corolla? Did he think it was threatening him? And if so, what with? Tetanus?"

"He was aiming at me. I think he was just having a bad night."

"Idiot rednecks! I told you to move out of that two-bit town. You get your ass down to my attorney's office this afternoon. He'll take a deposition. Scratch that. It's Saturday. He'll be on the golf course. Come down to the club, and give him your deposition there. We'll sue the policeman, the city council, the mayor, and the county sheriff's office. No one treats my baby brother's boy like that."

This time, Nick did sigh. "Please don't do anything to piss anyone off. I have to live here. I already talked to the mayor. He's paying to repair the Corolla. He even gave me a ride home last night. He would have rented a car for me, but I thought I could just borrow one of yours."

Reverend Collins walked around the living room, squirting water around, burning the incense in the foil tray, and praying.

"What's that noise?" asked Uncle Earl. "You have the TV on?"

"No, that's Reverend Collins. He stopped by to help me..." He still didn't want to explain the demon to Uncle Earl. He'd probably try to sue it. "He's here to help me with a little problem."

"You're into the whores, aren't you? Your father was the same way. The old apple doesn't fall far from the tree."

This was news to Nick. His mother had always talked about his father as a paragon of virtue, who if not for his early death, would have been canonized as a saint. "No, Uncle Earl, I'm not 'into the whores.' I just needed to talk to someone with ecclesiastic training."

"Well, tell that shifty son of a bitch preacher I said hello," he said in a jovial tone. "I'll send the boys over later with a car."

Nick winced at the thought of his cousins visiting. They had mellowed considerably since school, at least where Nick was concerned, but he still had trouble forgiving them for tormenting him. "You don't have to send them. You can just leave the keys, and I can get a ride—" Uncle Earl had already hung up the phone.

He walked over to Reverend Collins, who seemed to be inspecting one of the dining room chairs. "That looks nice and sturdy," the cleric mumbled. He turned and motioned to Nick. "Come over here and have a seat."

"Before I forget," Nick interjected as he lowered himself into the chair, "my Uncle Earl says hi."

Collins smiled. "How's that shifty son of a bitch doing?"

"He's good, I guess." Nick shrugged. "So, what are we doing now?" Despite Collins' insistence he didn't want anything from Nick, there would probably be an expectation of some type of favor. Nick was ready to agree to anything if his suffering was finally over.

"Just stay still for one moment." Collins reached out and hand-cuffed Nick's arm to the chair with plastic cuffs. Nick gazed confusedly at his right arm, giving it a tentative tug, while Collins similarly restrained the left. The old man could move pretty fast.

"I hope you understand," Collins said, as he squatted down to zip-tie Nick's legs to the chair, "the restraints are simply a precaution. I've done everything I can for your condo. But there is an off chance that the demon is residing inside your body. The restraints will make it safer for both of us. Sometimes, they play rough."

"Maybe we could stop here and see if things get better—"

Collins picked up his bible. "Nick, I want you to remember that no matter what happens, Jesus Christ loves you, and he finds you his worthy child."

Nick found his sudden bondage disconcerting, and in his anxiety the pot of coffee he finished before Collins arrived was starting to become a more serious matter. "Are you sure all of this is completely necessary?"

"Oh, yes," he said, rolling his hips. "We're going to knock the evil right out of you. Oh Lord." With the word 'Lord,' he made a pelvic thrust in Nick's direction. He lifted his Bible. "Now, steel yourself. We are about to begin."

Collins swung his leather-clad Bible, slapping Nick across the face with enough force to loosen his teeth. "In the name of the Father, the Son, and the Holy Ghost, leave this young man."

At first, Nick was too shocked to react. Salty tears ran down his face, or was that holy water? He was too confused to form rational thought.

He swung the Bible again, backhand this time. "Satan! I cast you from this man. He is righteous and filled with the love of God and Jesus Christ."

Both sides of his face stung, and his eyes and nose ran freely, maybe they were even bleeding. Through the pain and humiliation, something caught in Nick's mind, something Collins was saying. He had said, "great shepherd." The Lord is my shepherd. Why would demons care about shepherds, a symbol of the other side? Maybe it wasn't talking about the mini-game.

Someone knocked at the siding glass door, and Reverend Collins stopped mid-prayer. He looked momentarily spooked, like someone caught doing something embarrassing.

Seeing an opportunity to stop the violent exorcism, Nick said, "That's probably my friend, Rudy. I invited him over. He's really early."

"Excuse me for one minute," Collins said. He took the squirt bottle and sprayed Nick with room-temperature saltwater while making the sign of the cross, like he was spritzing a salad to prevent it from drying out.

Collins took out a handkerchief and dried his forehead. Then he walked over and opened the patio door. "You must be Rudy. I'm Reverend Collins. Please, come in and have a seat. Nick is busy at the moment."

Rudy walked into the condo and glanced around. He was wearing all black today, and he looked like he hadn't shaved in a week.

Rudy's eyes bugged out when he saw Nick strapped firmly to a dining room chair. "What the hell is going on here?"

"Um, hi, Rudy," Nick said from his chair of captivity, embarrassed that his atheist friend had found him in a scene of religious extremism.

Collins returned to Nick and pulled a folding knife out of his back pocket.

"Watch it, Nick!" Rudy yelled, hurrying toward them. "He's got a knife."

Nick closed his eyes, anticipating Collins's attack, not wanting to see the knife slide into his body. He heard a pop, pop, and his legs were suddenly free. He opened his eyes to see Collins putting away the knife.

From his breast pocket, Collins produced a key for the handcuffs. "Well, since you have company, that's probably enough for today. Call me if you have any more problems, Nick."

Standing, Nick automatically offered his hand to Reverend Collins. "Um, thanks for coming over."

Reverend Collins took his hand and held it. "Don't mention it, all part of the service. Speaking of service, I'll see you in church tomorrow. I hear your mother's got a little surprise for you."

"Oh, that sounds great," Nick said, wondering what horrible thing she had lined up for him. She probably wanted him to be on some committee for the new church building. "Would you mind showing yourself to the door?" Nick's knees felt a little wobbly. He wasn't completely sure he could make it that far.

"Of course not. You just sit there and rest for a moment." Reverend Collins strode over to Rudy. "It was nice to meet you, Rudy. I don't suppose I could persuade you to come to our church?"

Rudy shook his head. "No, sir. I'm Rastafarian."

For a moment, Collins looked like he didn't know what to say. Nick couldn't remember another occasion which had left the man at a loss for words, but Rudy often had that effect on people.

After a long pause, Collins said, "Well, then, I'll leave you boys to your afternoon." He showed himself out.

Rudy walked over to Nick and said, "So, are you going to thank me?"

"What for?"

"For saving you from Reverend Psycho," Rudy said. He seemed to be fighting a smirk. "Trust me, a moment later, and he would have gotten his dick out."

"That's Reverend Collins," Nick spluttered. "He's an old friend of the family. I've known him all my life."

"When you were little, did he touch you in your no-no place?"

"Shut up. Reverend Collins was a friend of my father, and I'm not going to let you speak about him that way." The exorcism hadn't been pleasant, but the old man had been trying to help him.

Rudy shrugged. "Whatever you say, but I haven't often seen that level of restraint outside of an S&M club." His tone implied that he was merely speaking the truth, and it wasn't his fault if Nick couldn't handle it.

Nick almost asked when Rudy had been in an S&M club, but on second thought, Rudy might have an answer. He settled for: "Could you wipe that smirk off your face?"

For ten seconds, Rudy opened and closed his mouth, he squinted, and his cheeks strained. Finally, his face settled back into a smirk. "No. So, you want to get some lunch?"

Two hours later, well fed, they returned to Nick's condo and started up their *Global Fight!* console.

FightOS kernel 8.5.1.3 ....loaded
Searching for updates .... Up to date.
Interfacing with GPS hardware ....done
Discovering Controllers
Primary ....Global Fight! Gold Headset Found (default)
Network ....Found
Loading Newest Textures............................done
Building Texture Cache.........done
Starting Game

In the real world, the world of Baker Dental Distributing, Nick Baker was a mere minion of his Uncle Earl, but in the world of *Global Fight!*, he was Nick Toxic, one of the deadliest men alive. With his sidekick Doctor Rude, Nick Toxic had dispatched countless foes, earning him the rank of number three in the Midwest region.

Moving to take cover behind a parked car, Nick lifted his AR-15 and scanned the street for activity, marveling at the accuracy of the version 8.5 rendering engine. If not for a slight flicker around the edges, the virtual reality experience would be perfect, like he was standing on the street outside his condo complex. Every detail was there, right down to the orange roof on Mrs. Coltrane's garden shed.

Nick sighed. Games like this were why he studied programming. He hadn't really wanted to work for Edutacular all his life. He had intended to use it as a stepping stone, applying at a bigger studio once he had some experience. He could probably still do that if he wanted to, but he'd have to take an entry level job and move halfway across the country. Besides, he'd miss Baker Dental. It was home.

Rudy popped into the game world beside him, and Nick turned to face him. "Why do we always start in Downcastle? It's dead around here." Above Rudy's head, Nick would see his player name and his health bar, which showed his character had taken no damage since logging on.

Rudy had a point. There weren't always players in Downcastle. They often ended up playing in Cedar Rapids or Iowa City. "Let's try the Old Capital parkade. There's always a good fight down there."

Nick brought up his menu and hailed a SecureCab. Within a minute, an armor-plated taxi pulled up at the curb. That was another way in which *Global Fight!* differed from the real world, you would never be able to get a taxi in Downcastle. The SecureCab dropped them in front of the Old Capitol, Iowa's former seat of government, now part of the University of Iowa campus. Someone had set the dome on fire, and it burned like a giant torch.

They moved down the street toward Old Capitol Mall, covering and advancing as best they could in their exposed position. As they reached the far end of the sidewalk in front of Schaffer Hall, they took fire from Panchero's Mexican Grill across the street. They dropped to the ground and returned fire, putting dozens of rounds into the storefront.

Nick held up his hand, signaling for Rudy to stop firing.

"Did we get them?" Rudy asked.

"Shh. I hear something."

They both listened intently for a moment. There was something just outside the limit of Nick's hearing, a low thumping sound. He could remember hearing it once before in the game, but what was it?

"Chopper blades," said Rudy.

There were helicopters in the game, but they were nearly as hard to steal as in real life. Usually, people would go for news-copters, or sometimes rob a hospital heliport. However, what rose above the roof of the biology building lacked the logos of the television news and the local hospital. It was a black Apache attack chopper fitted with rockets and a chain gun.

The chain gun burped, turning the sidewalk in front of them into gravel. Nick's display lit up, showing he was taking damage from shrapnel.

"Where do you think he found that?" Rudy said, without moving. "How can that even be fair?"

Nick managed to find his voice. "Take cover!" He rolled behind a parked car. He zoomed in on the cockpit and read the player's name. The pilot was Cof!nF!l3r, the top-rated player in the east coast region, currently ranked third in the world. As Nick wondered what Cof!nF!l3r was doing in Iowa City, the helicopter fired a rocket at the car Nick was hiding behind.

In the real world, Nick would have already been dead. With the *Global Fight!* physics engine, he had a split second to turn and take a step before the shockwave of the blast carried him thirty feet into the small stand of trees in front of Schaeffer Hall. He kept his head down as the helicopter's chain gun turned the trees around him into matchsticks.

He looked up just in time to see Rudy take aim at the helicopter's tail section and fire a full magazine of rounds into it. Black smoke erupted from the helicopter. It started to spin and lurch drunkenly until it finally crashed into a bank across the street.

The scene reminded Nick of the game's ad campaign from the previous year: *"Global Fight!* It's a violent game." The campaign had won an award for accuracy in advertising.

"Nice shot," Nick said, standing up and walking out of the trees.

Rudy pumped his computer-generated fist in the air. "Yeah, I just racked up a major kill. I'll be rated higher than you soon."

"Um, yeah," Nick said. He tried to sound like it wasn't a big deal, but in his display, he brought up the real-time game rankings. Dr. Rude had indeed crawled up to fifth place, within reach of Nick's position. Nick's nemesis, DeathChick82, was still in the coveted number one slot for the Midwest region.

They did their run-and-cover move past the front of the shopping mall and reached the parkade. Using the low, concrete wall of the first level as cover, Nick scanned the parked cars with his weapon. Then he saw something awesome. Parked on the first level was a World War II era Jeep with a mounted machine gun.

They were both silent for a moment, and then Rudy said, "Do you see that?"

While Nick's smile didn't carry over to his Nick Toxic game avatar, he couldn't hide the expression in his voice. "Want to play Rat Patrol?"

"Oh yeah." Rudy jumped over the wall, ran up to the Jeep, and slid into the front seat.

Nick followed him across the wall, and jumped into the back. Grabbing hold of the Browning M2 submachine gun, he locked in a chain of ammunition.

"Where should we go?" Rudy yelled as the engine of the Jeep roared to life.

"Who cares?" Nick yelled back. "Just go."

Rudy backed out of the space at high speed and slammed on the brakes, throwing Nick out of the back.

Nick rolled across the pavement a few times before coming to a rest. He looked up to see the Jeep speeding away. It got all the way to the other end of the parkade before Rudy realized Nick had fallen off. The tires of the Jeep squealed, and it reversed, backing to where it had left him.

He jumped back into the Jeep, and they started going up the levels of the parkade at high speed. To get the hang of the .45, he fired shots into the parked cars lining the lanes, and twice they ran across some lower-level players, literally.

They crested the top of the parkade and broke into daylight. Rudy slammed on the brakes, and they squealed to a halt. Not fifty feet from them, against the back wall of the parkade stood Nick's nemesis, DeathChick82.

The sun was at her back, giving the appearance that a halo of white light emanated from her black body armor. She was surrounded by a bunker of sandbags, and she was aiming a M134 7.62mm General Electric mini-gun, capable of firing up to 6,000 rounds per second, the favored weapon of Terminators, and capable of cutting a WWII-era Jeep into tiny pieces.

"Good afternoon, boys. Did you miss me?"

"Ready to die, bitch?" yelled Rudy.

She leveled the mini-gun at them. "You first."

Rudy whispered, "Get ready." He jammed straight into second gear and pushed the accelerator to the floor. The tires squealed and then took hold.

Nick tried to hold his machine gun steady, but the sudden acceleration made it hard for him to concentrate his fire. His tracer rounds pounded harmlessly into the sandbags or flew over DeathChick82's head.

DeathChick82 released a torrent of hot lead into the engine compartment of the Jeep, which lurched and died before covering the fifty feet to the sandbag bunker. Nick dived right, and Rudy dived left as the stream of bullets climbed up the Jeep. Rolling behind a nearby parked car, Nick tried to think of a strategy.

The noise of the machine gun stopped. "I should thank you," called DeathChick82 over the roar of the fire consuming their Jeep.

"What for?" Rudy yelled.

"For taking cover so close to the line of claymores I hid under the parked cars."

Nick dropped to the ground and looked under the car he had been hiding behind. Under it was a green-painted metal box with "FRONT, TOWARD ENEMY," written on it. "Oh, shi—"

Nick's view became red tinged, and then went black.

You have died. You can re-enter play in five minutes.

4:59

4:58

"That whore!" Rudy pulled off his headset and threw it to the floor. "Can you believe this shit? We were in game for what? Twenty minutes? It was like she was waiting for us."

"Actually, she was probably waiting for Cof!nF!l3r, but we were the next best thing."

"Now we have to wait a whole five minutes to re-spawn."

"I don't think that's going to be an issue," Nick pointed out, calmly setting down his controller. "I think you just broke your headset. I've told you not to throw it around like that."

Rudy picked up the headset. It had split down the middle and hung in two pieces. "Shit. I swear that one of these days, I'm going to nail that bitch."

4

Drinking Tea

"Calm down, Rudy." Nick took the broken controller from his friend. "We can always try to tape it back together, and even if you did permanently break it, we can get a new one. The game store is open until nine."

"Yeah, I guess so," Rudy said, obviously pouting.

"If you're interested, I have a new formula I've been working on."

Rudy's eyes lit up. "Why are we just standing around then?"

"Aren't you interested in what it is?" Nick asked.

"You're the mixmaster. If you say it's good, it will be good."

"Okay," said Nick, heading for the kitchen. "But this recipe takes a while."

Nick spent the next hour heating and straining. He worked with three varieties of tea, only two of which were truly tea and one that wasn't strictly legal. At one point, he so overheated his cheap teapot that the spout went from erect to flaccid. He would have to remember to buy himself a sturdier pot. When the tea was done, it was thick, like sludge.

Rudy sniffed it tentatively. "It's very aromatic. I'm a little worried it might give me anosmia." He made a face and poked the thick tea with his finger, failing to break the surface tension.

"What?" Nick asked.

"Anosmia, it's the loss of smell."

"Ah."

Rudy tipped up the cup and waited for the tea to reach the lip of the cup. As the tea oozed, he tried to open up a bag of Doritos with his free hand, managing to spill half of them on the carpet. "Oops." When some tea finally found its way into his mouth, he bit off the end and chewed. "What's in this stuff, Toxic?"

When Nick finished chewing his own tea, he said, "I wanted to create something that would let us game all night. I'm still experimenting with the formula, but this one is the strongest batch yet. I start with this Kenyan tea, which looks more like ground coffee, then I add some Peruvian Chacruna—"

Nick was interrupted by squealing tires in the parking lot outside. He turned to look through the patio door and saw a giant, red truck in front of his building. As it slowly maneuvered and parked, he got a look at who was driving. "Oh, shit. It's my cousins."

Soon, Carrey was walking up the sidewalk. He looked sharp, wearing a tailored sport coat over a V-neck shirt, giving a simultaneously dressy and casual look. He knocked on his sliding glass door. When Nick slid it open, Carrey threw open his arms. "Cousin Nick!" he said, like they had not seen each other in years. "It's good to see you, but what are these bandages?"

Nick could not have answered at that moment if he had tried. Carrey's hug was like a stress test to determine whether his ribs or his spine would shatter first. Nick had just a moment to breathe in as he was passed to Larry, who gave him similar treatment, but lacked the strength to kill with an overenthusiastic hug. The smaller, but still quite large, brother was wearing a button-up shirt emphasizing his slim figure.

"Yes, Cousin," Larry said. "Why are you hurt?"

"It's nothing really," Nick explained, "just a scratch."

Carrey nodded. "Fine then. You be more careful in future. We don't want anything to happen to our favorite cousin. Speaking of which, why do you never come to our house?"

"Well," Nick said. "Uncle Earl keeps me pretty busy, and we do see each other at Sunday dinners." To change the subject and follow proper protocol, he continued with, "Could I get you guys a cup of tea? It's a special brew, my own recipe."

"Certainly," Larry said. "We will be patient and wait."

Larry and Carrey made their way across the living room, crunching the spilled Doritos into the carpet on their way. They sat down on either side of Rudy, making him look tiny.

Nick went into the kitchen and used a wooden spoon to scoop some tea into cups. He returned from the kitchen and handed them out to his cousins before sitting in a chair across from the couch.

The two big men lifted their cups and waited for the thick, brown liquid to reach their mouths. Maybe Nick had made it too strong. He'd heard stories of people overdosing on energy drinks. Could his tea actually be dangerous?

When Larry finally got a taste, he lowered his cup and said, "Is good."

"Yes, is very good, Cousin," Carrey agreed. "Very strong."

"This tea," said Larry, "reminds me of the old country. They used to serve good, strong tea in orphanage. On many days in the long winter, it was the only way to stay warm. It tastes of sad memories and loss."

Carrey nodded. "Days of darkness. Thank you, Cousin Nick."

For a second, Nick wasn't sure if they were being sarcastic. Then Larry added, "We owe Papa and all the Bakers a gratitude for bringing us to this country and welcoming us as family. Papa is a good man for taking us under his wing."

Nick was surprised both by the outpouring of emotion from his cousins, who he still remembered as his childhood tormentors. They had probably meant well, but hardened in the cruel orphanages of Eastern Europe, they had lacked the sensibilities of American children and failed to realize the effect their actions had on him.

Larry raised his tea glass and said, "*Noroc.*" Everyone took another drink.

When they finished chewing, Rudy set down his cup. His focus shifted to his right hand, and he wiggled his fingers, gazing at the movement in disbelief. "I seem to be experiencing optical hallucinations. Cool." When he looked back up, his pupils were black voids.

Nick felt something shift deep inside him, not a gastric something, more like someone was turning his volume knob from two to ten, making him hum with potential. He felt hot and cold at the same time. He looked over at Rudy, who was digging his fingers into the couch cushions.

"Is it hot in here?" Rudy asked in slow motion. Was space and time starting to warp, right here in Nick's apartment?

"Well," said Larry, somehow avoiding the time warp Rudy had been caught in, despite sitting right next to him on the couch, "isn't this nice. It is Saturday and the nighttime, and here we are with our favorite cousin and friend..."

"Rudy," Rudy supplied.

"We should go out," Larry continued, "hit the town."

Even with their statements of affection, Nick wasn't crazy about going out with his cousins. He was sure their ideas about what constituted a fun Saturday night were different from his. "I don't know, Larry. We planned to play *Global Fight!* tonight. We were actually on our way to get Rudy a new game headset." Nick held up the broken controller to demonstrate their need.

Carrey nodded. "We need to show him Dong's."

Before Nick could ask what they meant, Rudy started laughing uncontrollably. "Twice in one day," he said between gasps. "Why does everyone want to show you their dicks?" His laugh went on quite a long time, doubling him over as if in pain.

"Not show him dicks," Carrey said, agitated, "show him Dong's, our favorite electronics store. Trust me, it's a good place. You will get good deal."

Nick looked back and forth from Larry to Carrey, enjoying the 3D effect of real life. "We were just going to go to Mega Buy—"

Larry stood. "We would not hear of it. Please, come with us, and if Dong doesn't show you something you like, we will take you to Mega Buy."

Nick stood too, and swayed. His ears didn't seem to be working right, and his vision had narrowed down to a small point.

"Oh," said Rudy. "I definitely want to see what Dong's has to show us." He hopped up from the couch, clearing the coffee table and landing in the middle of the living room.

"I think I made the tea too strong," someone said, and Nick realized he was the one speaking. That made sense. He was the one that had made the tea, so he would be the one who had made it too strong.

Larry grabbed Nick's hand and led him out to the Hummer, talking excitedly the whole time. At least, Nick assumed he was talking. His lips were moving and he was gesturing with his free hand, but the volume seemed turned down, and Nick couldn't make out any of the actual words.

Nick was happy Larry held his arm, as Nick had achieved the buoyancy of a helium balloon, making him worry about drifting away on a sudden gust of wind. He had to be at church tomorrow morning, and it wouldn't do if he got caught by a sudden gust and snagged on a high tree branch.

As Larry was tucking Nick into the back of the Hummer, Nick gave him a hug, as thanks for not letting him fly away.

"You are in a good mood tonight, Cousin," Larry said, holding Nick's head down like a police officer would, so he wouldn't hit it on the roof of the car. Before Nick could answer him, he shut the door.

Nick watched colors shift outside the Hummer's window, and he realized he was watching headlights of other cars. They were simultaneously multi-colored and black-and-white at the same time. Things shifted oddly, and Nick realized the show outside his window had become a still life. He stared at it until Larry opened the door. He blinked for the first time in quite a while.

"What's going on?" Nick asked, trying not to yell, but feeling like he was failing.

"We are at electronics store." Larry said, helping him out of the back of the Hummer.

Nick felt cool air on his face. Gravel crunched under his feet. He blinked a couple times until his eyes focused. They were standing in a dark alley outside what seemed like an abandoned warehouse.

Carrey led their group to an unmarked metal door and knocked. As they waited, Nick tried to peer into the inky-blackness behind the windows, but realized they had been painted that color.

The door opened, letting out a waft of cold air. An Asian man, maybe Chinese, with a spider web tattoo on his neck stood in the doorway, wearing a heavy coat. When he saw Carrey, he bowed, and then stood aside to let them enter.

Carrey patted the man on the shoulder. "Good to see you again." He stepped past into the building, and everyone followed him.

Once inside, the warehouse feel did not dissipate. The first thing Nick noticed was the chill. Despite the coolness of the night, it must have been at least twenty degrees cooler in the warehouse. Hung up along a stretch of wall were a number of white coats. Larry and Carrey both put one on, although in Carrey's case, the one-size-fits-all didn't fit that well. Nick and Rudy followed suit, acquiring coats for themselves.

They walked down a long hallway lined by metal shelves. On the shelves were stacked boxes with "USDA Grade A Beef" written on them, as well as things like, "Angus Beef fresh from Iowa." Every few steps, Nick would start shrinking or growing, or at least going uphill or downhill as the hallway stayed level. Once in a while, they would pass a door filled with similar boxes or hanging sides of beef. Nick concentrated on putting one foot in front of the other and staying the same height. The hallway ended in another large metal door, and when they went through, the air was abruptly warm.

The room reminded Nick of his Uncle Earl's office, except everything had an upscale-Chinese-restaurant feel. At the far end, a Chinese man sat behind a high, polished desk. He was flanked by two scantily-clad young women, one was giving him a manicure and the other was actually fanning him with an oversized fan, like in a movie.

When Nick was twelve, recovering from his panic attack, he had gone for a walk in the hospital. About halfway through his meandering, he'd needed to use a restroom. Finding a men's room, Nick opened the door and walked in. Two steps inside the door, he realized two things. The restroom was spacious but meant for one person, and it was already occupied. He was frozen in place. He didn't know the protocol. He was, after all, in a public restroom, and the man hadn't locked the door. Plus, backtracking now meant opening the door and exposing the room to the hallway a second time. Being that it was a public restroom, and the door had been unlocked, Nick opted to wait casually looking the other way and pointedly ignoring the close quarters. To this day, he wasn't sure he'd made the right decision. He counted the incident as one of the most awkward moments of his life. For some reason, watching the Chinese man be pampered by nearly-naked women reminded him of that experience.

"Ah," the Chinese man said as they entered, "the Baker boys. Please come in, won't you?"

Larry bowed. "Fang Dong, I didn't know you would be in tonight."

"In my native China, management relationships tend to be hierarchical in nature. However, when working in the West, I believe a hands-on management style encourages loyalty. I want to be thought of as more than an employer."

"Fang," Carrey said, "let me present to you my cousin, Nick Baker, and his friend, Rudy."

Fang's face lit up in recognition. He came around the desk to shake Nick's hand. "Nick Baker, I was a good friend of your father, James. We did some business many years ago in Vietnam."

Through the fog of Triple Tea, Nick tried to fathom this. Maybe Fang Dong wasn't Chinese. Hadn't they fought on the other side? Was it racist if he asked? Also, he was pretty sure his father had been twelve when the Vietnam War ended. "Oh, that's nice."

"He was instrumental in designing my toothbrush factory in Kon Tum." He looked closely at Nick. "You have injured yourself?" He raised a tentative hand toward Nick's forehead.

Nick took a step backward. "I'm fine, Fang Dong. Just a scratch."

Fang Dong nodded. "Very well. Now, what favor can I do for the son of James Baker?"

Rudy stepped forward. "I need a *Global Fight!* controller." To Nick, he looked a little off. His eyes were dilated, and he was swaying slightly. Nick wondered if he looked as bad from his tea experimentation. Larry and Carrey seemed unaffected.

"Ah, I think I can accommodate you." He dialed a number on the desk phone and shouted a short burst of what Nick assumed was Chinese, which echoed through the building on an overhead speaker system. After he hung up the phone, he said, "I will need fifty dollars."

"That's actually a little expensive for just a controller," Rudy complained. Rudy was always short on cash. He was still in college, after all, and probably would be for life.

Carrey slapped his hand over Rudy's mouth and whispered something in his ear.

Larry stepped forward and bowed again. "I am sorry Fang Dong. We did not mean disrespect. This one has... shit-talking..."

"Diarrhea of the mouth?" suggested Fang Dong.

Larry nodded. "Yes, that is what I was looking for."

Fang Dong slowly drew his hand from the attentions of his manicurist and stood, although with the size of his chair, this did little to add to his height. Nick estimated him at around five-four. He walked around the desk, and Nick could see Fang Dong's shoes also added a couple inches. Fang clapped his hands and barked two words in, assumedly, Chinese. The women fled the room.

Walking up to Rudy, Fang Dong put his hand on Rudy's shoulder and stood on his toes to better look Rudy in the eyes. "For fifty dollars, I am giving you a full console system with two platinum controllers and headsets. Is that too expensive?"

"No. That's a great deal," Rudy said, somehow looking smaller than the tiny Asian man. He pulled a credit card from his wallet.

Fang Dong shook his head. "This is a cash only deal. If you want a paper trail, then I will direct you to Mega Buy."

Rudy lowered his gaze. "I'm sorry then..."

Larry pulled a large roll of money from his pocket. After searching through several hundred dollar bills, he found a fifty and handed it to Fang Dong. "Here you go. I am sure Cousin Nick's friend is good for money."

"Thanks, Larry," Rudy said. Nick mentally added the fifty to the rest of the money Rudy owed him. He knew he'd probably never get it back, but if he did, maybe he'd buy a nice computer or something.

Larry poked Rudy in the chest with a thick finger. "When you get it, give the money to Cousin Nick."

Rudy nodded quickly. "Of course. Consider it done. I wouldn't dream of not paying Nick."

An asian man walked in from the refrigerated section carrying boxes. He set down his burden, then plucked the top one from the pile and offered it to his master.

Fang Dong poked at the contents for a moment. "Excellent." Fang Dong took the box from his minion and held it out to Nick. "Son of James Baker, I believe you will find everything here promised to your friend."

Nick wondered what he should do with the box. He passed it to Rudy. "Thank you, Fang Dong."

The underling passed the second box to Fang Dong, who held it out to Nick. "Out of respect for your father, and in hopes that you and I will one day do business, let me present you with this gift."

Nick took the box from Fang Dong. There was a pause, which started to go on for a moment. Larry put his hand on Nick's shoulder and squeezed. Nick realized he was supposed to say something, but he was at a loss on exactly what to do. What would Captain Picard do in this situation? "I am honored by your gift, Fang Dong."

"In this box you will find both top sirloin and T-bone steaks. I am very enamored with the quality of your Iowa beef. I export large quantities back to China."

"Thank you," Nick said, feeling awkward accepting a compliment on behalf of Iowa's beef-producing industry. As he stood, holding his meat, he watched the little man's aura, a great dragon, dwarfing everyone in the room. He attributed this to the effects of the tea, as he did the tendency of the florescent lights to wander around the ceiling.

Fang took hold of Nick's shoulder and stood on his tiptoes to whisper in his ear. "This is not the time, but I have a business proposition of great value to offer you."

"Oh," Nick said, "that's nice."

Balancing his box of *Global Fight!* paraphernalia in one arm, Rudy picked up a magazine off Fang Dong's desk. "Crochet Rocket? Do you crochet, Fang Dong?"

"Yes, I have recently made a toilet paper roll cozy that looks like there is a little squirrel peeking out of it. In a high-stress job such as mine, I find it helps me find order in a world of chaos." He clapped his hands. "But excuse me. I'm keeping you from enjoying your evening, and I need to return to my mani-pedi."

The scantily clad manicurists, perhaps summoned by his hand clap, returned to the office and held the doors open for them.

As they were walking out through the sides of beef and boxes of frozen meat parts, Rudy said, "That was the weirdest experience of my life."

"Why," Nick asked, "because you were nearly killed by a Chinese gangster?"

"No, because the florescent lights kept crawling all over the ceiling."

Nick nodded. "Next time, I'm not going to steep the tea as long."

For some reason, the trip down the hallway was all downhill this time. In fact, Nick had gained so much momentum by the time he reached the end, he tripped on his way out the door. Larry's big hands caught him. "Careful there, Cousin."

"I think I made the tea too strong." Nick blinked several times. "I think I should go home."

"Nonsense," Larry said, tucking him back into the Hummer. "I doubt you could sleep anyway. Now is the time to party."

After Carrey crawled into the front seat, he handed Nick a bottle. "If you don't feel good, take two of these."

Nick fished two pills from the bottle. They were red, with a Soviet hammer and sickle imprinted on them. "What are these?" he asked.

"They will make you feel better." Carrey took back the bottle and popped two of the pills in his mouth. "See, not problem, or are you chicken?"

Not wanting to look like a wimp in front of his cousin, Nick downed the pills, barely managing to choke them down without water.

"Can I see those?" Rudy said, snatching the bottle out of Carrey's hand. He tipped the bottle up to his lips.

Carrey hurriedly took back his bottle. "Whoa, let's slow down there, cowboy. These are very strong, not even legal in the US."

Rudy and Carrey continued to talk back and forth, but Nick felt like he had water in his ears. He looked back and forth as Carrey and Rudy talked, but he heard only the gentle waves of the ocean.

Sometime during the car trip, everything shifted into fast motion. There was cool night air on his face. They were outside in a parking lot. Then they were inside, and Nick was dancing with a beautiful blonde woman in a tiny black dress, the kind of pretty girl he was afraid to talk to when he was in college. The fast motion slowed, and he realized they were grinding pelvises on the dance floor, her dress riding up, showing him the lace around the top of her stockings, pushed so tight he could feel her body through their clothes, and he was sure she could feel his rock-hard erection. This contact did not, however, deter her, instead, she seemed more intent upon rubbing up against him in ways that would drive him insane with lust. She was extraordinarily gifted at this.

Time started to bend again, and Nick was lying on the side of a hill in a field. Everyone else was there, including the blonde woman, who was still all but attached to him.

He seemed to be lecturing her. "I come from a long line of wealthy and noble men, who singlehandedly made their fortunes by stomping on those less fortunate. I just want to be my own person, a normal guy, you know, not some scion tasked with regaining my family fortune. We need more equality, not dynasties protecting their giant fortunes across generations."

"You know," said Larry, "the Soviets took over our country and tried to make everyone equal. We didn't like it that much."

"More equality does not mean absolute, state-enforced equality. I think there's probably a happy middle ground." Nick had a liquor bottle in his hand. He took a drink, and it tasted like licorice. "Where did we get this?" He asked.

Carrey pushed himself up on his shoulder. "Little man give it to us, a little man with a pointy beard."

Nick tried to focus his memory through a haze of alcohol, pills, and tea. "Wait, did the little guy have a beard? Was he really tiny, and was his beard red, like brick red?"

Larry nodded. "Sounds like the guy."

The blonde woman sat up and straightened her dress. "Well, it was lovely, Nick, but I have to be in church tomorrow morning, and so do you." She stood up and started walking gracefully down the hill, barely staggering.

"She makes a good point," said Larry. "We all have to be in church tomorrow."

Nick tried to stand up, and fell back down. "I seem to have lost the use of my legs."

"Do not worry," said Larry. "I've got you, working class hero."

Nick fell asleep in Larry's arms as he was carried down the hill. His memory was a little sporadic after that. He vaguely remembered throwing up, taking the keys to the Hummer, and promising Carrey he would drink lots of water.

Nick's phone rang at 7:00 AM the next morning. He slapped his alarm clock, and when the phone didn't stop ringing, he slapped it hard enough to knock it off his night table. Determining the actual source of the noise, he leaned over the side of his bed, reaching for his pants. Too late, he realized he was already wearing his pants and fell off the side of the bed. Lying on his back on the floor, his head hurting so much he didn't want to live anymore, he answered his phone.

"Nicholas, this is your mother speaking. I believe I left my umbrella at your house. Could you please bring it to church with you this morning?" She paused. "Are you there, dear?"

Deep within the crevices of pain within head, Nick managed to say, "Umbrella. Bring to church."

"You sound odd, dear. Did I wake you?"

"Of course not, Mother. I just finished my first cup of coffee. Just feeling a little groggy." According to the etiquette taught to him by his mother, admitting you were inconvenienced was impolite to your caller. Then again, he was pretty sure you weren't supposed to call people at seven in the morning either. Maybe there was an exemption for Sundays, when you were supposed to be getting ready for church.

"Oh, good. I love you. See you at church."

"Love you. See you at church."

Nick considered lying on the floor for the rest of the morning, or at least until he died, whichever was sooner. Deep down though, he knew he would have to get up. Sooner or later, he was going to be sick. Probably sooner.

Standing up, he found a glass of water on the nightstand along with a pair of aspirin and a set of keys. A note was stuck to the glass of water, reading "take aspirin and drink." By the lack of fancy stationary and the scrawled handwriting, he inferred the note had been left by one of his cousins. He picked up the glass and drank the contents, which tasted like water, only more painful. He picked up the keys, which had "H2" inscribed into the plastic grips.

He staggered into the bathroom and threw up. This made him feel considerably better. Then he took two more aspirin to replace the pair he just hurled into the toilet. He continued his morning rituals until, an hour later, he was showered, dressed, and coffeed.

The marks on his forehead looked worse. They were turning puffy. He was pretty sure this was a bad thing. Probably some kind of infection which would get into his brain and kill him. He hoped it hurried up.

Larry and Carrey had left him the red H2. It was a little conspicuous for his taste, and it didn't get the gas mileage of his Corolla—he liked to think of himself as a green person. Still, he couldn't complain. His cousins were just trying to do him a favor, and his only other option was the bicycle someone had left on his patio. He was in no condition to ride a bicycle.

His legs were shaking with fatigue, and it took him two tries to crawl up into the truck. The gigantic Hummer immediately made him miss his little car as he tried to get used to the immense thing by backing out of a parking spot without destroying the cars to either side of him or the garages behind him. He tried to use a three-point turn, just to be safe, but it turned into more of a twelve-point turn.

He arrived at the church on the late side, and hustled into the building as they were shutting the doors. His mother was in the second pew from the front, the one long-established as the Baker pew. As Nick walked up the center aisle to join her, he felt like everyone was watching him and judging him, like they knew how hungover he was.

Larry and Carrey were also in the Baker pew, composed as ever, showing no ill-effects from the previous night. Uncle Earl was absent, of course, as it was the middle of golf season.

Next to Nick's mother was a woman Nick had never seen before. She was blonde, and had a pretty face. The rest of her was hidden under a floppy hat and a voluminous dress.

On the other side of Nick's mother, sat her dog, David. Of course, everyone knew that dogs shouldn't come to church, but rules were there for lesser people than Esther Baker. Reverend Collins would never dream to exclude the dog of his biggest donor, and if the little David was all right with Reverend Collins, no one else dared say anything.

"Good morning, Mother," Nick said, sitting down on the side of the dog.

"I don't suppose you remembered my umbrella?" his mother asked.

Nick rested his aching head on the pew in front of him. Even through the bandages, his forehead made a solid thump against the oak, startling the people sitting ahead of them.

"Nicholas Randall Baker!" his mother whisper-yelled and hit him on the arm. "What is wrong with you today? Sit up straight and proud. Everyone can see us. And why do you have those ridiculous bandages on your head?

Nick sat up straight and proud. "Yes, Mother. I'm sorry about the bandages. I hurt my head."

"Well, be more careful. If it's a serious wound, I hope you saw the doctor. I don't want to be known as the woman with the disfigured son."

"Yes, mother," Nick said, knowing that this was her way of showing affection, probably.

"Now be quiet. Reverend Collins is about to begin."

Reverend Collins approached his podium and spoke. "Good morning, everyone. Before we get started, I want to mention the great sale we are having in our garden center." He lifted up a white, plastic bag. "How much would you expect to pay for this high-quality organic fertilizer? Twenty dollars? Fifteen dollars..." Nick zoned out as Collins continued his sales pitch. "...And finally, all dry cat food is twenty percent off for the rest of the month."

When the reverend finished with the sales, he gave the church an update on his ever-continuing fight with the IRS. It included several references to Washington D.C. as a modern day Sodom and Gomorrah. This gave Nick pause. Surely Washington couldn't embody both Sodom *and* Gomorrah. Maybe Sodom could be Washington, and Gomorrah could be Baltimore?

Collins settled into his sermon, which went smoothly until the Bible reading. "Today," he said, "we read from the Book of Samuel, a tale that reminds me of our own small church's fight with the federal government, the story of the colossal Philistine Goliath, and a tiny shepherd named David."

On hearing his name, David raised his head, and spoke. "*Woof.*"

Nick looked over at his mother. Her face had gone red. The blonde woman beside her seemed to be struggling to hide a laugh. His mother buried her face in a hymnal.

"The shield bearer of the Philistine army, the giant Goliath, approached David."

"*Woof.*"

"The giant looked David—"

"*Woof.*"

"...over and saw only a boy. He instantly disliked David—"

"*Woof.*"

"...and said to him, 'David—'"

"*Woof.*"

"'...am I a dog, that you come at me with sticks?'" Reverend Collins seemed to be a little lost, like he had been thrown off his game by the barking corgi. "The Philistine cursed David—"

"*Woof.*"

"...by his gods. 'Come here,' he said, 'and I will give your flesh to the birds and breasts.'" This brought an involuntary chuckle from the congregation. "Excuse me. The birds and the beasts."

The reverend cleared his throat. "David—"

"*Woof.*"

At first Nick had enjoyed the chaos ensuing from the little dog, but now his head was throbbing with every bark, like a hammer striking him in the back of the head, always hitting the exact same spot. All he wanted to do was get out of the pew and breathe fresh air. He sighed loudly, and called out, "I think we all know this story, can you skip ahead?"

There were a few murmurs of disapproval and a momentary silence. Then, Collins said, "Perhaps that would be for the best. Thank you, Nick." He cleared his throat and continued.

"As David—"

"*Woof.*"

"...triumphed over the Philistine with a sling and a stone, so will we save our church from the armies of the Internal Revenue Service. They have armies of Philistines ready to attack us, but like King David—"

"*Woof.*"

"...we have God in our hearts."

After a couple more songs, another commercial, and final prayers, Collins wrapped things up. As they left their pew, Nick waited to escort his mother. Instead of taking his arm, she escorted the blonde in the floppy hat out of the church, leaving Nick to follow behind them.

"Reverend Collins is a visionary man," his mother said to the blonde woman. "Wait until I show you the plans for the new facility."

Nick realized that she must be buttering up the woman for a donation to the church. She was probably some rich trophy wife, looking to join a cause to keep life interesting. Now, everything made sense.

They walked outside to the strip mall parking lot, where people were congregating before going home, or heading to the church's store to shop for their weekly groceries. When they had cleared the doorway by a considerate distance, Nick's mother turned to him and said, "Nick Baker, allow me to present you to Penelope Stafford Jennings." When Nick didn't immediately show a sign of recognition, his mother said, "Of the *Philadelphia* Stafford Jennings. Her grandfather and your grandfather often did business."

With the ache in his head, Nick couldn't have cared less, but he didn't want to seem impolite. "Of course, the Philadelphia Stafford Jennings. I'm very pleased to meet you, Penelope."

"Actually," she said, in a boarding-school accent which grated on Nick's hangover, "we've already met. Last night. A little guy with a bright red beard came up to me, and said he was your friend. We danced for about an hour."

"Um..." Of course. Nick hadn't recognized her with so many clothes on. Again, the demonic creature was messing with his life. Why had he been targeted by this minion of evil?

Nick's mother clasped her hands in front of her heart. "Oh, how wonderful, I do enjoy a formal dance, but I wasn't aware there were any functions last evening."

Penelope smiled. "It was a less-than-formal venue, Mrs. Baker."

"Oh," Nick's mother made a face, "a dance hall. Well, I suppose you're both at that age."

"Don't worry, Mrs. Baker. I have met young men from America's finest families, and I can assure you that, despite our surroundings, Nick conducted himself like a true gentleman."

Nick blushed at the thought that less than eight hours ago, he had been thrusting his trouser-clad erection at Penelope in a tea-fueled frenzy.

She winked at him.

Reverend Collins waddled up to them. The big man was already sweating in the mid-day sun. He blotted his forehead with a handkerchief. "Esther, who is this enchanting young lady you've brought to us?"

The Reverend and Penelope did all their introductions and hellos. Then Collins said, "Of course, I've seen the awful things they write about you in the tabloids, but I don't believe a word written in those nasty things."

"Well you should," she said, "because they're all true."

There was a moment of awkward silence, and then Penelope put her hand to her face and let out a little chuckle. Suddenly, everyone was laughing. Despite his less-than-jovial mood, Nick added a couple chuckles to seem like he was in the spirit of things. Penelope winked at him again.

"You're very lucky to be here today," the reverend said. "This afternoon is the groundbreaking for our new church…"

As Reverend Collins talked at Penelope, Nick's mother walked him a few feet away for some private conversation. "What do you think of Penelope?"

Nick tried to clear his mind of the image of Penelope's stockings. "She seems nice enough."

"I want you to make a good impression on her. She comes from the right kind of family to be suitable for the Baker heir. The prominence of her family will help restore the Baker name to its former glory."

Nick wondered where she was headed with this line of thought. "So, like for publicity reasons, you want me to be seen with her?"

His mother put her hand on his arm. "Nicholas, I don't want you to get upset."

"Upset about what?"

"You have to understand that as the heir, you have responsibilities. Your Uncle Earl has worked really hard negotiating this deal."

Nick still didn't understand. "What kind of deal are you talking about?"

"It's all for the greater good," his mother said. "To extend the Baker legacy into the next century, we have arranged for Penelope Stafford Jennings to be your bride."

5

DEDICATION

At a young age, Nick Baker had learned things about the Universe that made him seem insignificant. He knew the Earth traveled around the Sun for a period of time called a year. Also, the Moon traveled around the Sun in about a month, causing varying amounts of nighttime illumination and tides, and, by extension, moonlit strolls on the beach. Nick knew the Sun, or Sol, sat in the spiral arm of a grouping of stars called the Milky Way galaxy that, somehow, caused candy bars. He knew all of these phenomena were governed by the force of gravity, mass, and inertia of a magnitude that could only be called astronomical. None of these facts were as immutable as the reality of a Baker Sunday Dinner.

Nick really wanted to go home and nurse his pounding head. Instead, he was escorting the stranger, soon to be his bride, to Baker House. He glanced across the cab of the H2 at Penelope. She looked like fashion models did after the photographer was done photoshopping them to perfection. Nick found it kind of horrifying, especially the way her long blonde hair stayed perfectly still, like calm waters before a hurricane. However, she was fidgeting ever so slightly, picking at her lavish dress as if she was uncomfortable, and this seemed to make her a little more human.

"Is your dress bothering you?" Nick asked, wondering if this was too intrusive a question for polite company.

"Oh, no. I'm just not used to wearing clothes like this. I feel so over-dressed and frumpy."

He looked back just in time to see the nearest stoplight had turned yellow. Immediately, a group of college students stepped into the crosswalk, forcing Nick to stand on the brakes to avoid jellifying them with the three ton Hummer. Oblivious to their narrow escape from the laws of inertia, the students proceeded unharmed across the street. This kind of chicken-game was a University of Iowa tradition, and Nick had to admit, he had been guilty of it when he had gone to school.

"Are you attending the groundbreaking ceremony this afternoon?" He asked as they sat at the light, hoping for some kind of conversational segue.

"That's what they tell me." She said no more.

When Nick parked the Hummer outside his ancestral home, his nerves were frazzled from the dual stress of unobservant pedestrians and impending nuptials. His voice shook as he said, "Welcome to Baker House."

Penelope gave the house an evaluating look. "How quaint."

Nick didn't know how he felt about the opulent old house being called "quaint." He actually felt obligated to defend his ancestral home. "We've always liked it. It's really more than the family has needed. We don't even use the third floor anymore, and the attic..."

"Oh, it's quite lovely," she said in a way that somehow communicated, "I'm sure it will make a lovely funeral home someday."

In keeping with his upbringing, Nick tried to stay positive and polite, "Well, shall we go inside then?"

"Look, Nick, I'm sure you're a nice guy, but I'm only here because my grandfather wants on the Board of Directors of Baker Dental. So you don't have to be nice to me or anything."

"Well, as long as we're here, we might as well make the best of things. I think you'll enjoy Sunday dinner. My mother's housekeeper is a pretty good cook."

"I'm *sure* she is," Penelope said. Nick wished she could at least try to keep the sarcasm out of her voice.

Opening his door and sliding to the ground, Nick walked around the vehicle to open Penelope's door. She rotated in her seat, which pulled her dress up above her knees. Nick tried to look away, but he had to offer her his hand to help her step down to the curb. As she slid from her perch, the dress pulled up further, revealing impractical underwear under her practical dress. He told himself it would be sleazy to look, but he looked anyway. Somehow the illusion that he was sneaking some forbidden peek was more titillating than the intentionally revealing outfit she had worn the previous evening.

Nick was a little disappointed in himself for his attraction. Penelope was beautiful on the outside, but he didn't even know if they had anything in common. He knew she was devoted to keeping her inheritance, but he didn't consider that a virtue.

Still, there was no reason to be impolite. Nick offered her his arm to escort her inside.

Penelope looked at his arm like he had tried to hand her a dead eel. "I'm sure I can manage by myself."

Nick sighed and let his shoulders slump. "Okay, whatever." He closed his eyes for a few seconds to relieve the burning and let out a groan.

"Just how hungover are you right now?" Penelope asked.

Nick shook his head. "Don't worry about me. I'm fine."

"Nonsense. I was with you last night. You drank half a bottle of ouzo, and that was on top of whatever you'd taken earlier."

"Yeah." Nick felt his face redden. "I was really out of it. I'm sorry."

"Oh, no. Don't apologize. You're a lot of fun when you're wasted." She reached into her purse. "Take these. They're some experimental painkillers Stafford Pharmaceutical is working on. They're great for hangovers."

Nick took the pills, but didn't put them in his mouth. "Are these even legal?" he asked. The last time someone has given him unidentifiable pills, things had not gotten better.

Penelope shrugged. "You'll live. Aren't you going to take them?"

"When I get some water."

Penelope rolled her eyes. "Don't worry, they're coated."

"Oh, okay." Nick still wished he had some water, but he didn't want to look weak in front of his assigned fiancé.

"Why are you making that face?" she asked.

"Just trying to work up some saliva."

"Take the pills, Nick. They taste like candy."

He popped the pills in his mouth and swallowed. They tasted like old gym socks and burned going down. "Ug, that was like eating athlete's foot."

Penelope looked rather amused. "Do you just believe anything anyone tells you?"

"No, but I didn't expect my fiancé would try to poison me."

Penelope gave him a look like she was sizing him up and considering possibilities. "Good to know." She turned and started up the sidewalk.

Uncle Earl met them at the door. He had dressed for dinner, which meant he'd probably cut his morning golf short and only shot nine holes. He must have wanted to impress Penelope. "Welcome to our home, Miss Stafford Jennings. I'm Nick's uncle, Earl, so you can call me Uncle Earl. I've been speaking with your grandfather so often these days, I feel like I know you already. How's everything going?" He held out his hand.

"I'm doing quite well... Uncle Earl," Penelope said, taking his hand and allowing him to lead her inside, "and you simply must call me Penelope. I believe my grandfather is quite fond of you as well. Sometimes, I think maybe the two of you should be the ones getting married." She paused for a moment, and then snatched her hand away from Uncle Earl, presumably to raise it to her mouth and let out a little giggle.

Uncle Earl let out a huge guffaw. "My, you're a witty girl."

Penelope smiled. "That's what they tell me."

"You should have been out on the links this morning, Nick. I'm going to go finish the back nine when dinner's over. Do you want to come along?"

Nick shook he head. "No. I'll be escorting Penelope to the groundbreaking."

Uncle Earl shook his head. "You know, you don't have to do everything your mo— There you are, Esther."

Nick turned to see his mother walking into the foyer.

"Welcome, Penelope," she said. "Please join us in the main dining room. Dinner is served."

Larry and Carrey were already seated at the large mahogany table inset with the Baker coat of arms, a horror show of dental tools and appliances. Carrey was holding his table knife as if judging its ability to kill. David was also seated at the table in a booster chair, to the right of his mother. He wore a doggy dinner jacket.

They took their assigned seats, Uncle Earl assuming the head of the table. As the guest of honor, Penelope sat to the right of the lady of the house, or in this case the dog of the lady of the house, and Nick was seated next to Penelope. Gladys had used the eight-piece table setting rather than the thirteen piece, which meant Penelope was already being considered family and, thankfully, dinner would be served in only three courses.

When enough pleasantries had been made and soup had been served, Nick's mother cleared her throat. "Everyone," she announced, "and by everyone, I really mean Larry and Carrey because everyone else already knows, may I introduce Penelope Stafford Jennings. She and Nick are to be married."

Up until now, Nick had hoped he could somehow talk his way out of the wedding. This announcement around the ancestral table, however, cemented the family's position. He now had two choices. He could go against his mother and heritage or marry a sexy billionheiress. Still, maybe if he protested immediately, he could somehow reverse this decision.

"Actually, Mother, I really think we should talk about that—"

"What is there to talk about?" she asked.

"Well... No offense to you, Penelope. You're a lovely girl, but I don't even know you. This isn't the nineteenth century. People get a say in who they're going to marry."

His mother shook her head in disappointment. "Oh, Nicholas, things were going so well. This marriage is so important to the family. Why do you have to spoil things for everyone?"

"Nonsense!" Uncle Earl boomed. "It's natural for the boy to want to know his future bride. I think we're all curious about this young lady." He turned to Penelope. "So, Penelope, why don't you tell us what you think of the Midwest?"

"Well, it's the first time I've been here. It kind of reminds me of Eastern Europe." At the mention of Eastern Europe, Nick saw Larry and Carrey perk up.

Uncle Earl, who no doubt equated any comparison between the "commie" part of the world and the fertile, blessed plot of Iowa with an act of treason, raised an eyebrow. "Why do you say that?"

"Everyone eats so much meat," she said.

"In orphanage in Romania," Carrey said, knocking his accent up three notches, "we only had gruel, and whatever we could dig from garbage. I do not remember meat. Do you remember meat, Brother?"

Larry shook his head and turned his accent up to eleven. "No, no remember meat. To live in such bountiful place is true blessing."

Penelope actually looked horribly embarrassed. She hadn't exactly gone pale, but her tan had slipped a couple shades. "Oh, I'm sorry. I didn't realize. I mean..."

Penelope was saved by Gladys the housekeeper, who chose that moment to roll in a cart loaded with food, the cart being a concession to Gladys' age and the reluctance of Nick's mother to hire more help. Nick noted it held both a platter of ham along with a platter of roast beef, perhaps vindicating Penelope's accusations of meaty excess.

Carrey smiled. "What a beautiful meal. We are blessed to receive such a bounty, eh, Penelope?"

"Speaking of blessings," said Uncle Earl, snatching the conversation away from Carrey, "Esther, would you do the honors?"

Nick's mother bowed her head. "Oh, heavenly Father, thank you for the food you have brought to this table at the lowest prices available anywhere. Let it sustain us as we go forth and make more heavenly purchases in your name.

"Also, bless Nick and Penelope, whose marriage will not only unite two beautiful, young people, but also unite the families controlling two of America's leading dental manufacturing and supply companies. Amen."

As Gladys carried the platter of beef to Nick's mother, Carrey turned and used his dinner fork to harpoon a large chunk of greasy, dripping meat. He slammed it down on Penelope's plate. "Here. Eat. Is good."

No doubt used to impeccable displays of table manners, even the quick-witted Penelope seemed caught off guard. "Um... I don't really—"

"Eat," Carrey said insistently.

Nick might not want to marry Penelope, but neither did he want to see her accosted at the dinner table. "Please, Carrey," he said. "Leave Penelope alone. She doesn't want your meat."

"Maybe so, Cousin." Carrey again stabbed the hunk of meat and moved it to his own plate. "But question is, does she want yours?" He smiled mischievously.

"Now, Carrey," Penelope said. "There's no reason to be like that. Nick and I have just met each other. We have to get to know each other."

Uncle Earl crossed his arms. "I don't know why. The deal is done. The contracts are written. All we need to seal the deal is the wedding."

Carrey pointed at Nick. "And what about you? Do you like this spoiled rich girl? She has skinny hips, not good for breeding."

"Carrey!" Nick's mother yelled. "Please, we are at the dinner table." From the tone in her voice, Nick was glad she wasn't carrying a gun.

Larry, sitting quietly the entire time, decided to add his two cents. "Can we eat now? Meat is getting cold."

A brief cease-fire was called so Gladys could serve the meal. Once they had started eating again, Penelope threw out what might be considered an olive branch, "Carrey, I get the impression you don't like me."

Carrey nodded, and when he stopped chewing, he said, "I think spoiled girl like you doesn't deserve Cousin Nick. He is good man." Nick was a little surprised and flattered by this pronouncement.

"Now, Carrey," Nick's mother said, "there's no reason to be rude. Penelope is Nick's fiancé."

Penelope raised a skinny hand to quiet the table. "Please, Esther. I'm not a child. I can speak for myself." She turned to Carrey. "You call me a spoiled, rich girl, but Nick drove me here in an H2. I'm pretty sure he didn't do back-breaking labor and save up for it."

Carrey nodded. "Is true. Car is mine."

"And did you work hard to own such an expensive vehicle?"

"No, I win contest."

"Contest?"

"Yes. Reality show. They put ten people in a house. Whoever can convince others to leave gets one million dollars." His voice turned cold. "I can be quite convincing if I have to be."

"That must have been quite difficult. Why haven't I ever heard of this show?"

Carrey shrugged. "I was a bit too convincing. Everyone else left in first week. Not enough footage for a series. Producers were quite upset."

"Oh," Penelope said softly.

At that moment, David, who had been quite well-behaved today, only licking himself occasionally while waiting for his food, jumped up on the table, grabbed what was left of the roast, and ran away.

"David!" Nick's mother said. "Bad doggy!"

All in all, Nick reflected later, as he ate his pie and watched Penelope pretend to eat hers, this was the best family dinner in a long time.

Tall trees lined either side of the highway, trees Nick now knew belonged to his family, part of the same land parcel which included the Baker Administrative Complex nearly a mile down the road. Many cars were already parked on the gravel shoulder on the way to the proposed church site, making the lane seem narrower and forcing him to concentrate hard to navigate the large Hummer. Amongst the cars, he even saw vans bearing the insignias of local news crews.

He found a parking space reasonably close to the groundbreaking. He stopped in the road a few yards behind the space. "Do you want to get out here?" he asked Penelope. "So you don't have to step onto the gravel shoulder in your heels."

"That's most thoughtful of you, Nick," Penelope said. She sounded pleasantly surprised, and she gave him a genuine-looking smile.

Nick smiled back and got out of the Hummer, so he could walk around to her side and help her out of the big vehicle. Again, her dress slid up and gave him a good view of her underwear.

Penelope raised an eyebrow. "Like what you see, Baker?"

"What?"

"Did you just run round here to get a look up my dress, like a junior-high-school boy?"

Nick shook his head. "No. I just thought you might need some help. I hate this giant thing." He waved his hand, indicating the Hummer.

"Trying to convince me you're a real gentleman, huh? It's not going to work after last night."

Nick flushed. "Hey, I was just trying to help you—"

The car waiting behind them on the highway honked.

Penelope stepped carefully onto the shoulder. "Looks like you need to move the car, Galahad."

Nick pulled the huge car into the spot. He had slightly underestimated the size of the vehicle, metal screeched and branches snapped as he wedged it into place against the trees. When he got out of the Hummer, he offered his arm to Penelope, and to his surprise, she took it without a single sarcastic remark.

They walked a couple hundred yards to a large clearing which had been mowed in preparation of the groundbreaking. A large audience was already gathering on the close cut grass, and past them, Nick could see a podium already inhabited by Reverend Collins, Nick's mother, and the church's outdoor sound system.

A couple hundred yards behind the cleared area, through some trees, Nick could see the edge of the Coralville Reservoir, over which their church would loom. His mother and Reverend Collins couldn't have chosen a more beautiful place to put the church. It was a shame how many old trees they would have to cut down to accommodate the big, ugly building.

As they stepped onto the grass, Penelope gripped his arm a little tighter. "Thanks for the escort, Nick, but you may want to take cover."

She nodded over to the podium where the gaggle of local news people had stopped setting up and started quickly making their way to where Nick and Penelope were standing. Nick sidestepped away and ducked behind a row of spectators. From this vantage point, he watched as the media descended on his fiancé, snapping pictures and enthusiastically tossing out unimportant questions.

"Miss Stafford Jennings, why are you attending the ground-breaking today?"

"Esther Baker asked me to attend. She's an old family friend."

"What are your views on the controversy surrounding the Church of Great Savings?"

Penelope blinked. "And who are they?"

"We're here for their groundbreaking today?"

"Oh! That's what all this is about. You know someone probably told me, but I'm such a fluffhead." In front of the cameras, she was like a completely different woman. How much more of her public persona was just an act?

"Will you be staying here long?" another reporter called out.

"In this field you mean? I don't know. Will there be drinks? I'm liable to stay for quite a while if there are drinks. And then who knows what will happen."

"Are you here for business or pleasure?"

"Pleasure, of course." Penelope waggled her fingers at the reporters. "Aren't you all supposed to be covering a groundbreaking? I don't want you to get distracted."

The star-struck reporters laughed along with the on-looking audience members. Still, one of the reporters pressed on. "So you refuse to comment on your business in Iowa?"

Penelope gave them a confused look. "I'm in Iowa? I must have partied too hard last night."

Nick had just met Penelope this morning, or rather last night, but he had quickly pegged her as quick-witted. He watched on in amazement as she continued to answer questions as if she didn't have a brain in her head.

Eventually, the members of the press seemed to be getting tired of Penelope's vacuous answers. She read their moods perfectly, and said, "So, are you all ready to go meet my friend Esther? I believe the podium is this way." They walked after her as if in a trance, hypnotized by her lack of depth.

Nick felt a little dazed himself—both by the voracity the press had displayed at seeing Penelope as well as by her methods of avoiding their scrutiny. If they were married, would he be attacked by the media everywhere he went? Would he have to act like an empty-headed idiot just to get rid of them?

Someone tapped on his left shoulder. He looked left and closely examined the Asian teenager standing there. She seemed uninterested in him. Behind him, someone said, "Nick."

Nick spun around and found JenJen standing behind him. She poked the end of his nose. "Boop."

"JenJen!" Nick said with perhaps a bit too much enthusiasm. Then, realizing she had done it again, he said in a more discouraging tone, "Would you stop booping me on the nose?"

JenJen gave him a look like she was seriously considering it. "No. I don't think I will."

Nick sighed. This latest trend of JenJen booping him on the nose was probably the last nail in the coffin of her ever seeing him as a man.

She nodded to the podium. "Shouldn't you be up there with the rest of the Bakers? And is that Penelope Stafford Jennings?"

"Yes, but I'm trying to avoid them. I'm trying to avoid Penelope as well."

She raised an eyebrow. "I knew your family was loaded, but I didn't know you travelled in those circles. On a first name basis with her as well?"

"Well, you know, old friends from back when the family was more affluent... Can we talk about something else?"

"Sheep?"

"Pass."

"Actually, I was hoping you'd give me the scoop on what happened with the home invasion."

"Um, nothing much. I think it was some sort of weird prank." He wasn't going to discuss demons. She probably already thought of him as a religious nut. He tried to come up with an innocuous conversation topic. "What brings you to the new home of religious savings?"

"Well, I live just down the road, you know, and I figured you'd be here, so I decided to check it out."

"That's cool. Not all tech people are so open-minded about religion."

"Well, I have bad habits too. I play video games. I spend too much money on lipstick."

Nick opened and closed his mouth a couple of times. He hadn't expected JenJen to refer to his religion as a bad habit. He didn't quite know what to say.

She punched him in the arm. It made her boobs bounce, and he momentarily forgot what he was thinking about. "I'm just winding you up. You should see the look on your face."

Nick blushed. "I'm sorry. I'm having a bad day. I actually..." he lowered his voice. "I went out drinking last night."

JenJen patted his arm. "Poor baby. Is that how you hurt your forehead? Did you get falling-down drunk?"

"No, well yes, but that is not how I hurt my head." He decided to change the subject. "Where's Steve today, on the road?"

Before she could answer him, the amplified voice of Reverend Collins cut through the crowd. "Good afternoon, everyone! Thank you all for coming here to wish us well on our new endeavor. I know that, with your support, The Church of Great Savings will be here for a long, long time."

Sensing the opportunity to be in the public eye, all the politicians had filtered themselves to the front of the gathering, and they were now lined up behind the podium with Nick's mother. Some of the local politicians were pushed all the way over into the tall grass.

Nick's mother took over the microphone. "Before we start the groundbreaking, I have an extra-special announcement to make. Penelope, come on up here." Penelope joined her, and the reporters stopped looking bored for a moment.

His mother gazed through the crowd. "And where did Nick go? Get up here, Nicholas Baker."

"Hide me," Nick whispered, ducking behind her. Of course, he knew that some of his fellow parishioners could identify him from where he was standing. He would just have to hope none of them would betray his position.

"Hmmm," JenJen said. "Hiding you from the press. I think you'll owe me big time for this."

"I'll buy you lunch tomorrow."

"It's a deal."

Nick took a deep breath and lost himself momentarily in how spectacular her hair smelled. When he returned his attention to the podium, all the dignitaries were standing in their places; the Bakers, the politicians, the owners of the construction company, and Reverend Collins.

Nick's mother shook her head. "Oh well, we'll just have to save the other announcement for later. Let's get the other Baker boys up here. Larry. Carrey." She waved at her nephews, who were standing off in the tall grass smoking cigarettes.

Larry and Carrey shrugged, and dropped their cigarettes into the dry grass, which started to smolder. They stomped around the area for a second before joining the politicians at the podium.

Collins went into his usual spiel about the importance of saving souls and the practicality of saving money while doing it. Senator Dorsky spoke of the importance of continuing the tax exemption for religious organizations. Finally, the US attorney, rumored to be running for congress, assured the audience that churches were all that stood between the American family and anarchy.

JenJen yawned. "God, this is boring. Are all groundbreakings like this?"

"Yes," Nick said. "I've only been to a couple, but they're pretty much like this. At least I don't have to stand up front and pretend to look interested."

When the US Attorney had finished, Collins took the microphone from him. "I think we're ready for the shovels." As two men in suits supplied the group with chrome-plated shovels, the reverend added, "I'd like to thank our contractors, the Raynor brothers of Raynor Brothers' Construction, for being here today."

There was a momentary delay as the Raynor Brothers taught the assembled dignitaries how to put their foot on the ceremonial shovels and use their body weight to press them into the ground. In

Penelope's case, they needed to pre-loosen the area, as she wasn't heavy enough to break through the sod.

Collins held the microphone in one hand and his shovel in the other. "Now, the moment you've been waiting for. I want Esther Baker, our building committee chairwoman, to do the honors."

Nick's mother shakily raised her not-quite-practical shoe to the top of the shovel blade and stepped down with all her weight. The blade sunk in about half way, and she pried up a small chunk of sod. The local reporters surrounded her and took pictures. Then the other assembled dignitaries all took a shot at digging, but only Penelope and Reverend Collins got as much attention as Nick's mother.

"Oh boy," Nick whispered to JenJen. "My mother's picture in the paper again."

She shook her head. "At least it keeps her off the streets. You'd be amazed at how many older socialites are turning to crack these days."

"You're just making that up."

"As if. What do you think killed Lady Bird Johnson?"

Nick was ninety percent sure she was joking. "Okay, point taken."

He peeked over her shoulder to get a better view of the action. It looked like they were trying to establish the social pecking order so everyone would know where to stand.

"Could you stand next to me like a normal person? They're not looking for you anymore, they're too preoccupied with their shovels."

Nick stepped up beside her. "Okay, but if I get dragged up there, you're buying me lunch."

"I'll take full responsibility. What's PSJ doing here anyway?"

"What?" Nick asked. "Is a PSJ a sandwich? Like PB&J?"

"No. PSJ—Penelope Stafford Jennings."

Nick shook his head. "Oh, well, her grandfather knew my grandfather. It's really a long story. I don't want to talk about it."

A smattering of applause went up as the politicians, the Raynor Brothers, Reverend Collins, Nick's cousins, and Penelope removed their ceremonial clods of earth.

JenJen shrugged. "So that's it? I never would have guessed that so many people would come to something this dull."

Nick raised an eyebrow. "You actually thought something was going to happen? You poor misguided..." He stopped, his mouth halfway open. His mother seemed to be doing some kind of spirited dance. He gaped as Reverend Collins joined in.

"What the hell are they doing?" was all Nick had time to say before every newly-dug hole started disgorging a black and yellow cloud of hornets.

The hornets seemed especially attracted to Nick's mother and Penelope, who'd been standing beside her. In two seconds, they were enveloped. They waved their arms wildly, screaming and swatting. When this didn't work, Nick's mother grabbed Penelope's hand, turned, and fled, towing Penelope behind. She ran toward the woods, where a tiny man with a red beard waved at her. Penelope trailed behind her, perhaps lacking the leverage to break free from Nick's mother's grasp.

"No!" Nick tried to run toward the podium, but JenJen grabbed his arm, holding him back. He pulled against her. "Let go! That's my mother."

He looked back, but his mother was now nowhere to be seen. Only the politicians, builders, and Nick's cousins remained. Almost everyone had adopted the same strategy for dealing with the hornets, running around and waving their arms.

Only Larry and Carrey were keeping cool. As hornets landed on the two brothers, they were vigorously smacking each other with the flats of the light chrome shovels. Every blow would take out a dozen or more. Despite the wholesale carnage they were inflicting, their efforts were inadequate against the ever-growing number of insects.

Larry took a particularly wild swing, missing his brother and hitting the US Attorney in the temple, knocking him out cold.

Then, the ever-growing number of hornets turned on the crowd. They came not a few at a time, but in a mighty wave, like they had coordinated their attack.

The crowd, previously stunned into inaction, saw the threat headed toward them and went crazy. Some ran in circles. And some, perhaps out of confusion or terror, ran toward the hornets. However, most of the spectators ran for their cars, carrying Nick away from where his mother had disappeared.

JenJen yelled, "Forget your mother, Nick. We have to save ourselves." She tugged on his arm and gave him a dead serious look. "Come with me if you want to live."

Nick and JenJen joined those running away, but before he took two steps, he was clipped by eighty-five-year-old Agnes Milford, usually seen running the church kitchen with an iron fist, currently fleeing for her life.

Momentarily dazed, Nick got turned around and ran in the wrong direction. He didn't last long against the weight of the crowd. Someone elbowed him, knocking him backward, and he fell to the ground. Before he knew what was happening, someone had stepped on his hand. Another person stepped on his stomach, knocking the wind out of him.

Somewhere, deep in Nick's mind, he imagined a copy of the *Cedar Rapids Courier* with the headline, "Baker Trampled at Groundbreaking."

A small hand closed around his wrist and pulled him to his feet. It was JenJen. She pulled him through the crowd. "I thought I'd lost you for a minute, Nick." He allowed her to lead him, while wondering if he should somehow thank her for saving his life.

Holding each other for stability, they pushed sideways through the crowd. They reached the edge of the clearing and Nick pulled JenJen into the woods, away from the crush of people. After a few faltering steps, he found an animal trail and followed it, pulling JenJen behind him.

He saw a momentary flash of red obnoxiousness through the trees. It was the H2. A plan started to form in his mind. "This way," he said, pulling JenJen toward it. Nick hit the door unlock as they arrived at the behemoth vehicle.

"Is this yours?" JenJen asked.

"Get in!" he yelled at her.

Nick climbed into the driver's seat. There were already people running down the middle of the road, fleeing the hornets, so he put the H2 in low gear. He carefully pulled off the shoulder and drove toward the clearing, dodging people running down the middle of the road. Fortunately, most of the people who had made it to the road had the sense not to throw themselves under the H2.

When he pulled the H2 up to the clearing, many people were still running around the mowed field. He steered well clear of them when possible. He also avoided those that lay on the ground, not moving.

The podium wasn't even visible through the black and yellow cloud of hornets, so Nick just drove in the general direction, pushing the H2 into the wall of insects. The mass of hornets threw themselves against the side of the H2 making the sound of a hailstorm.

"My God," JenJen said. "Is this the apocalypse?"

"I don't think so," Nick said. "I think that's supposed to be locusts, not hornets. But still, this sucks."

Finally, they reached the remaining politicians, covered in hornets and writhing in pain. Nick parked the car and threw open the door. He wanted to follow his mother, but he had to help his cousins. "Larry! Carrey!" he yelled. "This way!"

The first person who arrived at the H2 was Commissioner Donaldson. This put Nick in a momentary quandary, because he knew he wasn't going to be able to help everyone. As big as the H2 was, they couldn't load a dozen politicians, relatives, and builders before hundreds of hornets flew through the door.

Nick didn't have to worry about the ethics of his situation for long. There was a loud ringing sound, and Donaldson's eyes went wide as Carrey's shovel hit him over the head. Donaldson went down. Larry ran to the vehicle, huffing and puffing, with over three hundred pounds of Reverend Collins thrown over his shoulder.

A moment after the back door was closed, JenJen slapped Nick across the face. Then she slapped him again. "Hornets," she said, matter-of-factly. And Nick noticed that Larry, Carrey, and Reverend Collins were all engaged in similar slapping of themselves and each other.

When the last of the stowaway hornets had been killed, Nick put the H2 back into gear and drove over to the edge of the woods, the last place they had seen his mother. He started to take off his seatbelt, but Carrey put his big hand on Nick's shoulder.

"You have done a good job, Cousin. Your work is done. It is time to go."

Nick shook his head. "We need to find my mother." A moment later, he added, "And Penelope."

"No cousin. We need to go to the hospital. Reverend does not look well."

JenJen turned to look at Reverend Collins. "It's true, Nick. We have to go. He's barely breathing. There's no way we can find her now. She's in the woods, and we can't search with the hornets still out there."

"I can go," Nick offered. "You take him to the hospital."

"Nick," gasped Reverend Collins, "your mother is a strong woman... perhaps the strongest woman I've ever known... If anyone can survive that... it's Esther Baker."

"No!" Nick shouted. "I have to go."

He threw open the door and started to run for the woods. He felt the armored bodies of wasps bouncing off his body, his face, his arms. He clamped his eyes shut and kept walking. He thought he was walking in a straight line, but the constant activity of the hornets was disorienting.

"Ow!" he yelled as the first stinger pierced his skin, and he immediately had to spit two hornets from his mouth. He clawed at his ear, where one seemed to be taking up permanent residence. Then something hit him on the head.

He fell to the ground.

6

Jump for Jesus

If Nick Baker were to make a list of all the places he didn't want to wake up, the Emergency Room would not be at the top of the list. However, the lack of prioritization would stand more as a testament to his imagination than any desire to be hospitalized. For instance, Emergency Room would take a back seat to options such as buried alive, in a shark tank, or during the Battle of Gettysburg.

"Mother!" Nick yelled, sitting up. He immediately regretted it. His head felt like he was spinning around in tight circles, quite quickly.

JenJen was there immediately, putting pressure on his shoulders. "You should lay back. You took a really nasty blow to the head. You're in the emergency room. They got you in right away since you were unconscious."

"What happened?" Nick asked, settling back into his hospital bed.

JenJen blushed. "Well, um... Carrey ran you down and hit you with a shovel. They're here too, you know, your cousins, being treated for stings." She paused, but then leapt ahead. "I'm sure he did it out of love. I mean, you don't know what might have happened to you if you'd gone out into that..."

"It's okay." He smiled. "It's not like you could have stopped him if you'd wanted to, and, well, Carrey Baker is one of the few people I know that could deliver a head wound out of love."

Nick's phone rang, interrupting them.

Hoping it was news about his mother, Nick answered immediately. "Yes? Hello?"

"Mr. Baker, I'm a reporter with *Citywide* magazine. Would you like to comment on whether you plan to continue your mother's legacy of giving to the arts?"

"What? No!"

"Do you mean you're not going to continue her charity work, or you aren't ready to comment—"

He hung up.

"Can you believe that?" he asked JenJen. "That was a reporter. She was acting like my mother was already dead. Aren't they supposed to wait before contacting family members when something horrible happens?"

JenJen shrugged. "I don't know. That reminds me though, do you think your uncle knows?"

Nick sighed. "Good question. He ignores most calls when he's on the golf course, and if Larry and Carrey haven't thought of it..." He selected Uncle Earl from his contacts.

Uncle Earl answered the phone, sounding only slightly drunk. "Nick! How was the groundbreaking? Did they give you a shovel?"

"There was—"

"Of course, your mother wanted me to come along. I gave an assload of money to build that damn thing, but I really wanted to try out this new club on the back nine. I had it specially made—"

"Listen, Uncle—"

"I had a great day on the back nine. You should have been there. I'm over at the clubhouse right now. You should—"

"Shut up!" Nick yelled into the phone. Uncle Earl shut up. "While you were out golfing, hornets attacked the groundbreaking—not just a few hornets, thousands of hornets. We are all at the emergency room. Mother is missing. She ran into the woods."

Uncle Earl was silent for a moment, then sighed. "Don't worry, my boy. I'm sure she'll turn up sooner or later. Don't worry about it at all. I'll take care of that dog of hers. That's what she'll be most worried about." He paused. "I hate to let you go with everything that's going on, but there's really nothing I can do right now. I'm sure the authorities are doing everything they can. Just a moment." His voice became muffled, and Nick could see his Uncle holding the phone against his chest, as he often did. "We'll take another round. I had an old fashioned and the Judge had a G&T." His voice then became un-muffled. "Okay, I'm back."

"You're staying at the club? Larry and Carrey are in the emergency room. What if something happens? They could end up in ICU, or worse."

Uncle Earl sighed. "Buck up, Nick. Larry and Carrey are made of sturdy peasant stock from Bulgaria, or Romania, or wherever the hell we found them. I just remember they were all a bunch of commies. But never mind that. If their condition changes, call me."

Nick lowered his phone from his ear. "Uncle Earl wants me to keep him apprised in the event one of his sons is put into intensive care or dies. Otherwise, he will continue to drink gin and tonic. Oh, and he said Mother could take care of herself."

JenJen put her hand on his shoulder. "Your family has an odd dynamic, doesn't it?"

The phone rang again. Nick answered, hoping it was word about his mother.

"This is Craig Winters from your Action News—"

Nick hung up the phone. He looked over at JenJen. She returned a concerned look, like she wanted him to share his feelings, but he didn't want to whine at her. After all, she had survived the attack, which was still traumatic even if she had only been stung twice. She wasn't having the best of days either. He held out for a whole minute. "I know what you're doing," he said.

JenJen gave him an innocent look. "What?"

"You are doing the if-I'm-quiet-he'll-start-talking thing. It is not going to work on me. I am not going to start blubbing about my mother, or how she was my only living parent, or how I felt when my father died."

She shrugged. "I'm not trying anything. How did your father die, anyway?"

"It was rather mundane. He and my Aunt Sonia, Uncle Earl's first wife, were coming back to Baker House from a bridge night. Apparently, they liked bridge, but Mother and Uncle Earl didn't. They hit a patch of black ice and lost control. Just the kind of run-of-the-mill accident that happens every day."

"How old were you?"

"I was twelve." Nick fell silent for a moment, wondering if he should say anything else. "Weird. I've now lived more of my life without him than I had with him."

Nick's phone rang again, and as eager as he was to hear about his mother, he had learned his lesson. He checked the caller ID. It was Rudy—he must have heard about the disaster and was calling to see if everyone was all right.

"Toxic! Flip on your TV to Channel Six. Some people were out at a church picnic or something, and they were attacked by bees."

"Rudy—"

"Are you watching this shit? They are saying five dead, four in critical condition, and over thirty went to the hospital. A US attorney was killed. And someone hit that old perv Commissioner Donaldson with a shovel."

Nick wanted to tell Rudy to go to hell, but he lacked the energy for an argument. He waited for Rudy to take a breath so he could speak. "Rudy, listen to me. That 'church picnic' was the groundbreaking for my new church."

"Oh, you were there? That's epic. Did you see that old bag run into the woods?"

"Rudy, don't you realize that this was a real, horrible thing, not some video game? These were real people with families? That old woman that ran into the woods was my mother."

"Okay, that sucks, but seriously, have you seen the video? It's gold."

"F-you, Rudy." Even at his current level of anger, Nick didn't want to use the F word in a public place. "My mother is missing, you jerk."

"No big deal. She'll come out of the woods when she gets hungry, unless she knows how to catch a squirrel and cook it over a campfire. Does your mother know how to skin a squirrel, Toxic?"

Nick literally saw red, and he really wanted to throw something. His arm pulled back and he threw his phone into the far wall of the examination room. It shattered.

"Um..." Nick said, feeling his cheeks heat to levels more often achieved via nuclear fission. "I guess that was pretty stupid."

JenJen shook her head. "No, Nick. You're under a lot of stress. It's okay to show you're upset." She walked over to the wall and picked up the pieces of his phone. She tried to put them back together, but eventually she gave up and stacked them on the counter. "You are going to need a new phone though. The control board is snapped and the screen is cracked."

Nick shook his head. "Well, at least I won't have to deal with people asking stupid questions. It's so frustrating. I just wish I could do something."

A doctor with thick glasses, stringy hair, and bad teeth walked into the room, reading something on a clipboard. "Hello, Mr. Baker. I'm Doctor Grenshaw. I understand you were caught up..." Looking up from the clipboard and seeing Nick for the first time, he stopped mid-sentence. "Oh, it looks like you've been treated already." He reached over and traced the edges of the bandages. Then he tapped the center of the right bandage and made a face. "What do we have here?"

"Just a bad scratch," Nick said. "It didn't need stitches or anything."

"I really should take a look," Doctor Grenshaw said.

Nick shook his head. "No it's fine, really. I was hit by a shovel earlier though. You may want to look at that."

"Oh, yes?" Grenshaw said. "That's odd. That's the second one I've seen today. Why don't you sit up then?"

After getting Nick to sit up and poking and prodding at his head a bit, Grenshaw flashed a light in Nick's eyes without warning, "Concussion, I think, a rather minor one, but I don't want you to be alone." He turned to JenJen. "Just make sure that if he does sleep, you wake him up every couple hours, just for tonight."

He patted Nick on the shoulder. "I don't know how you got hit by a shovel, but it's nothing to be taken lightly. In your case, there's no damage to the skull, and I don't think you'll even end up with a dent when all is said and done. You've been very lucky."

"I'm not a medical professional," JenJen said, "but wouldn't he have been luckier if he hadn't been hit by a shovel? I mean, it's just an odd phrase, 'you've been very lucky,' to say to someone who just got a lump on their head, simply because they didn't suffer severe brain damage."

Doctor Grenshaw looked like he was trying to decide how to answer, but then he just shook his head and turned back to Nick. "I'm going to prescribe you some pain killers, but I think you'll feel all right in a couple days. Still, if you have any problems after a few days—pain, dizziness, blurred vision, that sort of thing—make sure you see your family doctor."

Nick nodded. "I will do that."

Grenshaw turned back to JenJen. "And you, I assume you were at the groundbreaking also. Are you injured?"

"No." She gave Nick a very pointed look. "Some of us have the good sense to run away from impending disaster."

Again, Grenshaw looked like he didn't know what to say. He looked back at his clipboard, wrote something down, and passed it to Nick. "This is for the pain. You'll have to take this one to the pharmacy yourself. I've also added a topical steroid for your stings."

"Thanks," Nick said as the doctor was leaving.

JenJen snatched the sheet of paper away from him. "Nice." She handed it back.

Nick shrugged. "I'm probably not going to get them filled anyway. I just have a headache and a couple stings."

JenJen shook her head. "Yes you are. This is the good stuff. If you don't want it I'll use it."

"Umm. Okay." Nick didn't know if that was strictly legal, but if it made JenJen happy, what the hell.

What the *heck*, he corrected himself.

———————————

After being released, JenJen and Nick walked down a wide hospital hallway toward the lobby. "Do you know where we're going?" JenJen asked.

"Yes. This is the way to the lobby. I need to find Larry and Carrey. They have my keys."

As they approached, Nick became aware of a confluence of people. "There seems to be a confluence of people in the lobby," he said to JenJen.

"What the hell are you talking about, Nick? Confluence? Who talks like that? Do you mean crowd?"

"Well, yes, but crowd tends to denote a group of people standing around, while confluence means a group in the process of merging. Confluence was just the first word that came to mind."

JenJen shook her head. "Next time, Nick, just say crowd."

"Okay."

As they reached the crowd, Nick saw something bobbing up and down at the center. It turned out to be the well-rounded form of Reverend Collins doing jumping jacks. He finished, pumped his fist at the air, and yelled, "Praise Jesus!" A few people even cheered him on, and Nick recognized them as members of the congregation.

Reverend Collins yelled, "Almighty God, give me strength." He dropped to the ground and started doing pushups. He actually managed them pretty well, but every time he dropped to the ground, his belly would hit first, and he would grunt.

JenJen raised her eyebrows. "Now there's something you don't see every day. Or is it?"

Nick shrugged. "As far as I know, this is the first time he's publicly exercised. I'm kind of impressed. The old guy can move."

After twenty pushups, Reverend Collins jumped back up, perhaps because he was done with his set, or maybe due to the arrival of the local news. "Ladies and gentlemen, in case you're just arriving, we've had word from the county sheriff. They have not found any fatalities."

Rudy had told him, over the phone, that there had been six fatalities. He wondered which number was right.

The crowd cheered and applauded, but Collins held out his hand to silence them. "However, there have been some serious injuries, and two people are currently considered missing. I would like to say a prayer for the safe return of our own Esther Baker and Penelope Stafford Jennings, who was visiting the Baker family."

Collins raised his hands high. "Oh, Great God, please be merciful on your daughters Esther and Penelope. Keep them safe in the depths of the forest and protect them from the vicious hornets. They are humble servants of God.

"However, Great God Almighty, who does nothing without a reason, you clearly sent us a message today. You told us we should be physically fit, so that we can meet our challenges in life. You have shown us the way, and we are amazed by your greatness. I pledge to build a mighty shrine to you that will not only feature the best goods and services at low prices, but will also feature the grandest of health clubs—free weights, cardio machines, spinning classes, and if you see in your greatness and wisdom to grant us resources for a swimming pool, water aerobics, open 24 hours a day, and without teaching the unholy practices of strip tease, pole dancing, or boxing for women!"

"I didn't know female boxing went against God," JenJen said under her breath. "I wonder what God's opinion is on Tae Bo."

"The Church of Great Savings," Collins continued, "will be the healthiest congregation in Iowa. We will be the healthiest congregation in America. And we'll keep lifting weights, running on treadmills, and shedding pounds, for modest monthly membership fees, until we have the healthiest congregation on Earth. Amen!"

Nick noticed a little less enthusiasm, especially among the more sedentary members of the congregation.

Collins spotted Nick in the back of the crowd and waved at him. "Nick! Nick, my boy, get up here."

Nick tried to avoid eye contact and step back behind JenJen, but Collins had already spotted him. He gave up and walked over to join Collins.

Collins put his arm around Nick, enveloping him in the funk of sweat from his exercise. "Friends, this is Nick Baker. I know most of you know Nick, or his mother, our sister in Christ, Esther Baker, without whom our fantastic new church would not be possible. Nick's family has already given twelve million dollars to our building fund."

Nick wondered how that could even be possible. The family was well off, but in the grand scheme of things, they were rather garden-variety millionaires. The value of the oral hygiene businesses, the core of their family fortune, couldn't be worth more than twenty million. Compared to Penelope, they were practically paupers. No wonder they were trying to marry him to money. They'd leveraged everything to build the megachurch.

Collins continued. "I told you earlier that Nick's mother, Esther, has gone missing. Now, I know that you may be worried for her welfare, but Esther Baker is a strong woman. She has met every challenge that God has sent her, the loss of her husband and having to raise Nick alone."

Nick often heard statements like this about his mother. As always, he did not bring up Gladys, their housekeeper and cook, or Delores, who had babysat him whenever his mother dropped him off at work with Uncle Earl.

Collins continued. "I have no doubt she will survive this ordeal. And if she doesn't, she will be secure in the arms of God."

Nick wondered if Collins expected some reaction from him. Between the attack, the disappearance of his mother, and his suspicion that Collins had conned his family out of their entire fortune, he felt totally empty. He shook his head and walked away, making his way through the crowd at a good pace.

"That's right, my boy," Collins called after him. "Walk it off. Go home and get some rest. Don't hesitate to call me when you're ready to talk." Nick shook his head. Collins really shouldn't be allowed to counsel people.

As he walked out of the waiting room doors, JenJen caught up to him. "Nick. Wait up. Where are you going?"

"Away from here. Let's find Larry and Carrey. I want to leave."

She stopped and grabbed his arm, turning him to look at her. "Nick, listen, I'm sorry. I didn't know he could be so... horrible."

He sighed. "Actually, neither could I. Look, I'm not really mad at you. I just don't know how to feel right now." Every time he started to think about what had happened, he didn't feel sad or angry. He just felt sick to his stomach. "I just want to get my cousins and get out of here."

Carrey raised a spoon with a tiny amount of blue Jell-O to his nose and sniffed. He let out a little sigh of pleasure, and then slurped it into his mouth. He had only gotten halfway through his little plate of goo, and seemed in no rush to finish. Nick, Larry, and JenJen sat around the cafeteria table, watching him ritualistically consume the glob.

"Wow, Carrey," JenJen said. "You really like Jell-O."

"Yes," Carrey said, before returning to his dessert.

"When Carrey and I first came to America," Larry explained, "we travelled across the Atlantic with Earl and Esther Baker. They took us to a restaurant in the airport and told us we could have anything we desired. We were unfamiliar with the dishes, so Esther ordered for us. For dessert, we get Jell-O. Growing up in orphanage, we had never tasted anything so sweet. It was then we knew we were in America, and we would never go hungry again."

They waited for Carrey to finish the Jell-O.

After a trip to a nearby pharmacy to fill their various prescriptions, they returned to the scene of the groundbreaking. Nick didn't want to be reminded of what happened, but they had cars to retrieve, and if any kind of search party was being organized, he intended to volunteer.

A mile down the road, a deputy manned a roadblock made from his patrol car and yellow police tape. Nick lowered his window to talk to the officer, who had to look up into the H2. "Hi folks. I'm afraid I'm going to have to ask you to turn around. We've had an incident up the road, and we want to keep things clear for emergency vehicles."

"Hi, officer, my name is Nick Baker. My mother was at the groundbreaking today. I want to help search for survivors."

The deputy shook his head. "I'm afraid that's not possible. That whole area is still swarming with angry hornets. There's no way we can ensure your safety."

Nick pounded his fist on the dashboard. "I don't care about my safety. There are people still in there. We have to do something!"

The deputy pursed his lips and held Nick's gaze. "I'm sorry, Mr. Baker. I can't let you through. We're doing everything we can, and we'll let you know when we have any news."

"Just drive around him, Cousin," Larry whispered from the back seat. "He will not shoot upset son."

The deputy's face switched from sympathetic to annoyed. "We're doing all we can. If you want us to do our job quickly and efficiently, you'll stay out of the way."

Nick nodded, raised the window, and turned around the H2. Once they were headed back down the road, he slowed down and said, "Well, you heard it. They're not even going to let us in. What are we going to do?"

Larry answered him. "Take us back to Papa Earl's house. We will drive the Mercedes."

"No," said Nick. "Not 'what are we going to do about a car?' What are we going to do about my mother?"

"I am sorry, Cousin," Carrey said. "Your mother is probably dead. I do not want to say this. You do not want to hear this. But this is the case."

Nick sagged in his seat. He was kind of glad someone had just come out and said it. It was like a burden had been removed from his shoulders. There was really nothing he could do. Nothing would be expected of him. Now he could go home and grieve. He nodded. "Okay, I guess I'll just take you all home, then. I can drop JenJen off first; her place is on the way."

"That's okay," JenJen said. "Why don't you drop your cousins off first?"

"That doesn't make sense. You're on the way. You'll have to ride with me for an extra half hour, and it will add ten minutes to my drive."

JenJen shrugged. "I'm in no rush. Don't you think your cousins would like to get home sooner?"

"But we're closer to your place. I can drop you off in five minutes—"

From the back seat, Larry put his hand on Nick's shoulder. "Listen very carefully, Cousin. Take girl home last."

Nick shrugged. "If that's what you want, but it's not the most efficient route."

During the drive to Earl's house, JenJen found a radio news report on the groundbreaking. "North of Coralville, state and county police are coordinating with exterminators to contain what is now being called the largest hornet infestation ever found. The hornet's nest was found during a groundbreaking of the new Great Savings megachurch, covering parishioners and dignitaries in thousands of hornets. While no fatalities have been reported, local philanthropist Esther Baker and noted socialite Penelope Stafford Jennings are still missing—"

"I don't think skinny girl will make it," Larry pointed out, making no commentary about whether this was a good or bad thing.

"...Local authorities have asked everyone to stay clear of the site until further notice has been given. The Governor's office issued a statement today slamming the FDA for refusing the deployment of DDT."

After they dropped off Larry and Carrey, Nick drove back north toward JenJen's apartment. He tried to think of something to say, to ease their awkward silence, but he felt hollow inside, like someone had scooped all his guts out. Finally, they arrived, and he parked the H2 in the lot below her apartment.

"Do you need a ride to work tomorrow?" he asked.

"Yeah, I suppose." She paused. "Nick, how are you feeling? Are you going to be okay?"

"I guess. I don't know. I just keep thinking that if I would have been up there at the podium, I could have done something. If I had faced my responsibilities, my mother wouldn't be missing right now."

"Your big strapping cousins were up there. They couldn't save her. They could barely save themselves. If you'd gone up there, things would be worse, not better."

"I guess." Nick saw her point, but he couldn't bring himself to believe it. Maybe it was irrational. Maybe it was survivor's guilt, but he still couldn't stop feeling that way.

JenJen put her hand on his shoulder. "Look, you've had a stressful day. You're exhausted. Your head is all mixed up right now. I'm not sure you should be alone. Why don't you turn off the engine and come upstairs for a while?"

Nick nodded. "Okay."

7

MISSED MESSAGES

Nick followed JenJen up the rickety steps to her second-floor apartment, allowing himself to be soothed by the sway of her hips. Yes, she was just a friend. Yes, he still found it embarrassing that he couldn't be more mature about their relationship. But it had been a long day, the view was pleasant, and looking wouldn't hurt anyone.

When they reached the landing, JenJen unlocked the door and stepped inside. "You'll have to excuse the mess," she said, tossing her purse on an end table.

He followed her into the apartment with caution, aware that her well-muscled boyfriend, Steve, might be lounging on the couch in his underwear. Thankfully, the living room was empty of lounging, half-naked boyfriends.

The room was a bit dusty around the edges, but otherwise tidy. The decor was an eclectic mixture of feminine knickknacks, geek chic, and leftovers of dorm living, not yet discarded for more mature alternatives. Nick was surprised at the poor representation of Steve's possessions, such as baseball trophies or beer posters.

"It doesn't look that bad to me," Nick said. "I still haven't picked up the Doritos my cousins ground into my rug last night."

"You really should do that. You'll get ants."

Nick nodded. He was trying to think of something equally mundane to say, when he spotted something near and dear to his heart. "Is that a *Global Fight!* controller?"

JenJen rolled her eyes. "It is the most popular game on Earth. You aren't one of those guys who thinks girls don't game are you? I do work for a game company, you know. Don't you think I might be remotely interested in the number one selling game in the world?"

Nick blushed. "No. I just... Well, girl gamers are rare and beautiful things, like unicorns." He realized, in a roundabout way, he had just called JenJen beautiful. He felt his face get warmer. If it got any hotter, it would be able to peel wallpaper.

She smirked. "Don't get all embarrassed, Nick. I'm just giving you crap. Besides, you wouldn't be the first boy whose ass I had to kick in a video game."

"You're pretty good, huh?"

She nodded. "I think so."

He had been holding back, but now that she had bragged a little, he figured it was his turn. "You know, I'm ranked third in Midwest Region, and another member of my guild, Team Toxic, is ranked fifth."

She nodded. "Third? That does sound impressive." Only, she didn't really seem all that impressed.

"Yeah, my friend Rudy and I started the guild when we were seniors in college. We still play quite regularly."

"Uh huh."

Nick felt he was losing her. Time to ask her a personal question. "Do you have Mossman's book on the *Global Fight!* architecture?"

"No, but I did splurge and pick up Walberg's *Global Fight! Design Bible.* Have you seen it?"

"I flipped through it in the bookstore, but I'm more interested in gameplay than level design."

"You should look through the section on computer generated textures, though. And the section on real time bump mapping techniques is one of the best I've read. I hear they use the Walberg book as a textbook at UC Berkeley." She waved at her sofa. "In fact, just sit down. It's in the other room. Let me go get it."

Nick sat down on the dilapidated futon, which had probably resided in JenJen's dorm room. While he waited, he picked at a puddle of dried wax on the coffee table, seeing if he could pull it up in one chunk. He couldn't.

JenJen returned with the giant tome, Walberg's *Global Fight! Design Bible*. She sat down next to Nick and after moving a couple candles and a decorative flowery thing out of the way, placed the book on the coffee table. "It's not a bad book for understanding gameplay, either," she said. She leaned over to flip through the book. In doing so, she pressed her left breast into Nick's arm. "Look at these weapons stats."

Nick tried to ignore the feel of JenJen pressed against him. "Um, where's Steve tonight?"

"Oh, he's on the road. They have a training camp or something."

JenJen's boyfriend, Steve, was approaching forty and had never made it out of the minor leagues. In Nick's opinion, he was too old to have aspirations toward the pros. For that matter, Nick thought, Steve was too old to have aspirations toward JenJen.

Nick usually enjoyed discussing the merits of specific weapons in the game. But every time JenJen pointed to a gun or turned a page, her breast would rub against his arm. He was having trouble concentrating. It had been quite a while since he had felt real, live breasts. In fact, the last time it had happened had also been on a dorm-room futon.

JenJen nudged him. "I said, 'I think the game overrates the Arms Moravia CZ-G2000 in stopping power,' don't you?"

He shrugged. "Sorry. I kind of zoned out there. I guess I'm getting a little tired."

"If you think you're too tired to drive, you can stay here tonight."

For a second, Nick thought she was propositioning him, but he was being silly. She was just a good friend offering him hospitality after a horrible event. No matter how tempting the offer, there was no way he was going to get any sleep knowing she was just in the next room. He shook his head. "No thanks. No offense, but I don't think I could sleep on your futon."

"There's always the bed."

Again, he shook his head. "Actually, I have an awful time sleeping in strange beds." Besides, Steve slept in that bed.

She put her hand on his knee. "But you already said you were tired. I would feel awful if you fell asleep on the drive home. We could have a sleepover. It would be fun."

Nick shook his head. "What would we do? Give each other makeovers? Sorry, not my kind of fun." It was bad enough that she saw him as a girlfriend and not a real man. He didn't need his nose rubbed in it.

"Stay a little while longer," she said. "We can do other things."

With all the talk of being tired, Nick was genuinely feeling drowsy now. It had been a long day. "Nope. If I don't leave now, I really am going to fall asleep." He stood up, noticing JenJen had leaned so far into him that she had to catch herself to stop from falling over. It was weird how she lacked the techie aversion to being touched.

Following Nick to the door, JenJen said, "Are you sure you don't want to spend the night with me?"

Nick yawned and shook his head. "Like I said, I need to sleep in my own bed tonight. Besides, I don't think Steve would like me staying over."

JenJen put her arm around his waist. "Who says Steve has to know?"

Nick stepped away from her and opened the door. "Of course you'd have to tell Steve. If he found out I'd slept over and you were hiding it from him, then he'd really jump to the wrong conclusion. He'd probably kick my ass."

"What if I told him you stayed over no matter what? You'd get your ass kicked anyway, so you might as well stay." She grabbed his wrist and pulled him back across the threshold. "Come in and have a glass of wine with me."

Nick chuckled and shook his head. Wow, was she being a tease all of a sudden. "No, JenJen. I want to make it home alive, not pass out on your futon."

JenJen sighed. "Okay. I guess I'll see you at work tomorrow."

"Cool, you still need a ride?"

"No, Nick. I can find my own way to work."

"Are you sure?" he asked. "It's no trouble."

For some reason, she turned red in the face. "I'd hate to put you through so much trouble." She slammed the door in his face.

On his drive home, Nick mentally went over his interaction with JenJen. If he didn't know better, he might think she'd just made a pass at him. He was sure that JenJen was not the type of girl who would see someone behind her boyfriend's back. One thing was clear, Nick did not understand women.

When he arrived home, Nick tossed his little bag of antibiotics on the kitchen counter and checked his messages.

BEEP! "Howdy, Nick. This is Reverend Collins. I wonder if you could make an appointment to meet with me tomorrow. I know this is a tough time, and I'm sure you could use someone to talk with. Also, we could go over my plans for the new workout center—" *MESSAGE DELETED.*

After he got ready for bed, Nick lay staring at the ceiling. He had been tired at JenJen's, but now, he couldn't get the image of his mother lying dead and covered in hornets to leave his mind. He alternated this vision with his anger at Reverend Collins for wanting to talk about a health center. At some point, late into the night, he finally fell asleep.

For the second day in a row, Nick woke up with a headache. He also possessed a vague recollection of dark nightmares. He crawled out of bed and staggered to the bathroom.

The bandages had come off his forehead as he slept. He needed to take a look at the wounds, and see if they'd gotten any better. Part of him wondered if he should have shown the bumps to Doctor Grenshaw. Still, they were just bumps. What harm could they do? He splashed some water on his face.

The bumps had grown. They now stood out almost a half inch from his forehead, and they were pointy. He tried squeezing one like a pimple, and found the sensation quite odd, like the skin was loose and moving over something hard. He put some pressure on the point, and wiggled his finger. The skin slid back and forth. He pushed down a little harder—

"Ow!" He pulled his finger away and looked at it. There was a drop of blood on the end. He sucked the drop of blood from it and examined his finger. Something had broken the skin.

He looked at the bump in the mirror. It had blood on it as well. Nick went to rub it off with his finger, and the skin around it tore. The hard mass looked like a pointy bone sticking out of his forehead. A horn?

Nick pinched the other pointy bump between thumb and forefinger and pushed. Another tiny horn popped out. He now had a perfect, if tiny, set of horns.

"What the F?" He really should have shown those bumps to Doctor Grenshaw. Just to be safe, he went to the kitchen and took a double dose of the antibiotics. As he stood at the sink finishing his glass of water, he wondered if he should call in sick for the day. Maybe he could wear a hat?

He sat down at the computer to do an Internet search for people with horns. In the middle of an article about a man in France who had a horn grow out of the back of his head, his phone rang.

"Hey, Nick," JenJen said. "You know how I said I didn't need a ride?"

"Uh huh." Nick was only half paying attention. He would catch up with the conversation when he finished the article. As it turned out, horns weren't actually made of bone. They were keratin, like fingernails.

"As it turns out, I could use a ride. Pick me up at seven thirty?"

"Yeah." Another site claimed that human skeletons with horns were found in a cave in Pennsylvania. However, Nick didn't know how much he should trust the "Top Secret UFO Files" website.

"Okay, see you then. Thanks, Nick." She hung up.

"Sure... Oh crap," he said, finally catching up to the conversation. It looked like he would be going into work today after all.

Nick went back to the bathroom and examined the horns in the mirror. As a programmer, he liked to think of himself as a problem solver. They weren't that thick, and the article he'd read said they were made out of the same material as toenails.

He opened up his drawer and pulled out his nail clippers. They weren't just any fingernail clippers. They were Stanford Fatboy

XXXL nail clippers, guaranteed to cut cleanly through a steel finishing nail. He carefully fit the end of the clippers over the horn on the right side of his head and pressed the lever. Nothing happened.

He pushed again, harder, forcing the lever to flex. His hand shook with the effort. And then came pain, shooting down the little horn, like someone hammering a hot rivet into his skull.

Easing off the pressure, he set the clippers down carefully and leaned forward over the sink. Tears streamed from his eyes. His nose ran like a faucet. Saliva poured from his mouth. The room dipped and swayed around him while he waited to see if he would be sick. After a long moment, he straightened up and examined his handiwork in the mirror. He hadn't managed to cut off the horn, but it did have two big dents in it.

He thought about trying again, but he was running out of time if he wanted to pick up JenJen on the way to work. He quickly showered, careful to wash around his horns. When he emerged from the shower, they seemed to have grown more. He poked several little holes in one of his towels trying to dry his hair around them.

With everything that had happened over the weekend, he had neglected his laundry. He was forced to wear a pair of boxer shorts that were too small and liked to gape open in the front, a shirt with a collar that wouldn't stay down, and a wrinkled pair of pants. At least the pants were a good fit. He wondered why he didn't wear them more often. Probably because they wrinkled easily, and he never had time to iron them.

After dressing, Nick went to the hall closet and selected a wool stocking cap from his winter gear. After some careful arrangement, the horns were hidden inside the thick weave. He ran back to his bedroom to grab his keys out of yesterday's pants and saw a piece of parchment on his pillow.

Take the bike.

Nick assumed the creature meant the old bicycle that had mysteriously shown up on his patio. But where was he supposed to take it?

Just in case it might stave off his imminent death by hellish torture, he announced loudly, "I received your correspondence. I will take the bike today." He paused, waiting for some kind of response.

When none came, he said, "I'm going to finish dressing and go. I don't mean you any harm." He slipped the nine iron out of his golf bag, which reminded him he hadn't put away the driver. He more or less finished dressing, not taking time for niceties like buttoning his shirt of zipping up his pants.

"Okay, I'm going to go now." Holding the driver in front of him, he walked quickly down the hall. "I'm walking past the laundry closet. I'm *not* going to look inside." Fortunately, he'd left his shoes by the sliding glass door to his patio. He left the nine iron, grabbed the shoes, and slipped outside. Locking the door behind him, he turned around to find Mrs. Coltrane, Officer Kevin's mother, watching him.

"Um, hi, Mrs. Coltrane."

The old woman looked unhappy, as per usual. "I hear my boy gave you a bit of trouble the other day."

"I guess you could say that…"

"I told my boy never to pull his gun on anyone again."

Nick nodded. "Thank you, ma'am."

Suddenly, the old woman perked up. She even gave Nick a little smile. "Speaking of which, you might want to do up your trousers. I can see your willy," she said, pointing at his crotch.

Nick reached down and zipped up. "Um, yes, ma'am. Sorry about that. I guess I was in a bit of a hurry."

She shrugged. "That's all right. You don't want to come inside for a cup of coffee, do you?"

Nick shook his head. "No ma'am. I'm late for work."

She nodded. "Well, maybe some other time."

Before he left, Nick loaded the old bicycle into the back of the H2.

Nick parked the H2 in the lot of JenJen's apartment building. She hurried down the stairs. Like Friday, she was dressed for success: heels, jacket, and skirt. So he got out and helped her into the passenger seat, being careful not to look up her skirt.

They were already a bit late, so Nick concentrated on getting the H2 turned around and back on the road. Once they were underway, he wondered if he should say something.

Before he could think of a topic, JenJen broke the silence. "Have you heard anything about your mother?"

"No. I suppose it's a little soon though. Honestly, I doubt there will be good news."

They rode in silence for a few more minutes, and JenJen asked, "Why are you wearing a stocking cap? Are you cold?"

"No, I'm just having a bad hair day." To some extent this was true, as he had forgotten to comb it.

"Nick, about last night..."

Nick knew she would mention it sooner or later. He was ready with an answer. "Don't worry about it. I'm not upset."

"*You're* not upset?"

Nick thought he was being magnanimous, but for some reason she seemed quite annoyed. "Yes, I understand that slamming the door in my face was just your bad reaction to a stressful day."

They rode in silence the rest of the way to work. It was nice how they didn't feel it necessary to make chit-chat. When he parked, JenJen got out of the H2 without saying a word and headed for the building at a swift pace, only pausing momentarily to dodge an airborne coffee filter.

"Aren't you going to thank me for the ride?" Nick called after her.

JenJen kept walking. Without turning, she raised her hand and displayed her middle finger to him.

"Now you're flipping me off?"

"Screw you, Baker!" she yelled as a flotilla of fast food wrappers sailed by.

Nick shook his head, wondering what he had done to make her so mad. Would she still want a ride home?

Amongst the morning emails was a note from Uncle Earl reminding Nick to apply for the Creative Director position. The long diatribe contained Uncle Earl's views about the importance of Nick's advancement, the responsibility of being a Baker, and the need to keep a family comfortable. A postscript at the bottom asked, "BTW, have you heard anything about your mother?"

Nick deleted the email.

A company-wide email from Delores stated the company's—therefore Uncle Earl's—views on garbage removal had changed. However, they needed help in estimating the volume of accumulation and needed anyone with a courtyard office to measure the height of the refuse. Nick didn't know what had changed Uncle Earl's mind on this issue, but it gave him hope that possibly Uncle Earl had softened in his old age.

He opened up a desk drawer and searched through old papers and sundry office flotsam until he produced a twelve-inch ruler dating back to his first day of employment. He also grabbed a dry-erase marker, so he could make a mark on the window every twelve inches until he reached the top of the garbage.

He walked the ruler over to the floor-to-ceiling blinds that covered the entire office wall. He hesitated, his hand inches from the chain. The last time he'd opened them, it hadn't gone well. He steeled himself against seeing the demon with the beard, perhaps even waving his penis around. Taking hold of the little chain, he pulled the blinds open. Instead of the demon, he found something even more unbelievable.

He dropped the ruler and stared. Outside the glass wall of his office, a magical woodland had appeared. The garbage was gone, and in its place was a clearing surrounded by old growth forest. Where the far wall of the courtyard should have been, a small stream meandered.

Nick yanked the chain, pulling the blinds closed.

He needed caffeine. In his haste to deal with his horns and pick up JenJen, he hadn't gotten his coffee. He was way too under-caffeinated for dealing with multi-dimensional forests.

Just in case, he opened the blinds again. There was no garbage, only a woodland scene so beautiful it looked more manufactured than grown, like a computer-rendered scene of the perfect forest.

He closed the blinds, walked out of his office, and wandered down the hall to the next door. The three graphic-designers who shared the office—Sherry, Reg, and JenJen—looked up from their work.

JenJen stood. "What's going on, Nick? You look a little spooked." He must have, as she seemed genuinely concerned.

Nick shook his head to snap himself out of it and tried to play it cool. "Nothing. I'm fine." He loped across the room. "I just need to check something out." He jerked open the blinds. Outside the glass wall was nothing but a knee-high pile of garbage, even though both offices shared the same courtyard.

JenJen walked up behind him and put her hand on his shoulder. "Are you sure you're all right?"

"Um, I'm fine. I'll go back to my office now."

He went out her door and turned to go back to his office. Halfway back to his office, he changed his mind, walking to the break room where he hastily drank two Mountain Dews. After a burp that made his eyes water, he returned to his office and opened the blinds again.

Something—no, some *thing*—had bent the laws of reality. Nick knew he should wash his hands of the whole thing, but how many chances would he get to experience this sort of phenomenon? This was some serious *Star Trek* shit.

Then again, wasn't Nick caught in the ultimate *Star Trek* conundrum? Would he go forth and explore the unknown, or would he stay in the safety of his office? Once he had weighed the pros and cons, he realized that the biggest thing he had to fear was the garbage smell.

Scrunching up his nose, still expecting a lingering stink, he pushed the door open a crack. Despite his pessimistic expectations, no virulent smell of decay assaulted him. The air smelled fresh and clean. Smellvis had left the building.

Pushing the door open farther, he stepped into the courtyard-forest. The sun felt warm on his face. He took a few tentative steps and turned back. Behind him, he could see the sliding door, the glass wall, and through them his office. The rest of the Baker Dental building had disappeared.

He walked to the far end of the clearing, where a gradual slope met the little stream. Rocks had been strategically placed to allow someone to walk across, so Nick walked to the other side, where a grassy path led off into the woods. He followed the path until he reached another clearing.

Something about the grassy area was familiar. Had he been here before? No, that wasn't quite right. He'd seen the clearing before, when he was a boy. His eyes wandered along the trees ringing the clearing, following the leaves and branches of the trees toward the center.

His entire body started trembling, and he realized he had been here. He had seen this clearing before. It was etched forever in his nightmares. This was the painting. This was the clearing from the painting.

Nick ran.

He sprinted down the soft earth of the grassy path. Not being a big runner, by the time he reached the stream his heart was pounding and his lungs were struggling to pull in enough air. He didn't even slow down for the stream, he just ran though the ankle deep water. He struggled up the gradual slope on legs made of wet cement and his office came into view. It was still there.

Letting his momentum carry him the last few steps, concentrating on keeping his legs underneath him, he lurched through the door. Before he allowed himself to crumple to the carpet, he closed and locked the door and closed the blinds.

Then he crawled to his garbage can and threw up two Mountain Dews.

He lay on his side for a few minutes, gasping for breath and letting the sweat dry into his business-casual. When he caught his breath, he kicked off his wet shoes.

The clearing, the thing of his nightmares, was a real place. What did this all mean?

His office phone started to ring, so he heaved himself up off the carpet and walked around his desk to answer it. The pneumatic cylinder in his chair echoed his own sigh as he sat.

"Nick? Is Larry. We need to run errand. Need the big truck. You bring. Chinese buffet restaurant by First Avenue. You know? One with fish pond."

"Well, I'd love to help, but I have to work—"

"We okay everything with Papa. He said we have you for afternoon."

If Nick did spend the afternoon with them, only the sheep herding mini-game would suffer. He didn't really want to hang out with his cousins, but it beat doing actual work. "I can be there in thirty minutes."

8

CHINESE SECRETS

Nick drove the H2 out of the Baker Administrative Complex parking lot, squelching the tires over a sizable pile of refuse on his way out. The smell would probably stay with him for his entire drive downtown, but hopefully, his sacrifice meant some other employee with a lower-profile vehicle would not get stuck in the muck.

Despite Uncle Earl giving permission to leave, Nick felt guilty. While he might be planning to half-ass the mini-game, he hadn't actually done any work on it in five days, including the weekend. There were benchmarks to be met, and sizable penalties to be paid if Edutacular failed to finish on time.

Nick sighed. He needed to put work out of his head. How could he concentrate with his mother probably dead somewhere in the woods? And there was Penelope too. Should he feel sad about her? Should he feel guilty that he didn't feel sad? He didn't really know her, after all.

He parked outside the Great Wall Chinese Buffet just before 10:00 AM, leaving the radio on so he had something to do while he waited for his cousins. Of course, if he hadn't smashed his smartphone, he could have been surfing the Internet or reading a book.

As he listened to the radio, he looked at the shrubbery surrounding the building. The plants were typical Midwestern varieties with a little bit of creative sculpting to make them look Asian. Between the shrubs were small decorations such as ceramic Buddhas and temples. Also, something big seemed to be moving through the bushes. It stood up. It was Carrey. Through a series of gestures, Carrey indicated that Nick should drive around to the back of the building.

Nick started the H2 and drove around the building to find Larry standing by the back door. Next to him, a Chinese man in an apron leaned against the wall smoking a cigarette. Larry waved Nick over.

When Nick pulled the truck over and rolled down the window, Larry told him, "Back up to the door here. There will be loading." He looked in the back of the H2. "We may have to move the bike, but I think everything will fit."

As Nick was turning the big truck and lining it up with the back door, Carrey came around the side of the building. When Nick slid down from the H2, Carrey patted him on the shoulder with a steam-shovel hand. "Cousin Nick, good to see you this morning. Why you wear stocking hat? Are you catching cold?"

"Bad hair day," Nick explained.

"Good, you must have health. For without health we have nothing." Larry paused as if considering his words. "Is there word about Aunt Esther?"

Nick shook his head. "No. They're going to do a wider search today, but they don't have high hopes. I'm thinking about going over there later. I know I probably can't do anything, but I just don't want to sit around doing nothing."

Finishing his cigarette, the Chinese man standing next to Larry walked over to Nick and gave him a very thorough pat down.

"Yes," Nick said, "those are my balls."

Ignoring Nick, the Chinese man knocked twice on the metal door and barked something in what Nick assumed was Chinese. With a loud clunk, the door opened. Motioning to Nick, Carrey followed the Chinese man into the back of the restaurant. Nick followed and Larry brought up the rear.

"What's going on?" Nick asked Larry.

"We need to pick up some things," Larry answered, offering no more explanation.

"Oh, okay." Nick wondered if Larry and Carrey had ordered enough Chinese food to fill the back of the H2.

Nick had never been in a commercial kitchen before. Amongst three rows of stainless steel countertops and gas stoves, a half-dozen Chinese men wearing aprons were preparing for the noon meal, chopping vegetables, folding big noodles around meat pastes, and grabbing utilitarian pans and utensils from overhead racks. One wall was lined with heavy insulated doors, probably walk-in freezers.

Carrey approached a Chinese man in an Italian suit. When the man saw Larry, he yelled a few words in Chinese. The kitchen staff dropped what they were doing and ran into one of the freezers where they started picking up skinny boxes and carrying them out to the H2.

"What's in the boxes?" Nick whispered to Larry.

"Televisions. Direct from manufacturer. The restaurant owner, we call him TV Guy, his brother works in factory that makes screens for Panasonic. He make sure they make too many. Ship them here so we can sell."

"Is that legal?"

Larry shrugged. "Maybe not in China, but here we are okay as long as we say, 'same screen as Panasonic,' instead of 'Panasonic.' We are just buying a TV and selling a TV."

"Or in this case," Nick said, counting the TVs, "a dozen TVs."

"Baker's dozen," said Larry, "because we are giving the thirteenth to our good cousin, Nick Baker, for helping us out today."

"Uh, thanks."

"You will like. Forty-six inch screen, 3D technology."

Nick nodded. "Great." Maybe helping his cousins out wasn't so bad if it scored him cool toys to play with.

As they had been talking, the Chinese kitchen staff had finished loading the televisions. Nick noticed Carrey and TV Guy shaking hands. Carrey handed the man an envelope, but when he took it, he shook his head. He pulled a small stack of hundred dollar bills from the envelope. "What is this shit, Baker?" he said in a New York accent. "We agreed on small bills that had seen circulation. I can't wash these in my cash register."

"What is problem? Is good money," Carry said. "Straight from bank."

"Yeah, that's the problem. Too good." TV Guy seemed to be getting agitated. He threw the stack of money at Carrey's chest.

Nick glanced down the hallway toward the door. The Asian cooks had finished carrying TVs. Now they stood in a huddle between him and the H2. They looked scared.

Carry held up his hands in surrender. "Okay, you don't want money. I can't force you to take." He reached down and picked up the stack of hundreds. "But I am not leaving without the TVs."

"Run," Larry whispered.

"What?" Nick whispered back.

Larry grabbed Nick's arm and pushed him toward the door. Just before Nick turned, he saw Carrey hit TV Guy in the face.

Nick took a few faltering steps forward, still off-balance from Larry's shove. Then he heard the first gunshot. He sprinted for the door, running headlong into the Chinese cooks. He almost broke through the men by his momentum, but one of them caught hold of his arm. The man had a grip of steel, but he suddenly let go. Then he let go of a terrible shriek of agony.

Nick looked down and saw a knife stuck deep into the man's arm.

"Run, Cousin," Larry yelled again, as if he had to. Nick ran, and heard more screams and gunshots behind him.

He ran all the way through the alleyway and reached the street before he realized Larry and Carrey probably wanted him in the H2. He backtracked to find Larry and Carrey sauntering out the back door of the restaurant, as if they hadn't just initiated a bloodbath.

Nick jumped into the driver's seat and started the engine. He resisted the urge to stomp on the gas long enough for Larry and Carrey to get into the H2. Before they even closed the doors, he floored it. The Hummer shot out of the alley, squealing its tires and somehow managing to cut across three lanes of traffic without hitting anyone.

From the back seat, Larry patted Nick on the shoulder. "Slow down, Cousin. No need to call attention."

Nick eased off on the accelerator, but he was still shaking. "They were shooting at us."

Carrey nodded. "Unfortunate."

"Did you..." Nick tried to think of a better way to ask his question and failed. "Did you kill all those people?"

"We were merely defending ourselves, and you, Cousin," Larry said. "Besides, they were all bad people, Chinese gangsters, very nasty people."

"So," said Carrey, "are you going to marry skinny girl? If they find her."

Nick decided to change the subject. "I noticed the press seemed quite interested in her the other day. What's the big deal with her?" He turned on to Iowa Ave.

Carrey turned to look at him, surprise on his face. "You don't read *People* magazine? She one of most eligible bachelorettes in country. She turned down proposal of marriage from Jason Scotmoore, the actor in the new boxing movie."

A vision of Jason Scotmoore's perfectly chiseled abs flashed through Nick's mind. "I think I've seen the trailer for that movie."

Following Larry's directions, Nick pulled the H2 into a gravel alleyway and parked behind what looked like an abandoned warehouse. "Have I been here before?" Nick asked.

Larry nodded. "Yes, Cousin. This is Fang Dong's electronics store. We are going to resell televisions to him."

They exited the H2, and Carrey rapped on the door three times.

Nick jumped. He was still shaking from the earlier gunplay. As an afterthought, he casually brushed the front of his Dockers with his hand. Good—as far as he could tell, he hadn't wet his pants.

The man with the spider web tattoo on his neck answered the door again. He bowed to them and then motioned for them to come inside.

They walked down the large hallway, past boxes marked "USDA Prime" and hanging sides of beef. This time, Nick wondered how many of those boxes actually contained beef and how many held *Global Fight!* controllers or pirated videos.

Fang Dong sat behind the desk, crocheting what looked like a toilet-paper roll cover with a squirrel peeking out of it. In one corner of the office, a wizened Chinese woman sat smoking a cigarette and watching The Price is Right. When he saw Nick and his cousins come in with the TV box, Fang set the partially-finished squirrel on his desk and stood up.

"The Baker Brothers." He beamed. "And Cousin Nick. To what do I owe this honor?"

As he lowered his side of the television box to the ground, Larry said, "You know why we are here, Fang. We bring you televisions—forty-six inch screens, newest standard. We have a dozen to sell at five hundred per." As they talked, they unboxed the television they had brought in.

Fang walked around the TV and nodded. "Reasonable. And TV Guy?"

Carrey shrugged. "I've heard he was involved in an altercation this morning. I don't think we will be hearing from him again."

"Excellent. I will take the televisions. Please feel free to find some of my lazy employees to unload your vehicle."

"Thank you, Fang Dong," Larry said. He and Carrey started walking to the door. Nick followed.

Suddenly, the old woman appeared in front of Nick. She said something in Chinese. Larry and Carrey were already walking into the hall, and Nick tried to sidestep the woman. She stepped back into his path.

"Wait a moment, Nick Baker. My mother wants to tell you something." He called out to Larry and Carrey. "You guys go ahead and unload. We'll catch up."

The old woman took hold of Nick's wrist and led him to one of Fang Dong's office chairs. She motioned him to sit down, and when she saw he was going to comply, she sat down beside him.

She held out her hand, and Nick reflexively offered up his own. Instead of a gentle caress, she roughly took his hand and turned it over, gripping it in her stone-like fingers. As she traced the contours and lines of his palm, she mumbled disapprovingly.

"What's she saying?" Nick asked Fang Dong.

Fang shook his head. "She says that you are being followed by a *yaksha*, a nature spirit. The *yaksha* wants something from you. You also have many blocked meridians." He did not seem overly impressed by this information.

"Is that like a demon?" Nick asked.

"No, if she had meant demon, she would have said *yaoguai* or *oni*. She specifically said *yaksha*." He shook his head. "Look, my mother is well-meaning, but she is a foolish old woman."

Superstitious old woman or not, she seemed to get a sense of what Fang was saying, and she started yelling at him in Chinese. When she was done with Fang she turned to Nick, leaned forward, and said in careful English, "You. Have. Seen. Them."

Nick stood up and took a step back from her.

She stood and walked forward, pointing at Nick. "You. Have. Seen. Them."

This was too freaky. Nick made for the door. "Well, thanks for the advice, Fang Dong, Mrs. Dong."

"Mrs. Fang," Fang Dong corrected.

"Sorry, Mrs. Fang." Nick turned and jogged through the office door. As he speed-walked down the hallway of boxes and beef sides, he could still hear the old woman yelling. "You have seen them. You have seen them!"

Someone grabbed his arm, and Nick turned, bringing up his hands to defend himself.

Carrey held up his hands in mock surrender. "There you are cousin. We are unloaded and ready to go. Are you all right? You look not so good."

Nick shook his head. "I'm fine. Let's get out of here."

As they were leaving, the man with the spider web tattoo walked up to them and bowed. He handed Nick a package. "Compliments of Fang Dong."

"What is it?"

"Four pounds of T-bone steak. Thick cut. Plenty of loin."

"Um, thanks."

The man wasn't done talking. "Fang Dong regrets that his mother's words disturbed you."

"Um, tell him 'no problem' and thank him for the steak."

The man bowed again and opened the outer door for them.

Driving away, Nick kept turning the old woman's words over in his head. 'You have seen them.' Not a demon, a nature spirit.

After a few minutes, Carrey asked, "Why are you so quiet? Still upset about what happened at restaurant?"

"Well, maybe a little." Nick got shot at in *Global Fight!* all the time, but it was considerably different when it happened in the real world. "What do you know about Fang's mother?"

Carrey shrugged. "Don't know much. Just old Chinese woman. Why?"

"She sort of said something disturbing to me, about nature spirits."

"Don't worry about it," Larry said from the back seat. "Sounds crazy to me."

"Um, thanks," Nick said. A few minutes later, he parked behind Carrey's Mercedes, two blocks away from the Chinese restaurant.

Larry stopped halfway out of the car and asked, "You sure you don't want help carrying in the TV? We could follow you back to your apartment, unload TV, have a few drinks? Maybe call a few girls? Fun time to take your mind off Aunt Esther?"

Nick shook his head. "Thanks, but I'm not really in the mood. Anyway, I need to get back to work. Too much to do."

Carrey sighed. "I should tell our father to give you less to do. Then you could come on more adventures with us."

If there was one thing Nick didn't want, it was more adventures with his cousins. "Please, don't. I know my work isn't glamorous, but I enjoy it."

Larry nodded. "It takes different strokes to move the world, Cousin. Take care."

As soon as he had dropped his cousins off, Nick drove back to the Baker Administrative Complex. When he parked the H2, he didn't even take his hands off the steering wheel. He just sat staring straight forward. Then a fully intact, and wet, copy of *Elderly Golfer* magazine, open to a centerfold of Arnold Palmer's balls, landed on his windshield. This jarred him out of his state of shock. After he turned on the wipers to get rid of the offending magazine, he went inside.

Delores waved him over to the reception desk and handed him a slip of paper. "The sheriff's office called." It was odd that she was suddenly taking messages for him. They had a perfectly good voice-mail system. She looked at the package Nick had set on her desk. "What you got there, kiddo?"

"T-bones, thick cut, plenty of loin. Want them?"

Her left eyebrow rose. "Seriously?"

"Yes, a friend of my cousins gave them to me, but I'm not really into steak. They'd just sit in my freezer."

Delores bit her lip. "You sure you don't mind? That's an expensive package of meat."

Nick shrugged. "Go ahead."

"Thanks, Nick. I owe you one. Your timing couldn't be better. You know I've been dating Tony down in shipping. Well, he's getting back from a warehouse run to Florida tonight. I can't wait to see the look on his face when I serve him a giant T-bone."

Nick smiled. "Great. Enjoy." He walked back to his office hoping to get some coding in, but when he got there, JenJen was at his desk.

As soon as he saw her there, his eyes jumped to the blinds covering the far wall of his office. They were open, showing off his perfect, multidimensional courtyard. Didn't JenJen know that they shared the same view?

"Hi, JenJen. What's going on?"

JenJen gave him a disapproving look indicating she was still annoyed with him. He still didn't understand what she was mad about. He'd given her a ride to work. "I'm working. Some of us regular folks do that because we don't have rich families and we enjoy things like food and shelter." Yes, she was definitely still annoyed.

Nick sighed. "Why do you have to give me such a hard time?"

"The computer and monitors are bad enough, but I had no idea you had this kind of view." She looked up from the monitors. "I'd always thought we shared the same courtyard."

Nick shrugged. He was still hesitant to involver her in the whole supernatural creatures thing. "It seems like we should, doesn't it?

Some quirk of the architecture. I'm not sure how they did it."

"But we're just around the corner from each other."

"Like I said, it seems that way. Someday I'll show you the building blueprints and it will all make sense."

"I've actually seen you open the blinds from your side before." She didn't sound very convinced.

"Maybe it's Ron's office on the other side of your courtyard. I water his plants when he's away."

"Whatever. It's not that important." She stood up. "Do me a favor and log me out when those renders finish."

"Um, sure." He watched the sway of her hips as she walked out. He wanted to reach out and touch her. He sighed. She had a boyfriend, and he had a fiancé who was missing.

That reminded him. He pulled the message slip out of his pocket. It had the name "Deputy Randall" and a phone number written on it.

Nick called Deputy Randall. "Hi. This is Nick Baker, you left a message at my work."

"Yes, Mr. Baker. I'm sorry you weren't contacted earlier. We've been trying to reach you on your cell phone and not having any luck. I just wanted you to know we're still looking for your mother and Ms. Stafford Jennings. The National Guard has taken over the site, and they're dealing with the infestation, so we should be able to go in with our search teams soon."

"Would it be possible for me to help? I could be in a search party."

After a long pause, Randall said, "All right. You can join the search party, but wear some sturdy boots and dress in layers. I don't want you slowing us down."

"Yes, Deputy. I'll be there."

Nick hung up the phone. Shepherding code and the mysterious forest in his courtyard were going to have to wait. Maybe it was foolish optimism or just the need to do something useful, but he wanted to be personally involved with the search for his mother.

And Penelope, of course.

On his way up Highway 965, Nick drove the H2 past several detour signs. Eventually, he got to a barricade he had to drive around. A half mile after that, a deputy sat in a county sheriff's car in the middle of the road. Nick stopped the H2 and waited as a deputy got out of his car and walked over.

The deputy tapped his clipboard. "I'm sorry, sir, but I'm going to have to ask you to turn back."

"Deputy Randall asked me to come out," Nick said. "My mother is missing."

The deputy didn't even look at his clipboard. "Of course, Mr. Baker. We've been expecting you. Could I just have a look at your driver's license?"

Nick passed over his license.

The deputy examined the picture on Nick's license. "Would you mind taking off your stocking cap?"

"Yes."

The deputy looked quite annoyed at this lack of cooperation, but he didn't press the issue. "Okay, drive ahead. You'll see a tent about a half mile up the road. That's where you'll find Deputy Randall."

Yesterday, the road had been lined with the cars of church members and local media. These had presumably been towed. Now, the vehicles were marked by the logos and badges of many state and federal agencies, or painted with the camouflage of the National Guard.

Nick parked the H2 between two military humvees, which made his enormous truck look rather mundane. He walked through knots of people in various uniforms on his way to the site of the groundbreaking. Many of the soldiers were carrying M4 carbines, which Nick recognized from *Global Fight!*, but he didn't think they'd be much help against the hornets. Through the clutter of people, he could see the top of a tent and kept moving toward it. When he reached it, he found a group of men and women, also wearing suits and uniforms.

Before Nick even saw it, he heard the constant buzzing of the hornets. He stopped in his tracks and just stared at the black and yellow wall. It definitely didn't seem natural.

One of the men in a law enforcement uniform spotted Nick and walked over. "Nick Baker, right? They've been showing your picture on the television. I'm Deputy Randall." After they shook hands, Randall introduced Nick to a man in green jumpsuit and a beret with an eagle pinned to it. "This is Colonel Price Devlin of the Iowa National Guard."

"Mr. Baker," Devlin said. He held out a cellphone to Nick. "You have a call."

Nick took the phone. "Hello?"

"Nick, this is Governor Branstad. You know, I have nothing but admiration for your mother. I want to promise you that you'll be kept in the loop. And I've personally asked Colonel Devlin to answer any of your questions." Nick hadn't known that his mother even knew the governor, but that made sense. She made a point of knowing important people.

"Thank you, sir."

"And I also want you to know that the same goes for Penelope Stafford Jennings. You know, I really get a kick out of her, when she guest stars on *Celebrity Mistresses*."

"I'll, be sure to tell her that, sir, if we find her... alive." Nick hung up on the governor.

"So," Nick said, handing the phone back to Devlin. "What's the plan?"

"My first plan was using DDT," Devlin said, "but the FDA denied us permission to use it." He nodded over to the field. "We were just about to resort to more conventional means." Nick glanced over to the field, where a line of men stood wearing the chemical suits and tanks on their backs.

For a split second, Randall lost his composure, and his policeman facade slipped. He grinned and said, "You showed up at the perfect time. This is going to be really cool."

Devlin depressed the talk button of the radio velcroed to his collar. "Move in." There was a fwoosh noise, as the wall of men lit their row of flame throwers. They moved slowly forward, sweeping fire from side to side. A moment later, a wall of heat hit Nick, who was standing at least fifty yards away.

Chemical fire sprayed the wall of hornets, and the method proved devastating. Hornet corpses dropped to the ground like little burning Hindenburgs.

However, after the initial thrust, the hornets seemed to realize what was going on. They rallied.

The body of hornets split into two groups, circling around and flanking the soldiers. They closed the distance, flying too close for the flame throwers. Once they had them surrounded, they attacked the heavy garb and equipment of the soldiers, covering their face masks, taking away their vision.

The line held for another moment, but then, the formation broke. Men ran for their lives, slapping at hornets and flailing about in a way so reminiscent of the day before that Nick felt bile rise in his throat.

Devlin yelled unheard orders into his radio. Randall just shook his head and said, "My God. My God," over and over.

Between the running men and the pursuing hornets, a window opened, a hole in the carnage. Through it, Nick saw the little demon—or should he call it a nature spirit now? He was standing at the edge of the tree line, stroking his beard. The creature danced a little jig and finished with a flourish, bowing to Nick. He stood and motioned for Nick to come to him.

A calm came over Nick. All the stress which had been pressing down on him—his mother's disappearance, his fear of the demon, the fleeing soldiers, the wall of hornets—seemed to evaporate. He took a step forward and then another. Before he realized it, he was striding forward, through the fleeing soldiers, through the burned hornets, though the burning vegetation, ignoring the shouts of Deputy Randall and Colonel Devlin. He didn't receive a single sting as he walked through wave after wave of hornets and followed the demon into the forest.

9

THE PATH TO GOD

The demon, or nature spirit, or whatever, walked down an animal trail, and Nick followed him, wondering with every footfall if he was doing the right thing. His logical side said no, but if he put all logic aside and went with his gut, his gut said, hell no. Still, he kept walking.

Eventually, he worked up the nerve to speak. "What do you want of me, demon?" Of course, Nick knew he was probably a nature spirit, but, "What do you want of me, creature who is probably a nature spirit?" just didn't have the same ring.

The creature stopped so suddenly, Nick almost fell over it. He backed up two steps.

"I'm not a demon. I'm a faun. My name's Leopold."

"A fawn, like a baby deer?"

"Not a fawn, a faun, a child of Pan, a genuine nature spirit. Not to be confused with satyrs, which are bacchanalian creatures."

"Bacchanalian?" Nick asked. "You mean they're drunks?"

Leopold shook his head. "No. Well, they do like a drink or two, but they are mainly bacchanalian in terms of being servants of the god Bacchus. To tell a family secret, my grandmother was a satyr, but let's keep that between the two of us."

Nick was left speechless, which was just as well, as the creature turned and started walking again. This just couldn't be happening. There had to be a logical explanation. "Did Rudy put you up to this?"

The faun stopped in his tracks, turned, and gave Nick a withering look. "What?"

"Sure, I met guys like you at school. Alternative lifestyle types with all the body modifications, into all the heretical religions. Let me guess, you come from somewhere in southern Iowa, like Muscatine, and Mommy and Daddy are spending all their pig farming money to buy you a 'higher education.' You're majoring in drama, and your name is Cody or Jesse, but you got drunk, stoned, or laid for the first time during the first week of school, and for the last year, you have been calling yourself 'Starchild.' You took a class on mythology to get you out of a real class, and you learned about all this Pan junk, right?"

Leopold motioned to Nick. "Come down here, please."

After a moment's deliberation, Nick knelt down. "Why do you want me down here?"

Reaching over, the faun ripped the stocking cap from Nick's head to expose the two small, but sturdy horns. "Can you tell me how a drama student can accomplish that?" He grabbed one of Nick's horns and pushed his head back and forth. It was firmly attached. "That's genuine old-fashioned magick," he said in a way that made Nick think that magic would be spelled in some exotic way, if it were written down. Leopold waited a moment to see if Nick would retort and said, "Okay, let's keep walking. We don't want to be late."

"Late for what?" Nick asked as he started trudging after the creature again.

"We're going to see the boss."

"The boss?" Nick asked.

"You know, The Great God Pan, The Goat God? He's the god of goats, sheep, shepherds, stinging insects, music, panic, defiling maidens and nymphs, nature, meadows, forests, forest beasts, and general carnal lusting. He also serves as the god of the sea, but only when all the other sea gods are on vacation."

Somehow, this didn't add up. "I'm sorry, Leopold, but I just don't believe you. I was raised Christian, and taught that the only gods were the Father, the Son, and the Holy Ghost. Not the Holy Goat."

"Well, hang on to your socks, bub, cause you're about to meet one."

"Did you just call me bub?"

Leopold turned back around and started walking again.

After heading through the forest for what seemed like a significant time, Nick spotted a formation of three toadstools on the side of a tree, which he swore he'd seen before. "Have we been this way already?"

Leopold whipped round to face him. "Are you questioning my sense of direction? I'm a bona fide nature spirit. When was the last time you even went hiking?"

"I was just trying to be helpful," Nick said. "I thought I'd seen that tree before."

"How about you keep your opinions to yourself?"

"All right. Are all nature spirits so touchy?"

Leopold shrugged. "Hey, I'm a faun, not an angel." He turned and started walking again. At least their short conversation had given him a chance to catch his breath.

They walked through the woods for another twenty minutes. Despite Leopold's claims of being a nature spirit, Nick wondered if he was being taken to some kind of portal to Hell. Then again, the middle of the woods did seem more like the place to find nature spirits than demons. Demons would probably be more at home at insurance companies, or maybe telemarketing offices.

Leopold stopped suddenly again, causing Nick to stop short.

"Why are we stopping?" Nick asked.

"We have arrived."

"Oh God," Nick said. They hadn't just arrived at a clearing. They'd arrived at *the* clearing. The clearing in his great-grandfather's painting. The clearing somehow attached to his office.

"That's the point," Leopold said. "Now, open your eyes."

"My eyes are open," Nick said.

The faun shook his head. "No, not like you look at your computer screen. Really look at what's in front of you." The little creature reached up and patted Nick on the elbow. "How are you doing, sport?"

Nick had heard the phrase "beyond terror" before, but the concept had never really sunk in for him. After walking through a wall of hornets and following a mythological creature into the deep woods, he didn't feel anything, like his fear tank was empty. He closed his eyes and took a deep breath. "I don't know. I just feel kind of numb."

"That's good," Leopold said. "I think you're ready to meet the boss. Now, open your eyes."

Nick felt like he was a little boy again, gazing at the painting, shifting his gaze inwards, following the leaves and branches of the trees toward the center, the subject of the composition, and suddenly he was looking at the god Pan.

Nick opened his mouth, and a croaking noise came out.

Leopold patted his elbow again. "You're all right, big guy. Just give it a minute."

Pan stood eight feet tall, counting the horns. His hips and legs were heavily muscled and covered in thick fur. Like Leopold, he had hooves instead of feet. Other than the fur, Pan was completely naked, and he had an enormous penis pointing skywards. The tip was about eye-level with Nick.

The clearing was not empty at all. There were fauns and naked men and women everywhere. They were engaged in a variety of sex acts. Nick tried to avert his gaze. At Pan's feet sat a naked, middle-aged woman playing the flute...

"Mother!" Nick said. "Put some clothes on!"

His mother shook her head. "The human body is a beautiful thing. There is nothing to be ashamed of. Stop acting like such a prude."

"Oh my God." Something was seriously wrong. "Mother? What have they done to you?"

She smiled at him. "Nick, I'm so happy you're here. Allow me to introduce the god Pan." Typical of Nick's mother, she couldn't resist making a formal introduction, regardless of her nudity.

"Greetings, Nick Baker." Nick had expected Pan's voice to boom, but instead, it was lyrical and smooth.

"Um…" Nick was unsure how to address a god. He decided to stick with a classic. "Hello."

"Why are you so timid?" Pan asked. "Do you fear me, Nick Baker?"

"No… It's just…" Nick pointed to the god's preternatural penis. "Could you put that thing away somewhere?"

Nick's mother looked up at the otherworldly organ. "It's perfectly natural, Nick."

From where Nick was standing, there was nothing natural going on.

Pan chuckled. "In the religion to which you were born, I have been vilified as the root of all evil. Yet you worry about such a trivial thing as this?" For emphasis, Pan flicked the end of it, causing it to wobble back and forth.

Nick was paralyzed for a moment, a cobra watching the snake charmer's flute. When he regained his composure, he said, "Let's just stop talking about it."

"Very well," Pan said. "What would you like to discuss?"

He might as well go for broke. "Well, I'd like my mother back," he said. "And Penelope as well."

"Nick Baker!" his mother said, standing up. "I am my own person, and I will go where I want. I'm with Pan now."

Nick eyed Pan's otherworldly organ. "Define *with*."

Before anyone could answer, Penelope Stafford Jennings stepped up beside him. "Hello, Nicholas. How are you?"

Nick turned to answer her, only to be struck speechless. Like his mother, Penelope was also naked. However, Penelope was, for the lack of a better word, perfection. The first time he had seen her, he had been in an altered state. The second time, she had been wearing conservative church clothes. Now, she stood before him, free from both body hair and tan lines, she looked as much a goddess as Pan did a god. How did she do her makeup and keep her hair so straight in the forest?

"Nicholas Baker, stop that," his mother snapped.

"What did I do? You said the human body was a beautiful thing." And Penelope's was a ten-out-of-ten.

"Not when you look at it like that, it's not," his mother said haughtily.

As much as he hated to do it, Nick decided it would be best to avert his gaze from Penelope. He looked over at the goat god. A butterfly had landed on the tip of Pan's penis, like a scene from an erotic Disney movie. This was too much, so he returned to looking at his mother, trying to keep his view above her neck line, especially in consideration of the tightness in his pants after looking at Penelope.

Pan took a few steps forward, and said something Nick was not expecting. "Walk with me, Nick." He put his hand on Nick's shoulder and led him out of the clearing and onto a path through the woods. Nick tried to keep his eyes straight ahead and not look at Pan's massive erection swaying back and forth, not far from his face. He was definitely going back into therapy after this.

After they had walked for a short time, Pan stopped. They were back at the same clearing, but it had been transformed. The pine needles scattering the ground had been covered in red paint. A gigantic red circle outlined the clearing and a pentagram had been inscribed inside it. Five torches sprouted from each point of the pentagram, and crouching by each one was a naked woman. In the center stood a man, naked and erect. At first Nick thought he was covered in blood, but then he realized he had covered his body in Greek writing. Three scrolls lay at his feet. For some reason, the naked man looked familiar.

"Great-Grandfather Earl?!" Nick had seen the man before in a hundred family pictures. After his Great-Great-Grandfather Clayton Earl Baker had moved the family to Iowa City and almost lost the fortune building the factory and Baker House, Great-Grandfather Earl Prescott Baker Sr. had restored the family's prosperity.

"I've brought you back in time," Pan explained. "So you can see why I returned to your family."

Earl Sr. held up the first scroll and read some bad-sounding poetry. Then the women stood up and started walking toward him.

"Oh, no." Nick shook his head. "I don't want to see that."

"Are you sure?" Pan asked. "It's quite a show."

"No. Definitely not. Can we skip ahead or something?"

Pan snorted. "If you insist."

The whole world flickered and Nick nearly fell. He grabbed hold of Pan to steady himself, and realized he had grabbed hold of the deity's ding-a-ling. Nick was horrified by what he was holding, but rather impressed that it could resist his weight. It was as stiff as an oak branch. He let go, cleared his throat, and said in his manliest voice, "Sorry," as if it weren't a big deal.

Now, the women laid still around the interior of the pentagram, hopefully exhausted from the orgy and not dead from some kind of ritual sacrifice. Great-Grandfather Earl was back in the center, surprisingly still erect—maybe that was something to do with the magic. He picked up the second scroll and read another bad poem. Pan appeared before him, not the one standing beside Nick, but the one from the past.

The Pan before Earl Sr. looked identical to the one standing beside Nick. Randall fell to his knees before the god. "O Pan, great and powerful god."

Pan contemplated Nick's ancestor. "Please, stand up. You put together a nice orgy here, Baker."

"Thank you, great god."

"Just call me Pan. So, you wanted to speak to me?"

Earl Sr. hesitated for a moment, and then said, "My family, once wealthy, has fallen on hard times. I understand that you can grant boons of prosperity."

Past Pan nodded. "That is true. However, I only grant boons to those who do a service for me. Why do you believe yourself worthy of my attention?"

And then, something changed in the demeanor of Earl Sr. He seemed more comfortable. He picked up the third scroll and held it out to Past Pan. "This is the abstract to this land, three thousand acres of virgin forest which I own outright. Right now, this country is a vast, untamed wilderness, but you have seen the rate at which human society has expanded. How many years before this forest is converted to brick and concrete, factory and farm? Where will you and the creatures of the forest live in one hundred years, two hundred years? How long do you really have?"

Past Pan scratched his goatee. "You make an interesting point."

"If you grant prosperity to my family, I pledge to keep these lands untouched by human interference. As long as there are Bakers, this land will be kept pure."

"This is a generous offer. However, what guarantee do I have? How do I know that some descendant of yours will not break this deal?"

Great-Grandfather Earl stood proud for a man wearing not a stitch of clothes and facing a gigantic dong. "We Bakers are a proud family. We understand the sanctity of a fair deal and take pride in honoring our ancestors. I will leave instructions for my successive patriarchs. I trust them to honor our deal."

Past Pan nodded. "Very well, I accept your offer, but be warned. Breaking this deal will result in ruination instead of prosperity."

Current Pan put his hand on Nick's shoulder and guided him away from the clearing. "Now you know why I have taken an interest in you, Nick Baker. Earl Baker the Third, your uncle, has broken my pact with your ancestor. As his heir and successor, you must set right what he has done."

As they returned to the present, some of the stranger things in Nick's life started to make sense. Pan must have been the figure in his great-grandfather's painting, the one that caused the panic attack all those years ago, his mere image causing a break in Nick's mind. "Do you cause all the garbage to fall on the Baker Administrative Complex?"

"Oh yes," Pan said. "I'm particularly proud of that one. I'm surprised your uncle didn't give up after I dropped the first ton of garbage on his construction project."

Nick shrugged. "What can I say? Uncle Earl is stubborn."

"Just make sure he doesn't stubborn you out of your legacy." At the moment, this seemed like pretty good advice.

"I guess I'll do what I can," Nick said. "Now that I'm on board with your plan, can you do something about these?" Nick carefully took off his stocking cap to show his little horns.

"What do you want me to do with them?" Pan asked.

"Could you get rid of them?"

"Oh, well, I guess so. If you're sure. Personally, I think they look good."

Nick nodded. "I'm sure."

Pan reached over and Nick heard two little snaps. "There you go."

Nick reached up and felt his forehead, perfectly smooth. "Thanks," Nick said, stuffing his stocking cap into his jeans pocket.

After they walked a little farther, Pan produced a set of pipes, and started playing and dancing along the path. Nick was quite sure the melody Pan had been playing before was something from Pink Floyd, or maybe Jethro Tull. As he followed the prancing god back to the clearing, Nick found he had a spring in his step and his mood had greatly improved.

They returned to the clearing. Leopold, Penelope, and Nick's mother were still there. They sat on the grass talking and laughing. If they had been eating Oreos and marshmallows, Nick would have sworn they were stoned.

They stood at the edge of the clearing for a few moments, and Nick felt compelled to break the silence. "So," Nick said to Pan, "you are a god. What is that like?"

"You are a man, what is that like? I am as I am. The vision people have of me changes between cultures and millennia, but I am fundamentally just what I have always been."

"Is that why your penis was smaller in the past?"

Pan nodded. "As I said, I am shaped by the expectations of others. I blame Internet pornography."

"Um, Pan, I don't want to make you angry, but can I have my mother and Penelope back?"

"That depends, Nick Baker." He walked into the center of the clearing, where Nick's mother and Penelope were chatting with the faun. "Penelope and Esther, Nick Baker has asked that you return to the mundane world with him. What say you?"

Nick's mother spoke without hesitation. "I'm staying. I'm not going to go back to church boards and Sunday dinners knowing there is a bigger world out there."

Pan nodded. "Very well, and you Penelope?"

"Oh, I'll go back with Nick. No offense, but sitting around and listening to the flute is okay for a few days, but it's really not for me."

Pan walked over to her and took her in his arms. Nick noted that Pan judiciously angled his penis so it didn't hit her in the face. Pan kissed her deeply.

Penelope let out a moan and closed her eyes, going limp in his arms.

Pan lowered her to the ground. "Nick Baker, take her from this place and return her to the land of men. She will remember none of her experience here."

"All right," Nick said, "but there's one other thing I have to ask before I go back. What's the deal with the bicycle? Was that you?"

Leopold raised his hand. "Actually, that was me, Sport. I just thought it would be better for the environment than driving that big gas-guzzler. Think about it."

Penelope was skinny, but she was tall, making her not so easy to carry. Nick was forced to throw her over his shoulder, which meant his cheek was pressed against her naked thigh. He still wouldn't have been able to carry her far like this. Fortunately, on the way back, the path was flatter and considerably shorter. He was out of breath by the time he reached the groundbreaking site. His side had started to ache, and he was hyperventilating. But he didn't want to put her down, because he'd just have to pick her up again. He didn't even hesitate to walk through the curtain of hornets. They had let him through before, and this time, he had Pan on his side. He was too tired to worry about them anyway.

He emerged on the other side, the naked debutante thrown over his shoulder, and watched the assembled guardsmen and deputies as he walked back across the field. They were all going about their business, and none of them noticed him. Finally, a guardsman saw Nick walking across the burned landscape. To Nick's chagrin, he didn't immediately call for help, he took out his cellphone and started filming.

Nick finally got past the burnt ground and dead insects, and found a patch of earth that seemed suitably soft for Penelope's naked body. He carefully set her down and then collapsed beside her. He was vaguely aware of Colonel Devlin and Deputy Randall rushing toward them.

As he lay next to the very naked heiress, Nick thought about what Pan had told him. The goat god didn't want the mega-church, but why did he need to be involved? Even if Earl Sr. made some kind of deal with the god, that was none of Nick's business. There had to be a way to get rid of Pan.

Penelope opened her eyes. "Nick? What happened?" She rolled onto her side to look at him. "Oh, hello, what's this?" She squeezed the front of his khakis.

"There's a stocking cap in my pocket."

10

HOME INVASION

FightOS kernel 8.5.1.3 ....loaded
  Searching for updates .... Up to date.
  Interfacing with GPS hardware ....done
  Discovering Controllers
  Primary ....Global Fight! Gold Headset Found (default)
  Network ....Found
  Loading Newest Textures............................done
  Building Texture Cache.........done
  Starting Game

When he arrived home from the groundbreaking site, Nick found an email from Rudy. Rudy had been playing *Global Fight!* all day, as he spent many days, and he thought he'd found the lair of DeathChick82. After the events of the afternoon, a nice, relaxing game of *Global Fight!* was exactly what Nick needed. He read the message again to get the coordinates of DeathChick82's safe house.

Nick took a SecureKab to the coordinates Rudy had provided, a defunct warehouse not far from where Fang Dong's electronics store was located in the real world. The door opened, and Nick saw Rudy's avatar, Doctor Rude, motioning for him to come inside.

"You're late," Rudy said, as Nick came through the door.

"Dude," Nick said, "you don't even want to know about the day I've had. I am so ready to kick some ass." He looked out the window of the warehouse at the buildings across the street. "I don't see anything that looks like a safe house."

"That's the whole point."

Safe houses were places in the game where players had created their own customized lair, usually by taking advantages of glitches in the game's map design combined with a little custom programming—walk into a certain place in a wall and move quick to the left to find yourself in a hidden room. Players used them to hide equipment and gear. Players with money would sometimes pay the volunteer designers to build a glitch into an update, so they would have a hidden area to camp out.

Rudy sighed. "If you could see it, it wouldn't be a safe house." His avatar squatted down and lifted a metal grate that was built into the floor covering a drainage tunnel. Rudy hopped down and Nick followed. It was dark, so they switched on their flashlights, and she appeared.

DeathChick82 stood at the end of a 100-foot section of tunnel. She brought her gun up and said, "Who dares enter my lair?"

Before she even got off a shot, Nick started running. Rather than take cover, he decided to charge. With luck, he could fill her with more bullets than she could fire into him, an effective strategy in virtual warfare. Rudy was right beside him, shooting and running with him. They fell through the floor.

Of course, that was the problem with trying to track down a safe house. Anyone who could obtain a secret entrance could also hide a trap. After a minute, Nick said, "So, this was a trap."

"Looks that way," Rudy agreed.

"This hole is really deep."

"Yeah, I think she probably used a cheat to create this, which is against the rules, you know."

"Yeah." There wasn't much else to say.

After another few seconds, Rudy said, "If we keep falling like this, will we end up in *Global Fight!* China?"

"No," Nick said. "I looked it up. The opposite end of the Earth from Iowa is actually the Indian Ocea—"

CRUNCH.

After his truly embarrassing *Global Fight!* game, Nick sat down on the couch and turned on the TV. The local news had just started, and inanely happy newscasters talked rapid fire back and forth, as images flashed up behind them.

"Tonight on your Eastern Iowa News Source, learn how a little known crop has been making big money for one Iowa farmer."

"Then we'll go to the weather lab to find out if our unusually warm weather will continue into May."

A picture of Nick and a picture of Penelope flashed up on the screen. "We'll also have reactions to the dramatic rescue of Penelope Stafford Jennings by Nick Baker."

A picture of Kevin, Downcastle's town cop, flashed up on the screen. "In other Baker-related news, we'll find out why this local policeman will be spending the next month on suspension."

"Tonight on the channel..."

Nick winced and turned off the set.

"Not a big fan of the news, Nick?" said a clipped, boarding-school accent.

Nick internally winced. He knew that voice. He turned around to see Penelope. "Don't you wear clothes?" he asked.

She shrugged, which made her breasts move, making them impossible not to watch. "I don't know why, but since I've recovered from my time lost in the forest, clothing has felt even more constricting than usual. Besides, nudity doesn't really bother me. I've been to nude beaches."

"I know. I do have the Internet." Nick felt his cheeks flush.

"Ah, so you've seen the pictures."

"Of course I have," Nick said. "I Googled you after our forced betrothal." He got up and pulled the blinds shut. "But this is Iowa, you can't just go around naked."

"Call me a trendsetter." She walked over and poked her finger into his chest. "You know it's not very polite rescuing a girl from certain death and just leaving her to be picked up by the ambulance.

I had to sit in a hospital bed and be poked and prodded all alone. You could have at least stuck around. I was bored."

Now that she was standing closer, Nick caught the scent of her perfume. Normally, he wasn't a fan of perfume and colognes, but Penelope's scent was subtle, like the smell of a cool breeze on a summer day, refreshing and innocent. It made him want to grab hold of her and claim that innocence, which he intellectually knew was a fantasy. He took a deep breath to steady his nerves, only to find himself again captivated.

He took a step back, trying to escape. Maybe if he was confrontational, she'd back off. "How did you get in here?" he demanded.

"I knocked and you didn't answer, so I just came in. You were playing your game and you didn't even notice me, so I decided to make myself more comfortable. I must have walked past you three times." Penelope talked so fast Nick had to pause after she finished speaking to catch up. It made him feel off balance, like a boxer after a flurry of jabs. He sat down, putting more distance between them. "But why are you here?"

"You don't want your fiancé to stay in a hotel, do you?"

"Well... Wait, you're not my fiancé."

"If I'm not, then certainly nobody's told me about it. The last I heard, Grandpa Stafford is ready to cut me off if I don't go through with it. To be honest, I wasn't so hot about the idea at first. I've had my eyes on Prince Harry for quite some time, and to be quite honest, well, I thought you were a bit meh."

"Hey!"

"But when you carried me out of that forest, I was like, 'Oh, Nick.'" She said, "Oh, Nick," quite dramatically, flicking her long hair and holding her hand to her chest, drawing Nick's attention back to the chest which had launched a thousand tabloids. "You were like an action hero."

"Me? Action hero?"

Nick had seen Penelope naked before, but now, without his mother around, his eyes couldn't help looking up and down her body, examining her in such detail that a CT scanning machine would be impressed. She was flawless, like an airbrushed cover girl, or a centerfold for that matter.

"So, my hero," she said, sitting next to him on the couch. "What do you think we should do now?" She put her hand on his thigh.

Nick yelped and stood up. "I... I... I... really have to go." He started walking briskly, or as briskly as he could currently manage. He was feeling lightheaded, as if there was not enough blood in his body to fully power his brain. "I have an appointment I have to keep." He reached for the door.

"It's okay, Nick, we're engaged."

He closed the door behind him and leaned on it, catching his breath. Maybe he should see what Rudy was doing.

"Hello, Nick."

Nick looked up. "Oh, hi, Mrs. Coltrane."

"That's quite a tent you're pitching."

"Um... Thanks? I really have to be going."

He walked up the steps and opened the door just in time for Mrs. Coltrane to call out, "Try to keep that thing in your pants this time."

Nick nodded to Officer Kevin Coltrane, who had been watching them from the door. "Um, hi, Kevin."

––––––––––––––––––––

A half hour later, Nick eased the H2 into the narrow alley behind Rudy's house. He was getting a little better at driving the large vehicle, but as he slid out of the driver's seat, he cast a guilty glance at the bike lying on top of his 46" television in the back. It probably would be a better way to get around, for the environment, at least.

Nick walked through the alley, down the outdoor basement stairs to Rudy's house, and knocked on the door lightly, so he would not wake up Rudy's parents. After a few minutes, Rudy opened the door. "Hey, Nick, what's up?"

"You mind if I hang out for a while?"

"No problem. Come on in." Rudy got a silly grin. "I saw you on the news today with Penelope Stafford Jennings."

Nick nodded. "Yeah, that's why I am here."

"You get a piece of that yet?" Rudy raised his fist for a bump.

No bump was returned. "No. My relationship with Penelope is complicated. I don't even know her. Any attraction I feel is just superficial lust."

"What's so wrong with that? Why do you have to over-think everything?" Rudy tapped his chest. "In here, I hate you a little right now. Come on, let's watch TV."

They sat down on the couch. Rudy was watching some low-budget science fiction show about a small town terrorized by vampire cows. "This whole program is ludicrous," Rudy said.

"Why? Because cows as herbivores would be unlikely to turn into vampires?"

"No, it's ludicrous that they would take the time and trouble to film a vampire movie with no gratuitous nudity or hot lady vampires. And seriously, why would vampires go to Nebraska?"

"Rudy, do you ever get your mind out of the gutter?"

He shook his head. "No, I like it there. The gutter is a good place to be. You can meet some really interesting people. You should try it sometime. It could open you up to a whole new world."

"No thanks."

The program stopped for commercials and the hemovorus bovine on the screen was replaced by a black man with half of his face painted white wearing a black top hat. "Are you interested in life beyond the grave? Are you visited by supernatural creatures? Has any member of your family risen as a zombie? If you can answer yes to any of these questions, then perhaps we can help.

"My name is Papa Damballah. I come from New Orleans, and I bring with me many authentic Voodoo artifacts and charms. If you are just looking for some authentic New Orleans charm, come down to the Voodoo Hut, in the Pedestrian Mall in Iowa City, next to McDonalds."

Rudy turned off the TV and asked, "So, what's bothering you? Tell Doctor Rude all about it."

"Uncle Earl and my mother conspired behind my back to arrange a marriage with Penelope Stafford Jennings."

"Holy Shit! You're engaged to PSJ?"

"Oh, have you heard of her before? I guess she's kind of famous."

"Heard of her? I've memorized her nipple size. But I thought she was marrying Jason Scottmoore, the one with..."

"The perfectly chiseled abs. She turned him down."

"Actually, I was going to say, 'the massive wang.' He did some softcore independent films before he made it big. So, what's your problem?"

"Well tonight, she comes over to my place while I'm playing *Global Fight!* I log off from the system and she walks in wearing nothing at all."

"Nothing at all?" Rudy repeated.

"She starts telling me about how I'm a hero for saving her and everything. The engagement is still on, and she's moving in."

"And, what did you do?"

"I left and came here."

Rudy's jaw dropped. "You had PSJ in your condo, nude, calling you her hero, and you didn't do anything?"

Nick shook his head. "No. I don't even know her."

Rudy leaned forward and punched Nick in the arm.

"Ow! What was that for?"

Rudy shook his head. "I don't believe you. What's wrong with you? So what if you don't get along afterwards. It's better to have boned and lost than never to have boned at all. In fact, you know what?" Rudy stood up and pointed to the door. "Get out of my house right now. I can't make you bang her, but I don't have to sit here and watch you not bang her."

"Meaning you would watch me bang her?" Nick asked.

Rudy nodded. "I think I could get past the initial awkwardness. Now, I'm serious, get out."

Nick left.

He parked the H2 in front of his condo. When he got home, the condo was dark. He flicked on the lights. There were no naked women in his living room. He walked down the hall, opened the bedroom door, and froze.

Penelope Stafford Jennings was sleeping naked on top of his covers.

Nick backed out and closed the door. He took off his shirt and khaki's and tried to get comfortable on the couch. Usually, with a female houseguest, he would never have considered sleeping in his underwear in the living room. He knew his mother wouldn't approve, but he didn't really want to go back into the bedroom to get his pajamas, as he had seen more of Penelope's body than he had of his last two girlfriends, and his mother was currently taking naked flute lessons from Pan. It would probably be all right. Eventually, he fell into a deep sleep, until the screaming started.

Nick woke to the sound of screaming and fell off the couch. This would have been no big deal, except he was not the world's best housekeeper. He'd let some things go, such as picking up and vacuuming. The thin layer of sweat he had built up while sleeping acted as an adhesive, and when he stood, he brought with him some computer screws, a few Doritos, some candy corn left over from Halloween, and a remote control.

At first, he thought he'd had a nightmare, but then he realized the screaming was coming from his bedroom. He pulled the remote control off his cheek and gave the rest of his torso a quick brushdown to get rid of the worst of it.

Nick knocked tentatively. "Everything okay in there?"

Penelope's voice sounded shaken. "I believe there is a monster under your bed."

"What?"

"There's a monster under your bed."

Nick waited for a better explanation, but none was forthcoming. "Okay. I'll take a look." He walked into the bedroom. Penelope was nowhere to be seen, but the bathroom door was shut, and there was light coming from under the door. Nick got down on his hands and knees and looked under the bed.

Leopold looked back at him. "Howdy, Sport."

"What the hell are you doing under here?"

"I came in to give you your daily advice from Pan." Leopold handed Nick a piece of parchment. "I didn't know Penelope was going to be in your bed. By the way, are you hitting that, Nick?" He held up his fist to be bumped.

Nick ignored the fist. He was getting a little more than tired of questions about his sex life. "No, I am not," he snapped.

"There's no reason to get huffy. Anyway, she wakes up and starts screaming her head off. I duck under here, and she runs in the bathroom. I don't get it. She wasn't ever shy around Pan."

"She doesn't know what's going on. Pan erased her memory. It's not like she woke up to find some horned beast looking down at her. I couldn't possibly imagine what could have made her nervous."

"No need to get sarcastic. Now would you help me out of here? I have a horn stuck in your box spring."

As Nick was trying to lift and twist the mattress, Penelope's voice came from the bathroom. "Nick? It's quiet out there, are you all right?"

"I'm fine." Nick said in a voice hopefully pitched loud enough to penetrate a bathroom door. "Just stay in there for a few more minutes."

"Okay," Penelope said in a shaky voice.

Free from obstruction, Leopold pulled himself out from under the bed. "Those horns are a pain in the ass, but it is tradition."

Penelope's voice came from the bathroom. "Are you talking to someone? Can I come out now?"

"Um, one more minute, Penelope," Nick called out. Then he whispered to Leopold, "Let's get you out of here." Nick gave the faun a hand up and escorted him to the door. As they were walking, he glanced at the note. In fine calligraphy, it said, "Ride the bike."

Nick opened the blinds to his front patio and slid open the glass door. "Hey, Leopold? Why are you giving me a note telling me to ride the bike? You already told you wanted me to."

"And have you done it yet? Aren't you even a little interested in the environment? A better world starts with you. Pedal power gets much better gas mileage."

"Okay, I'll give it a try, but only if you promise to stop sneaking around my condo in the middle of the night," Nick said, showing him through the door.

"That would be fine. I have other business to attend to anyway." Leopold bowed. "I thank you, and Pan thanks you." Then the faun turned and started walking.

Nick shook his head. If they had wanted him to ride the bike, they should have just told him to instead of dropping off notes in the middle of the night. It was the twenty-first century after all. Maybe it was time for Leopold to drop the whole calligraphy and parchment thing and get an email account.

Nick walked back and knocked on the bathroom door. "All clear. No more monsters."

The door flung open, and Penelope stood right in front of him. He was only wearing his boxers, and she wasn't wearing anything. She was a little disheveled from sleep, but this made her no less attractive. It seemed the old adage was true. If you started with a beautiful woman and took away the fancy clothes and jewelry, took away the hairstyle, makeup, and perfume, all you would be left with was a gorgeous, naked woman.

"You're my hero again," she said. "And here we are both naked. How will I ever repay you?" She ran a finger down Nick's chest.

"I'm not naked," Nick said. "I'm still wearing my boxer—"

In one smooth motion, Penelope squatted down, pulling his boxer shorts to the floor, and popped back up to face him.

"Never mind."

Nick let instinct get the better of him. Letting go of all propriety, Nick grabbed Penelope and threw her on the bed in a move that would have made any caveman proud if they'd had beds back then or knew what they were.

Nick pounced on Penelope, somehow crossing the bedroom without touching the floor.

"Oh Nick, finally." She pulled him down for a kiss, and then quite a bit of kissing and some groping went on as well.

Deciding to be playful, he nibbled and kissed her on the neck. This drove her crazy. She dug her nails into his back. It hurt.

"Ow." Despite the pain, Nick was committed to action. He positioned himself for more intimate contact, and felt Penelope holding him back.

Nick tried to push forward again, but she raised her knee to block him. Somehow, she had also got an arm between them. She pushed him back. He got the horrible thought that maybe she wanted him to tell her he loved her. She got him back a couple more inches and lifted something to his face.

"Is this a Dorito?" she asked.

"Um, yeah, that's what it looks like."

"What is it doing stuck to your back?"

"Well, when you screamed, I fell off the couch, and well, I'm not the world's best housekeeper."

She flicked away the Dorito, and used both hands to press against Nick's chest. Due to the sweatiness of their situation, some of the various items stuck to Nick now stuck to her. "Ew, ew, ew, ew. Oh, my God, you are the most disgusting man ever." Nick shifted his weight so she was out from under him.

"So, what now?" asked Nick, as he tried to pull up his semi-attached boxers.

"Now, I am going to take a shower, and then I am going to pack a bag, and then I am going home to Philadelphia and think about things a little. I tried to give you a chance, Nick Baker, but ew." Nick barely heard her; he was too busy taking a look at her spectacular body, which he was quite sure he would never be able to see again.

The bathroom door shut and locked this time. Nick was reasonably sure it would not open again until he was on his way to work. If he wanted to go to the office, he would have to shower the chips and other detritus from his body. He hoped the water would be nice and cold.

Showering in the guest bathroom meant Nick didn't get to use his toothbrush. He peddled the bicycle a few blocks to the Downcastle Gas 'N Go and bought a new one, a Baker Javelin. Of course, he could have just walked into the promotional department or the warehouse and picked up a box of Javelins if he'd wanted to, but no one else in the company would have been allowed to do that, so neither would he.

Getting back on the bike at the Gas 'N Go, he already felt a little stiff. By the time he was halfway to work, he wished he had taken the H2. There was no bike lane on highway 965, and his fellow commuters didn't seem to understand that a bicycle had an equal right to the road. His legs were cramping, and the wounds made by Penelope's fingernails were throbbing. As he crested the last hill on the way to the complex, a plastic bag from the landfill ambushed him at high velocity. He lost control of the bike and ended up in the ditch.

Nick staggered into the lobby of the Baker Administrative Complex with a dirty, torn shirt. He made a half-hearted effort at waving to Delores before staggering down the hallway. When he opened the door to his office, however, JenJen was already at his desk.

"Hey, JenJen, could I have my computer back?"

Without looking up she said, "I don't see why I should. You're the one who's late. I should get the nice view. Besides, you left half the project files checked out yesterday. I needed to use your computer to do my work."

"Whatever," Nick said, dropping into one of his visitor's chairs.

"What, no argument?"

"No, no argument. Just let me sit here for a minute." Nick felt he should explain his physical exhaustion. "I'm trying to reverse the ecological impact of driving the H2. I rode a bike to work today."

"What is that, about five miles?"

"Twelve," Nick said defensively. "I used to think it made for a nice, short drive."

"And now?"

"I'm not really sure I can make it back." Nick stood up, feeling a little less wobbly. He picked up the toiletries from the convenience store. "I need to brush my teeth." He walked in the bathroom and brushed his teeth with the Javelin, turning his back on JenJen.

When he walked back into the office, JenJen had gotten up. She seemed colder. She headed for the door. As she left, she said, "You might want to change your shirt."

Nick wondered for a moment what she meant. He looked his shirt up and down and nothing looked wrong with it. He went into his bathroom and took the shirt off. On the back were bloodstains where Penelope's scratch marks had bled through.

Nick put his shirt back on and walked back into the office. Uncle Earl was waiting in his visitor's chair.

"Whoa there, tiger. It looks to me like you've been up to no good."
Nick blushed. "Well, kind of."

"That's my boy. I would wager to guess that you have been 'hooking up,' as you young people say, with Miss Stafford Jennings?"

As always, Nick winced a little when Uncle Earl called him "my boy," even though Uncle Earl had been his paternal role model since the death of his father. "Well, we did fool around a little this morning, but I'm afraid I am going to have to let you down, Uncle Earl. She got upset this morning and returned to the City of Brotherly Love."

"What?!"

"Penelope announced to me she needed to think about things. I have no doubt that by now, she is petitioning her grandfather for a reprieve, and if necessary, tears will be involved."

"Don't worry about the Stafford Jennings. The ink is dry on that deal." Uncle Earl passed Nick an overstuffed manila envelope. "Hey, speaking of ink. Take a look at these documents and sign off on them. They're proxy voting rights for your shares."

"Why do I even have to sign over my proxy? What if I wanted to come to the meeting and vote?"

"Come if you want—if you want to be stuck in a boring meeting all day. It's your stock and your right to make decisions for the company. But things will go smoother if I have control of the majority of voting stock. So, just sign off on this and give it back to me, okay son?" Every year, Uncle Earl made the same request for his voting shares, and usually he complied, when he remembered. Years ago, Earl and Esther had each given Nick a small portion of their stock, agreeing that he would be a tiebreaker in the case of family disputes with the company. Such a dispute had yet to develop, allowing Nick to happily avoid all responsibility.

"Okay, sure." Nick set the envelope on his desk.

The conversation lapsed for a moment and Nick's thoughts shifted to Pan. Maybe the land hadn't been transferred yet. If he could convince Uncle Earl not to give the land to Reverend Collins, Pan would be happy and he would be free.

He knew it was not necessarily the time to mention the church, but he didn't know any way to ease into the topic, so he pushed on.

"Uncle, I know I have steered away from management decisions in the past, but I am technically on the board of directors."

Uncle Earl looked surprised, but pleased. "Go on. I would be quite interested in any ideas you have."

Nick could feel himself sweating. He didn't like to poke his nose into the business side. "Maybe giving all that money and land to Reverend Collins isn't such a good idea. I mean, he's a good man and all, and I know Mother rallied for it, but maybe we should wait and see what happens with the whole Penelope issue. Without the cash from her grandfather, wouldn't it be dangerous to give up so much?"

"Don't worry. I know what I'm doing. Even if you don't get to marry Penelope, the groundwork for the merger is in and we can turn around and sue them for enough to keep the company going."

"The litigation might take years though. Maybe we could just hold back handing over the money until we know for sure."

"No worries, Nick. A guy like Reginald Stafford can write a check for what our company is worth, and he'll do it too if that's what it takes to keep him out of the papers."

Nick felt a little sick to his stomach at the idea of his entire relationship with Penelope getting into the papers, especially the part where his family married him off like an eighteenth century princess.

"Listen, son, we have a project meeting with some of the Stafford people later today. I want you to go get a clean shirt."

"Can I borrow your Lexus? I rode a bike to work today."

"Ah, I know the urge well, the open road in front of you, a hog between your legs. Maybe you and I can go for a ride sometime, up to the cabin in Door County for a weekend or something."

"No, Uncle Earl. I mean a bicycle."

"What are you, twelve? Does it have a bell and basket? Do you put baseball cards in the spokes?"

"Well, it is more environmentally friendly."

"Have you been hanging out with hippies?" Despite the accusation of hippie familiarity, a set of Lexus keys came sailing through the air. "Have her back before noon. I have to take the Stafford guy out to lunch, and I'd like to have you along." Uncle Earl stood up and headed for the door.

"You got it." Nick said as Uncle Earl exited his office. Then, he sat down and made sure he had released all of the project files, so he would no longer be stepping on JenJen's toes.

———————————————————

Nick didn't have any dark-colored dress shirts at home, at least not any clean ones. On a whim, he drove downtown to a menswear store his uncle favored and bought a red silk shirt. He even put it on his uncle's account. His errand completed, he still had a little time before he had to be back, so he decided to walk around the Ped Mall. Maybe he could find a new phone.

Iowa City's pedestrian mall was an odd mix of upscale shops, fast food, college bars, and homeless people selling braided hemp jewelry. Despite its proximity to Baker House, Nick didn't come here very often, except in *Global Fight!*

As he strolled down the street, he saw one of these hemp bracelet merchants starting to shamble in his direction. He hesitated for a moment, looking for somewhere to run. The man was so close now, Nick could smell patchouli. He turned and walked through the nearest doorway.

As soon as he entered the little shop, Nick was assaulted by a dozen clashing smells. A small bell above the door rang, and a black man with long curly hair looked up. He wore a white tuxedo with half his face painted white, contrasting violently with his deep ebony skin. The man grabbed a black top hat and put it on. "Hello and welcome to the Voodoo Hut. I am Papa Damballah." His voice was high and gravelly.

"Haven't I seen you on TV?"

"Yes. I have a commercial that runs late at night on cable. It is good to know the advertising is working."

"No, that's not it. Weren't you in a Bond movie?"

"You are no doubt thinking of Baron Samedi from *Live and Let Die*, whose costume I have emulated. It adds a sense of occasion and humor for the nervous customer." As a nervous customer, Nick found it added neither.

Nick looked around the little shop. Nick was sure Reverend Collins would not approve of his presence here. Collins would probably tell him that Jesus had a poor opinion of it as well. However, Nick spotted a crucifix on the back wall of the shop. He figured if the store was Christian, it was probably harmless.

Papa Damballah interrupted Nick's examination. "Is there anything I can do for you, today?"

"No, I was just..." Nick broke the gaze of the shopkeeper and turned to find a display of eyeballs looking at him. He turned back to the Baron Samedi clone and pointed randomly to an item. "I was actually looking for one of these."

"Oh, well-spotted sir. You obviously have a high affinity with spirit energies."

"I do?"

"This is a powerful juju, and a steal at only one hundred and seventy dollars."

"Um, yeah." Nick lived well within his means and had plenty of money in his checking account, but he didn't want to waste over a hundred dollars on a trinket.

"I can see you are unimpressed. I admit, it is a modest charm. It will bring you general good luck however..." The man's voice drifted off.

"What?"

"You have such powerful energy, for you I recommend something like this." The shopkeeper reached into the case and took out the velvet bag. He placed it in Nick's hands. There was something inside, but Nick didn't want to open it because it smelled funny. Then again, everything in the shop smelled funny.

"How expensive is it?"

"It is a rare piece, but for you, I could go as low as five hundred."

"Dollars?"

"This juju contains the mummified head of a baby alligator, thrice blessed by a high priest."

That explained the smell. "Does thrice blessed mean three different high priests, or did the same high priest bless it three times?"

"I'm not sure. Would you like me to call the company?"

"No, don't bother." Nick looked at the little bag. It didn't look like five hundred dollars worth. "What does it do?"

"It will protect you from evil spirits."

"What about just general nature spirits who are holding a grudge against you?"

Papa Damballah shrugged. "It could work."

Nick took out his wallet. "Five hundred dollars? Do you take Visa?"

"Four hundred ninety-nine dollars and ninety-nine cents. Plus tax. And Visa will be fine." Papa Damballah took Nick's credit card and ran it. He reached down under the counter and pulled out something long and skinny. "You will also be wanting this, sir."

"What is that?"

"It is a hemp necklace, made by a local craftsman, which will allow you to wear the juju around your neck."

11

FIRE RELATED DISASTERS

Nick returned to the office with time to spare. He handed Uncle Earl's car keys to Delores. "Can you give these to Uncle Earl?"

"Don't you want to go say hi to your uncle?"

"I don't want to bother him."

Delores raised an eyebrow. "I know for a fact the only thing he's doing right now is playing with his putter."

"It is not that I am avoiding my dear uncle, and I wish him well in perfecting his short game. However, for the first time in days, I have a serious chance to get some work done. If I walk into that office, he will want something. I just know it."

Delores dropped the keys on her desk. "Okay, get out of here."

"Thanks, Delores."

Nick walked back to his office. He checked out files for the mini-game and re-ran the last compile to see where he had left off. A virtual field appeared and sheep began to swarm around.

JenJen had done a considerable amount of work on the graphics. The sheep looked more sheepy, even if their movements were still a little fishy. Nick looked at the movement algorithms, but ultimately decided the sheep would have to remain fishy for the time being. He did, however, remove the tail fin code which made the sheep wag their tails in a suggestive way.

Glancing at his system clock, he realized he had worked for nearly forty-five minutes uninterrupted. The gears of his mind were firmly clicked in to coding mode. Now, all he needed was to turbo charge.

He got up and walked to the Edutacular break room. Uncle Earl set up the break room after Nick showed him studies that regular caffeine consumption increased the productivity of tech workers by twenty percent. Nick had been pushing for an in-house barista, but Uncle Earl wouldn't spring for a new employee. They compromised. Uncle Earl bought some used refrigeration units from the Church of Great Savings and Edutacular employees got all the soda pop, cold cappuccinos, and energy drinks they could possibly imbibe.

Nick keyed into the Edutacular break room and found JenJen sipping a Diet Coke and texting. "Hey, nice render on the sheepies."

JenJen looked up from her phone. "Well, one of us has to work around here. I've looked at your last compile. What the hell is up with your sheep AI?"

"Well, I had some trouble finding sheep movement information, so instead of getting bogged down, I mapped the movement of the sheep to the AI we did for the fishing game." Nick walked over to the clear refrigerator door and started looking for something to drink.

JenJen nodded. "I'm relieved to hear that. I saw the way they wagged their tails and I was worried about your sexuality."

Nick felt his face turn red from embarrassment. He should be used to this by now. He'd been getting sheep-boy comments for the last month, especially from JenJen. "Don't you think it's about time we drop the sheep jokes?"

JenJen tapped her chin like she was thinking about it. "Um... No. However, if you do me a favor, I might be willing to forget about it."

Nick sighed. "What do you want?"

"I have a new game console, and I want you to hook it up for me."

"Oh, come on. I know you know how to hook up a game console."

"It's a hardware problem. We work in software. Besides, I don't like crawling behind the TV cabinet, and I'm not sure if my receiver can handle any more stuff."

"Alright, I'll take a look."

"Great! And I'll make dinner."

Normally, Nick might have liked the idea of spending the evening with JenJen, but his life was a mess. All, he had wanted was one quiet night to unwind with his *Global Fight!* console. "Oh, you don't have to do that."

"What's the problem, Nick? Are you still seeing Penelope?"

"Oh, no, she's gone home to Philadelphia. I think the wedding's off."

JenJen gave him a friendly slap on the shoulder. "Good for you. Way to stand up to your family..." A horrified look crossed her face. "Oh, shit. I'm sorry, Nick. Is there any news on your mother?"

Nick shrugged. "I honestly think that if they were going to find her, they would have found her by now. I like to think she's gone to a better place." ...as the lover of a turbo-sexual fertility god.

"I'm glad you're starting to come to terms with it. Now, about dinner?"

"You don't have to go through any trouble for me."

"It's no problem. I'm getting kind of lonely without Steve around."

Without Steve around made the offer sound much better. "Well, okay. I guess."

"Great." JenJen got up from the table and pitched her empty can into a recycling bin. "I'll see you tonight."

"Great." Nick said again, immediately wondering if the second "great" made him sound too enthusiastic. He had been looking forward to a quiet night at home, but he couldn't turn down an evening alone with JenJen.

He took the rest of his Mountain Dew back to the office and started coding again. His phone rang and identified the caller as "Earl Baker III," so he answered. "Hello."

"Nick, you have to get down here." Uncle Earl's voice was slurred.

"Have you been drinking?"

"I'm with the corporate guy. We're at Driftwoods. You have got to get down here, we're having a blast."

"Driftwoods? You took the corporate guy to a strip club?"

"That's where he wanted to go for lunch."

"I really have a lot of coding to do."

"Stop making excuses and get your butt down here. The corporate guy wants to meet our most talented coder."

"I will be there as soon as possible." Nick hung up the phone and went back to coding. An hour later the phone rang again. "Hello."

Uncle Earl's slur had become so bad Nick could not understand what he was saying. "Um, could you talk a little slower? This is a bad connection."

It was still hard, but Nick could almost understand Uncle Earl this time. "...kicked us out of Driftwoods...old farm...bonfire...join."

Nick checked his watch. It was nearly five o'clock. "Sure. I'm just going to finish a few things here and swing by the church. Uncle Earl, do me a favor."

"Wassat?"

"Don't try to light a fire until I get there."

An incomprehensible string of gibberish came from the phone, but Uncle Earl seemed to be agreeing.

"Thank you, Uncle Earl."

Nick finished the class he was coding and checked all the files back into the control system. He left the building in a hurry, giving Delores a wave. He picked off the garbage that had covered the bike during the day and wiped the seat with a wet-wipe. He made it home by pedal power, stopping three times to catch his breath, but he planned to switch to the H2. He had no desire to ride the bicycle all the way out to the old farm.

When he got home, a workman waited outside his door. "Are you the owner of this unit?" the man asked.

"Yes," Nick said, unlocking the door. "Are you from the condo association?"

"I just have a work order for this address."

"Tell you what, I'm in a hurry. I just need to grab a shower and then I have to go. You'll lock up here when you're finished?"

"No problemo. You got it."

Nick went into his bathroom and showered off the sweat of the twelve-mile bike ride. After that, he followed his newest pro-shower ritual, and carefully examined his forehead for evidence of horns. They were still gone. After putting on some fresh clothes, Nick waved to the workman, who was doing some measuring, on his way out of the condo.

As he drove the H2 to the farm Nick reminisced about the family's Christmas tree farm. In the winter, it looked festive. In the summer, it smelled of fresh pine. Nick drove back to the fire pit to find Uncle Earl sitting around drinking beer with a diminutive man in a cowboy hat.

When Nick got out of the H2, he saw something disturbing sticking out from under the cowboy hat, a bright red beard. "Leopold?"

Uncle Earl chucked a beer at Nick. He failed to get his hands up quick enough, and the can ricocheted off his shoulder and bounced through the open door of the H2.

"I guess you can save that one for the way home," Uncle Earl said. He waved Nick closer, and considering he managed to wave without hurting himself, he must have sobered up a little since the phone call. "Nick, meet Matt Johnson from Stafford Corp., Austin."

"Matt Johnson?" It was Leopold all right, looking every bit the part of the urban cowboy in cowboy boots, blue jeans, a white hat, and a white button-up shirt. The only thing that looked out of place was the bright red beard.

Leopold gave him a very pointed look. "Yes, my name is Matt Johnson. Got a problem?"

Nick shook his head. "No. No problem here."

"I'm glad you're here," said Uncle Earl. "Sit down and have a beer and get to know Mr. Johnson."

"Call me Matt."

Nick started piling wood in the fire pit. "Oh, gee, I would love to get to know... Matt better. However, I have a previous engagement. I'm just here to make sure you don't blow yourself up."

Nick added the secret ingredient to start any Baker family bonfire: gasoline and waste oil. The secret ingredient was the reason Nick had worried about Uncle Earl starting the fire in his inebriated state. Nick would never forget the Great Christmas Tree Fire of 1997. "Everybody stand back."

Standing back ten feet from the wood pile, Nick threw a match. It bounced off a petroleum-soaked log. The flame flared for a second and died out. Nick waited. Just at the moment a normal person would be more tempted to examine the fire pit, flames shot ten feet in the air, releasing a small mushroom cloud. From where he stood, Nick felt a blast of heat. He licked his index finger and used it to stroke his eyebrows: still there.

"This concludes your fire lighting for this evening. I will see the two of you at work tomorrow. Good night, Uncle Earl. Good night... Matt."

"Good night, son, but you're going to miss an awesome night. Matt brought marshmallows, and I invited a couple of the Driftwood girls to come over after their shift." By "invited," Nick was sure Uncle Earl meant paid.

As Nick drove to JenJen's apartment, he had a horrible feeling like he was forgetting something. She did say she'd make dinner, so he really shouldn't go empty-handed. He ran through his shopping options between his current location and her apartment and sighed. He'd have to go to church.

The Church of Great Savings took up four storefronts in a strip mall: two for worship and two for grocery. Nick parked on the grocery side and entered the building. To his dismay, Reverend Collins was running the register.

"Nick!" said the reverend. "It's good to see you at church."

Nick found it difficult to get over the appearance of Reverend Collins. The minister wore a bright orange track suit with black piping and a large gold cross on the front. It made him look like a very religious basketball. "Good evening, Reverend."

"Tonight only, we have half off on dry pasta."

"No thanks, I'm just here for a bottle of wine."

"You should stop by my office. I want to discuss the new workout center."

Nick nodded. "I do want to speak with you about the new church. Do you think the building site you have chosen is suitable?"

"Of course it's suitable. It's a great example of God's natural beauty. Also, the price is right." He winked.

"Well, yes, and no. You will have to knock a huge hole in the woods to build the church. Just think about the number of trees that will be taken down. Isn't that ruining God's natural beauty?"

"Nick, you can knock down trees. It's ok. They re-grow. I have three volunteer trees growing in my backyard right now. Besides, don't you think God wants his house in a beautiful place?"

"But these trees are older trees..." Nick was obviously not getting through. He hadn't really thought out the argument. "I'm going to go get some wine."

The spirits section of the Church of Great Savings was small, but adequate if you wanted a bottle for a party. Not knowing what Jen-Jen was preparing for dinner and knowing she liked pasta, Nick picked out a Washington Pinot Grigio and a Chianti Classico.

As Reverend Collins ran him through the check-out line, he said, "You should tell your uncle to stop by my office too. I have a few details to go over with him."

"Yes sir, I will."

"Your Uncle Earl is a successful man, Nick. You could learn a thing or two from him."

Like how to get thrown out of strip clubs. "Yes, Reverend. I'm sure I could."

The Reverend Collins put each bottle in its own brown paper bag. "Have a good evening Nick, and say hi to Penelope. I'm sure she'll like what you picked out."

"I'm sure she will."

Twenty minutes later, Nick knocked on JenJen's door. She answered the door wearing an apron, but unlike the women in Rudy's Japanese fetish DVDs, she had clothes on underneath. Nick still found the domestic look alluring.

Before she had even greeted him, she was already walking back to the kitchen. "Come in, have a seat. My chicken is almost done."

"I brought wine." Nick saw something on the coffee table that looked familiar. "Holy crap! Is that what I think it is?"

"What are you looking at?" she called back from the kitchen.

"A NES console, still in the original box." The Nintendo Entertainment System had been the first console Nick had owned, and his great love for it had spurred his current career path. He owned several consoles since then, but he always held a special fondness for the NES. Sadly, Nick's mother had thrown away his console when he had graduated from high school, telling him it was "time to become a man."

"Take a closer look. It's a NES-T. It's a clone made in Malaysia, but the buzz is it has sturdy controllers with a comparable feel to the NES, and all the classic games are built in."

"Awesome. You just want me to hook this up then?"

"Yeah, but let's wait until after the food. I want to see the unboxing."

"What about playing some Mario later?"

"Sure."

As Nick waited for the chicken to cook, he looked longingly at the NES-T box. He flipped it over and read, "This box contains number 1 family bonding." He ran his finger down the seam of the plastic.

A spatula slapped his hand. "Bad boy. Don't make me have to punish you."

Nick couldn't help but think Rudy would have had a good comeback to that. "I was just testing the integrity of the seals."

JenJen eyed him warily. "Hands off." Then she turned her head to the side and sniffed. "Crap! The chicken."

A half hour later Nick finished scarfing down a tasty, if slightly overcooked, chicken Parmesan. He took a sip of the wine he had brought. It was good, but he had just one thing on his mind. "So, do you think we could…"

"Wait until I finish eating. I've never seen you so impatient."

"Sorry. I've just had a crappy week, and I really need the release."

JenJen set her napkin aside. "Let's go unbox that console."

They got a paring knife and a pair of scissors, and carefully unwrapped layer after layer of packing material. Under the plugs and controllers was the NES-T. Smaller than the original NES, it looked much like the original console, but without the functioning game slot, as all the classic games were saved on a ROM chip.

Nick pulled the entertainment cabinet away from the wall and took a look at the setup. "You are out of HDMI ports, but this system uses old analog connectors anyway. Hand me those wires. I'll crawl back there and pass them out through the front." He wriggled back behind the entertainment center and reached as far as he could. Jen-Jen passed the cables so he could plug them into the back of the TV. Then he plugged the console into the wall socket.

"Are we all ready to go then?" asked JenJen.

"Yes, there is only one problem."

"What's that?"

"I am caught behind this cabinet." Nick's shoulders were wedged in tight. He tried to wiggle himself out, and the TV above him wobbled alarmingly.

JenJen braced herself against the back of the cabinet and reached out to him. "Grab my hand." Nick reached up as far as he could and pulled.

She held her own for a few moments, then she started to loose her grip. She pulled harder, but lost first her footing and then her balance. She fell on top of him. "I guess I wasn't as well braced as I thought I was."

"Well, what should we do now?" Nick was highly aware of Jen-Jen's body pressed against his. While it wasn't considered a national treasure by the tabloids, he liked it just fine. It was soft, comfortable. "Maybe I can push you back up—"

"We could make out."

Nick laughed. "Yeah good one, but that won't get us out from behind here."

JenJen kissed him. "Shut up, Nick."

"But what about Steve..." he protested, but his protests only represented his brain. His body had other ideas.

She kissed him again. "Shut up, Nick."

———————————

This was the first time Nick had ever made out behind a TV cabinet. After several minutes, he said, "Okay, we have to stop. This is going too far."

"You're the one squeezing my ass."

It was a nice ass. It fit Nick's hands easily. Despite this, he removed his hands. "Better?"

"No. Don't stop."

Nick nearly complied. "No. We have to stop. One, because you have a boyfriend, and two, because there is a power strip digging into my right kidney." He silently added number three, because your boyfriend hits balls with a large club for a living.

JenJen rolled slightly to the side and looked up at the TV cabinet. "So, how are we supposed to get out of here?"

Nick thought about it for a minute, then he held his hands by his shoulders. "Okay, put your hands in mine and push."

JenJen pushed herself up with Nick's assistance. She had to move the TV and then pull the cabinet away from the wall before he was able to get out. Eventually, they actually managed to play *Super Mario Brothers III* on the NES-T.

It didn't take long for Nick to remember how to play the game. He deftly tapped buttons, making Mario jump over a goomba and hit a question block, scoring him the raccoon tail. Then he nailed a koopa troopa and sent the shell on ahead.

JenJen turned away from the TV to face Nick. "So, are you still feeling stressed?"

"Well, yeah, I guess. My mom's still gone and all." This made a ready excuse to explain why he was worried and stressed. It avoided any awkward discussions about Greek gods and kept the conversation away from the topic of commitment to a mental-health facility. "And Reverend Collins wants me to help design a fitness center." The koopa troopa caught him on the bounce. "Damn! Did you start me talking just to get control of the console?"

JenJen paused the game. "No, Nick. You seemed really freaked this afternoon. That's why I invited you over, not so we could make out while wedged behind the TV."

"Why did you do that anyway? Maybe I should ask what's up with you, Miss Steve-is-wonderful."

"I didn't do it all on my own. Gravity played a part. And, my relationship with Steve is..." She paused for a moment. "Well, relationships change over time."

"What's up?"

"You have your own problems. You don't need to hear mine."

"Even after we were behind the TV together?"

"Okay, hold on for a minute. This might take a while." JenJen went to the kitchen and came back with the Pinot and a pair of glasses. She poured two glasses of wine and put one in Nick's hand. "Now, you have to promise not to tell anyone."

"Mum is the word."

"Well, I don't know if I've ever told you this, but Steve is not very... intimate with me."

"You mean he doesn't cuddle."

JenJen thought for a moment. "Let me tell you a story. Last year, Steve was on a one-week bus tour, so I drove up to Madison to surprise him, and I found him sharing a room with his shortstop."

"Well, that is no big deal. I'm sure they save a lot of money that way."

"They were sharing a bed."

"Maybe the hotel ran out of doubles?"

"They were *in flagrante delicto.*"

"Is that Latin?"

"Are you trying to be obtuse? They were without clothes. They were naked. Steve was pitching and his shortstop was catching."

Nick had enough trouble picturing JenJen's macho boyfriend in bed with another man, but one detail really confused him. "I thought Steve was an outfielder."

"They were having hot gay sex, Nick."

"Oh." Obviously there was some terminology he was unaware of. "And you didn't know Steve did that sort of thing?"

"No. No, I didn't. I thought he was monogamous."

"Ah. I can see how that would be a problem."

The conversation hit a temporary lull.

"I mean," JenJen said to break the silence, "it came as quite a shock."

"It must have shocked the shortstop as well." He couldn't help but smirk.

She rolled her eyes. "It was consensual. Steve's not some kind of homosexual serial-rapist. They'd been seeing each other for years. The whole team knew about it. The problem was *I* didn't know about it.

"To make a long story short, now that he knows I know, he doesn't bother to keep up the pretense or anything else." She downed the last of her glass and poured another. "So, I've told you all the sordid things going on in my sex life; what about yours?"

Nick thought about not mentioning Penelope, but then he remembered JenJen had already seen the back scratches. "I nearly had sex with a famous debutante."

"You mean, like, everything but...?" JenJen added in a couple of hand motions to illustrate her point. Then, when she saw Nick's expression, she said, "Don't look surprised. You know what that means."

"Well, we were in... What was that word again?"

"*In flagrante delicto*? It means 'caught in the act.'"

Nick shook his head. "Whatever. We were naked. And she was digging her fingernails into my back and I was... making my final approach. She found a Dorito stuck to my back. It sort of ruined the mood. She packed her bags and went home."

"Poor baby." She seemed more amused than sympathetic.

"I thought so. Then I go to work the next morning and my best friend gives me a whole lot of crap."

JenJen had the presence of mind to look embarrassed. "Oh, sorry about that." She paused, "Wait a minute, best friend? What about Rudy?"

"You are at least my best friend at work. Rudy is... Well, Rudy is a hard guy to like sometimes."

"I've met him a couple times. I understand. How did you two become friends anyway?"

"Well, you wouldn't know it to look at him, but Rudy's parents decided public school had little to offer him and they sent him to the same private school as me.

"Rudy started in third grade, and by then, pretty much all the social groups had crystallized. He sat next to me in class that first day, and we found out we were both into video games, and he just started hanging out around me. I did not really plan to be his friend, he just never went away."

"Interesting. Did you ever stop to think maybe you were being too polite?"

"Kind of, I guess, but we do have common interests, and Rudy provides a unique perspective to my world. Besides, he is not stupid, just socially stunted. He's got like five PhDs and he'd probably be a professor or running some big company if he didn't play *Global Fight!* so much. I also think he's got some sort of testosterone imbalance."

"Fascinating." JenJen filled their glasses one last time and held the bottle upside down to show it was empty. "That's the last of the wine."

"If you want some more, I could probably come up with something. I just need access to your kitchen."

JenJen looked confused, or maybe the wine was getting to her. "What the hell are you talking about? You can't just whip-up wine. It takes years, and you need quality grapes and oak casks."

"It's a kind of gift I have. Some beet juice, some ketchup, a bottle of Jack Daniels, and some allspice and I could probably throw together a pretty decent facsimile for red wine."

JenJen sat up straighter. "Are you serious? How close could you get?"

"Given the amount we have had to drink, I think I could say with certainty that you wouldn't be able to tell the difference."

"I have to see this." She gave Nick a push off the futon. "Get thee to the kitchen." He stood up and was rewarded with a slap on the ass. "Go! To the kitchen!"

Nick grabbed the empty wine bottle off the coffee table and walked drunkenly yet enthusiastically into the kitchen. He started taking condiments out of the refrigerator. JenJen joined him in the kitchen just as he held up a bottle of ketchup and a bottle of Italian dressing. "Red or white?"

"Red."

He put back the dressing, and then squirted some ketchup into the wine bottle. "Where do you keep your liquor?"

"Cabinet at your knees."

After opening it, Nick paused. "Hmmm. You only have tequila and peppermint schnapps. This could be interesting."

"Are you welching?"

"No, no, let me think for a moment. Do you have any chili powder or cinnamon?"

When Nick was done mixing the wine, he strained it and poured two tall glasses. They took them back to the living room and sat on the futon. JenJen took a sip and made a face. "You know, this isn't really that bad. Maybe a pinch too much cinnamon."

"Told you. I have a talent. I wanted to be a bartender, but my mother didn't approve."

"Oh."

Nick realized the mention of his mother had put a lull in the conversation. Maybe because of the wine, he felt like being honest. "Actually, my mother has run off with a mythological figure."

"You mean someone famous, like Penelope?"

"Kind of like that. I have to keep up the charade because she does not want to be found."

"By the way, how did you score an engagement to the hottest young billionaire in the tabloids?" She took a sip. "Mmm."

Nick thought about it for a minute. "Well, it's kind of an odd story. You see, my family used to be rich."

"Used to be?" She raised an eyebrow.

"Trust me, after Uncle Earl and my mother get done donating money to the church, you will have more money in the bank than they do. But here's the deal, in his day, my great grandfather and Penelope's grandfather were business associates. They were self-made men. They were on the boards of the same companies. They basically traveled in the same circles.

"My great grandfather, the first Earl Baker, took a small toothbrush factory and built a dynasty. By the time he was thirty, he was a multi-millionaire. Now, fifty years ago, that was a lot of money."

"Really? I wouldn't have guessed."

"Well, fast forward fifty years. My Uncle Earl and my mother do their best to maintain the wealth, but Uncle Earl is not so good with it, and my mother is more concerned with maintaining her image as a philanthropist than her bank account. We are about to lose our collective shirts."

JenJen poured the last of the fake wine into her glass. "What about your trust fund?"

"Oh, that's safe, but it's chicken-feed compared to the money Mother has given away."

"And this is where Penelope comes in?"

"Right, so you are Reginald Stafford..."

"I am?"

"No, you are definitely not. I can tell. You're much prettier. However, for the moment, let us say you are. So you, meaning Reginald, have a wild granddaughter, an embarrassment to your legacy. You figure the best way to calm her down is to marry her off, but none of your super-rich friends want the embarrassing granddaughter in their family.

"Enter the Bakers. We have a high enough status to marry his granddaughter without him having to worry about us turning into low-class gold diggers, but he also knows we are hurting for cash, or at least we are hurting for cash to maintain our standard of living. Plus, how much trouble can she get into in Iowa?"

"So he approves of you because you are a higher class gold digger?"

"Well, when you put it like that, it sounds tawdry."

"But Penelope isn't going along with the deal?"

"Well, she had to make a show at trying because she doesn't have a trust like I do. She has an allowance. The old man can cut her off whenever he wants."

JenJen drained the last of her not-wine. "And here I am complaining about something so trivial as having a gay boyfriend."

"Stafford offered several million dollars, a seat on the board, and a good chunk of stock in his company in exchange for a controlling interest in Baker and my marriage to his granddaughter."

JenJen yawned. "Your problems are making me tired. Do you want to sleep here tonight?"

The offhandedness of JenJen's offer caught Nick a little off guard. After hearing her boyfriend was actually a batter for the other team, he wished he had not stopped their earlier make-out session.

Nick had never even considered JenJen as a mate before tonight—okay, he'd *considered* it, but he never thought it would actually happen because of her now-defunct devotion to Steve. However it suddenly occurred to him that down to the very core of his being, he wanted to do very naked things with JenJen. "I would like nothing more."

JenJen stood up. "You sound as ready as I am. I'll be right back." She patted him on the head.

Nick sat on the edge of the futon, nearly bouncing up and down with anticipation. After what seemed like too long a wait, JenJen returned.

She was wearing flannel pajamas and a robe. She threw a pillow and blanket at Nick. "Here you go. You can fold out the futon if you want to, but you'll have to push back the coffee table. See you in the morning. Maybe we can go out for breakfast or something." She left him there, sitting on the couch. At least he hadn't done something stupid like take off his clothes.

Nick lay down on the futon and covered himself up. He wanted to cry. For the second night in a row he lay on a couch while a nubile woman slept in the very next room. "I must be doing something very wrong with my life."

He lay awake and tried to think of some plausible reason for him to knock on JenJen's door. Twice he got up and nearly walked through her door just to see how she would react, but he never quite mustered the courage. Finally, out of drunkenness and exhaustion, he fell asleep.

12

ALLIGATOR HEAD GAMES

After maybe four hours of fitful sleep, Nick got up and let himself out. He felt almost sober enough to drive home, and he didn't want to stay that close to JenJen any longer. He kept thinking he should have knocked on her door, or even just let himself in. Every once in a while he would shake his head and say, "Stupid."

He parked the H2 in the parking lot outside the condo. All he could think about on the short walk to his unit was he wanted to sleep in his own bed for a change. He seemed too tired to lift his feet to walk down the steps from the split-level foyer to his ground unit. So, when he flipped on the light, his spirit was completely and utterly crushed.

Someone had vacuumed the carpet—or replaced the carpet; he'd forgotten what it looked like clean. Someone had removed his post-college furnishings and replaced them with more expensive and ugly pieces of furniture. His *Global Fight!* console was gone. And someone had taken down his Salvador Dali poster and painted a large mural on his wall.

The mural was large and unavoidable, a tropical beach with deck chairs, tables, and umbrellas. This was actually quite pretty and tastefully done. However, Nick didn't appreciate the two figures in the painting. One was quite definitely Penelope Stafford Jennings.

Penelope ran naked with a man who was possibly meant to be Nick, although he was tan in places Nick had never exposed to sunlight, and the man's abs were perfect. Was it Nick's head on Jason Scotmoore's body?

Nick's response to the mural was sudden and loud. He pointed at the wall and yelled, "What the hell is that?"

A light came on in the bedroom and Penelope came down the hall wearing a tiny robe that might as well have been invisible. "Darling, where have you been?"

Nick just shook his head. He couldn't believe this was happening. Maybe this was all a bad dream, and he was still sleeping on JenJen's futon. "Why is there a naked man with my face painted on the wall? Where is my furniture? Why are you in my apartment? Why do you walk around half naked?"

Penelope put on a playful look. "If being half naked bothers you, I'll take the robe off." She started pulling at the robe, exposing her right breast.

"Do not take the robe off," Nick said, but it was too late. Penelope's tactic had been all too effective. The sight of her undressing had stopped Nick's brain from working.

Penelope regarded Nick's faraway stare. "You look tired. Come to bed. We can discuss this in the morning." She turned and started walking down the hall on her delicious legs.

The anger that had been slowly filling Nick for days shattered his desire. He forced himself to look away. "Wait." He spoke with the dulcet tones of a man who has been pushed too far. Somehow, Penelope knew to stop and turn around. "The last I knew, you had left Iowa forever with the intention of begging your grandfather to spare you from the fate worse than death that is Nick Baker." He waved his hands up and down his body like a spokesmodel. "In addition to this fact, when I left this condominium ten hours ago, it contained functional yet affordable furniture, a *Global Fight!* console system, and what the hell is up with that mural? I'm sorry to use such strong language in front of a lady, but I'm quite upset."

"Don't you like it? I thought we could visualize what it might be like to be happy together, like a goal." She stopped playing with her open robe and balled her hands into tiny fists. "I mean, can't we just try to like each other for fuck's sake? I even had your apartment cleaned so it wouldn't be so gross. I'm just not good at being all shy and girly." She actually looked vulnerable, like she might cry. "Every man I've known has just wanted my money or my body," she said, ripping off the robe and throwing it on the floor. "The more aggressive I was, the more they liked it, but you're different. I don't like being vulnerable. Fuck!" Tears started welling up in her large, blue eyes and ran down her delicate face.

"Hey, I didn't mean to upset you." Nick walked over and hesitated, wondering if he should hug her or not. She was naked, after all.

Penelope grabbed hold of him and pushed her wet face into his neck. "I'm sorry. When my grandfather found out I left you, he cut me off, and I had to spend the entire fucking day flying back here from Philadelphia, and I just didn't know where to go."

"There, there," said Nick, while he awkwardly patted her on the back.

"I've been left with nothing."

Nick looked around his gaudy apartment. "Well, you had enough to redecorate my apartment."

She pushed him back. "What are you saying?"

"Well, I'm just saying, it must have cost some money to redecorate this place. You can't be that bad off."

Penelope went so quickly from remorse to anger, Nick wondered if she might have taken drugs as well. "I'm sorry, Nick Baker, if I'm not poor enough for your pity. I dip into the last of my savings to try to make your home livable, and this is how you treat me. You have no idea what it's like to be me. Nobody does."

Mentally, Nick conceded Penelope had a point. Very few people could claim to have lost a billion-dollar inheritance over a badly placed Dorito. "I'm sorry. You have had a very rough day and since I got in the door, I have done nothing but criticize you. I should have been a little more considerate." What the hell was he saying? Should he have been more considerate? It was his flipping apartment.

"Very well. I accept your apology. Now if you don't mind, I'm going to bed." She pulled him in for a final hug, released him, and headed off to the bedroom.

Nick wondered for a moment if he should follow her to the bedroom. Only a minute ago he seemed to be invited. Now, not so much. Penelope pulled the door shut behind her, answering his question. It was probably for the best anyway. Nick didn't know if he'd be able to control himself in bed with a naked Penelope Stafford Jennings.

"Okay, I'll just sleep on the couch then," Nick said to himself. He turned to where part of him was expecting the couch to be and saw something remarkably uncouchlike.

The monstrosity sitting in the place where Nick's couch used to be was vaguely couch-sized and had cushions. The familiarities ended there. With is polished wood curves, it looked like something from a future Ikea, or *Star Trek: The Next Generation*. Nick walked over and lifted the right armrest. Half of the armrest flipped over to become a writing desk. Ah, the device was configurable. Nick wondered if he could make it into something useful to sleep on. He had always liked playing with Lego and Transformers. He lifted the other half of the armrest. It popped loose and one of the upright cushions fell off the back. He pulled at the cushion, and a footrest popped out the front. He pulled at the footrest and revealed a drawer containing his *Global Fight!* console. He gave the drawer a shove back, and the whole monstrosity folded in on itself, leaving a thin and short footstool. He decided to leave it alone and sleep on this configuration.

Feeling urgency in his bladder, Nick awoke early. The thing he had been sleeping on had reconfigured into something larger, with multiple platforms. Once he had crawled off it and used the restroom, he realized the smell of coffee was coming from the kitchen. He followed his nose and found Penelope trying to kill an appliance.

The floor was covered in coffee grounds. Penelope was in the process of hitting Nick's coffee grinder with a large wooden spoon.

"Oh, you're up. I was going to wake you up with some breakfast."
She made a face. "It's not going very well."

Nick unplugged the coffee grinder. "The button sticks on the
grinder sometimes. All you have to do is unplug it."

"Oh, well, I'll buy you a new one."

Her offer may have been an attempt at kindness, but Nick's coffee grinder had been the first appliance he had bought on his own
and was now one of the few things in his apartment he still recognized. "Penelope, I don't need a new coffee grinder. Well, maybe I
do now that you beat the crap out of this one, but the point is that it
was working fine before you came along. Everything in this apartment was working fine before you came along. My life was working
fine before you came along."

"Well, I'm sorry. I've never made coffee before, but I thought that
was the kind of thing couples did for each other."

Nick shook his head. "Penelope, listen carefully. We are not a
couple. Now, I am going to go in my own bedroom and get ready
for work. If you can figure out how, you can clean up this mess.
Otherwise just leave it and try not to break anything or throw out
any more of my stuff." He went in the bedroom and, after pointedly
ignoring the changed decor, slammed the door behind him.

As he checked for horns in the mirror, he did not like what he saw.
Well, he liked the continued absence of horns, but everything else
was not as pleasing. His brow was crinkled, and his eyes drooped
over dark bags. In less than a week, he looked like he had aged a
decade. What did he do to deserve this?

All of these things started happening after Pan showed up. Was
the god somehow manipulating these events around him? Maybe
he had been too hard on Penelope earlier. Then again, she had
painted that awful mural on his wall.

Nick showered and then dressed quickly, trying not to look at the
avant-garde furniture that had replaced his bedroom set. So much
for sleeping in his own bed ever again.

On his way out of the condo, he stopped and looked through the
sliding glass door. The H2 and the bicycle were parked outside. He
would have to make a choice between the two vehicles. One would

physically exhaust him, and the other would draw the ire of a god. Decisions, decisions.

Penelope walked up holding his broom, which she had somehow snapped in half, probably not that easy for someone who weighed around one hundred pounds. "What ya doing?" she asked in her cutsey voice.

Nick was not impressed by the voice. "I am trying to decide which vehicle to take. One is ecologically the right choice, but the other is much more comfortable."

"Oh, that reminds me, some greasy guy stopped by last night with a rusty old car."

"A Corolla?" Nick looked out at the parking lot again. He couldn't see it.

"Yeah, that was it. I told him to keep it."

"You gave her away?"

"I'm not going to have any fiancé of mine driving around in a car like that. It would be embarrassing."

Nick took a deep breath to calm down. Then he took another. "Please add one more thing to your list. In addition to not breaking anything, could you please refrain from giving my things away?"

"You're really not happy with me here are you?"

"Well..." Nick didn't want to be impolite. "I am not one hundred percent sure if you moving in would be the best idea. Now, if you'll excuse me, I'm going to attempt to banish a god." Nick headed for the H2.

A half hour later, Nick parked the H2 and walked into his office like it was just a regular work day. Back at the Voodoo Hut, he had asked Papa Damballah how to banish a spirit with the juju. The procedure was simple. Nick just had to hold the juju out by its hemp necklace and yell, "Git spirit!"

Nick's courtyard was still an idyllic forest clearing. He opened the glass door and walked down the path. Soon after crossing the stream, he saw Pan. The goat-man danced around a tree while playing a haunting melody on his pipes.

Nick dangled the juju from the hemp necklace. Pan finished his song and looked at Nick in a curious manner. Nick twirled the juju on its cord faster and faster, and in that moment, he felt a little like David about to slay Goliath. "Git Pan! Git Pan! Git Pan!"

Pan plucked the juju out of the air. "Interesting. Thank you, Nick Baker, for your gift."

Nick had expected many possibilities from his action, including nothing at all. A "thank you" was not one of them. "Gift?"

The goat god opened the bag and examined its contents. "Wasn't that what you were saying? 'Gift Pan.' I am most grateful. It has been a long while since I have seen an authentic voodoo-style juju." He opened the velvet bag. "I particularly like the detail of the alligator head candle inside."

"Candle?" The shopkeeper had insisted the juju contained a real mummified alligator head. Nick had been too nervous to look.

With great strides across the clearing, Pan approached Nick. He plucked at something at the top of the alligator head and showed it to Nick. It was a wick. "Yes, an alligator head candle. I am not altogether knowledgeable of the modern concept of humor, but I believe this is quite amusing. Do you know they used to put real mummified baby alligator heads in these things sometimes?"

"Really?" He still couldn't believe he'd paid five hundred dollars for a candle.

"Yes." Pan raised his pipes back to his face. "Would you like me to play you a tune?"

While Nick's mother had taught him to be polite, he was in no mood. "I have to get going. I have work today."

"Yes, you must go work for Baker Dental. How is that favor we discussed? Is your Reverend Collins still planning to knock down these woods?"

Nick cleared his throat. "Um, well you know. I um... I have spoken to both Reverend Collins about canceling the project and my Uncle Earl about possibly not following through with the money."

"How well is that working?"

"Not very. If you let my mother go, perhaps she could persuade them? Or maybe Leopold. Do you know Leopold is posing as some executive for Stafford Corporation?"

Pan shook his head. "I want you to handle this, Nick Baker. Leopold is merely there to offer you support."

"So far, he's just gone drinking with my uncle."

Pan nodded. "Don't worry. Leopold has his methods. Oh, one more thing. Your mother wants me to ask you how David is doing without her."

He actually hadn't seen the dog since the day of the groundbreaking. "I don't know. I, um, guess he's doing fine. Uncle Earl said he would feed him."

"You should consider looking in on him, for your mother's sake. While she is enjoying her time in my realm, it is easy to see his absence bothers her. Now, if you'll excuse me, I have work to do." Pan started playing the song again and danced back to his tree.

The song was so light and invigorating, Nick had to resist the urge to follow Pan. "Well, I'll just look in on the dog then, shall I?" Nick yelled to Pan. The goat-god was already busy dancing to his song.

13

Business Meetings

As he walked back to Baker Dental, Nick wondered if the Voodoo Hut would give him a refund on his juju. Probably not, since Pan had taken his "gift." So much was Nick expecting to see JenJen using his computer, he actually looked twice to determine she was not there.

He got through all his email, checked out some code, and was just getting into the zone when Leopold opened the door to his office. "Hi, Nick." The faun walked through his office, discarding his cowboy hat and slipping out of his clothes. He opened the glass door and stepped into the courtyard without saying another word.

Nick got up from his desk and walked over to the glass door and watched the naked faun dance for a few more minutes, waiting for the creature to notice him, as his mother had taught him to be patient. Despite Nick's polite patience, his worry someone might enter his office and see the naked little goat-man won out. He opened the door and cleared his throat in a very pointed way.

Leopold stopped dancing and looked up. "Hey, Nick, what's up?"

"Just wondering what you were doing in my courtyard, naked and everything." Nick tried to casually motion at Leopold, without specifically looking like he was pointing at the faun's penis. It made him look like he was trying to dislodge something stuck to his hand.

"Don't you know what day it is, Nick?"

"Thursday?" Nick guessed. He had been so haggard lately he was losing track of the days. After a lifetime of waiting for the weekend, his new goal was making it to the next day without pissing off a relative or deity.

"It's the Beltane, Nick," Leopold said with great enthusiasm. When Nick failed to give any reaction, Leopold went on. "You know, May Day? Russian New Year? First of May, first of May, outdoor fucking starts today? Also, it's Wednesday."

"Yeah. So? I know what May Day is. Kids go around to all their little school friends and give baskets out with candy and paper flowers. What's the big deal?"

"This is a very important day, Nick. It symbolizes the beginning of spring and the start of planting season. It is a time to find new love and procreate with others indiscriminate of creed, color, or social status. This morning I am going to dance around trees and play my pipes, and then this afternoon, we will have a meeting about that shepherding game."

"Yeah, what's up with that anyway? You don't work for Stafford. So why are you here?"

"Well, I thought I might keep a tighter leash on you, but to do that, I needed an in. I found out that Stafford's company was sending up some hotshot to figure out who he could lay off after the merger. I got to him before he got a chance to meet with your uncle and fixed him up with a couple of loose wood nymphs; of course, that's redundant. I remember this one time I was..."

"Leopold, I'm really not interested in your sex life. What's this about laying people off after the merger? Stafford's going to lay off our people?"

"Oh, it's Stafford's standard operating procedure following a merger. Anyway, I got him a hot date with some nymphs and took his place." Leopold rubbed his hands together and raised his pipes to his mouth.

"So, I sit inside and write computer code all day while you pipe and dance?"

Leopold lowered the pipes. "Hey, making merry is my job, you know. It's harder than it looks. You have to be in peak physical condition to keep your wind up while dancing. If you don't believe me, slip off your pants and give it a try."

"I'll take your word for it. But Leopold, why the nudity? Just for me, can you put some pants on?"

Leopold shook his head. "No can do, buddy. Not on Beltane."

"You will be wearing them at the meeting this afternoon, won't you?"

He rolled his eyes. "Of course, I will put on some pants, but I won't guarantee I'll keep them on. If I manage to hook up with any of your coworkers, I may need you to cover for me."

"You mean you'd do it in the office?"

"Of course, first of May, first of May. You have your job, I have mine."

"I don't suppose you might find another tree to dance around? I know your values are all European…" Nick's mother had taught him that Europe was a lawless land of heathenism. "…but we Americans get nervous around frontal male nudity."

Leopold gave Nick a disgusted look. "I suppose, but I thought that as long as I was fertilizing the flora, I could start with your courtyard."

"Fertilizing?"

"Well, yes, after I finish dancing around the tree, I fertilize it with my seed."

Nick was pretty sure what Leopold meant by that and tried to block it from his mind. "I am going to have to ask you to take that elsewhere."

"Fine, your loss, but why do you think the courtyard is looking so good lately?"

"Nice to know." Nick was never entering the courtyard again.

"I'll see myself out." Leopold turned and walked behind a tree. After a moment, Nick realized he was not planning to come out around the other side.

"Okay," Nick said to himself, shutting the door. "Down to some serious coding."

Miraculously, he did get some serious coding done after Leopold left, stopping only occasionally to check for new cat pictures and interesting videos on his social aggregators.

Despite being out most of the week, things went smoothly, and by eleven o'clock, Nick had finished his demo for the afternoon product meeting, so he called up Rudy to kill some time.

Rudy answered. "Hey, what's up? You haven't been online for a couple of nights."

"Well, yeah, Penelope came back last night."

"Oh, I knew that."

"How did you know that?"

"I have the Internet, you know. I was on one of the Penelope Stafford Jennings fan sites. There's this guy from Bettendorf who's been staking out your apartment all week."

"That's completely disturbing."

"They have some pictures of you too. When did you start riding a bike?"

"It's kind of a long story."

"Do you want the address for the site?"

"No, no thanks. I'd rather not know."

"Suit yourself. So, you told me that Penelope's back, but what have you been doing? Have you seen her naked yet?"

"Of course I've seen her naked. She walks around naked half the time."

"Dude! I have got to come over. My parents want me at some kind of faculty reception tonight, but... Oh, screw it. I'll be over tonight."

"I do not think that would be the best idea."

"Oh come on, with the circles I travel in, there is absolutely no chance I'll ever see a girl that hot naked."

"Mainly because the circle you travel in is from the refrigerator to the couch to the bathroom. Besides, didn't you hook up with a Hawkeye cheerleader, like, three years ago?"

"Yes, but this is Penelope Stafford Jennings, not some college cheerleader, and that was three years ago. Besides, that's the exception that proves the rule."

"Not today, Rudy. I need some chill out time. Penelope's completely re-organized my apartment. I'm not even sure where my computer is."

"Okay, dude, but mark my words. If something happens to me, and I die before I get to see Penelope Stafford Jenning's pleasure mounds, I will not go into the bright light. I will come back and visit some serious shit on your ass."

"Rudy, I've got to go." Nick looked at the phone, which reported the time of the call as six minutes. Six minutes and he could barely stand talking to Rudy. Nick needed to find more friends.

"Okay. See you online tonight?"

"Maybe. We'll see." Nick hung up the phone.

"Was that Rudy on the phone?" asked JenJen from behind him.

"Um yeah." Nick tried to estimate how long JenJen could have been standing behind him and what he might have said to incriminate himself. He should really move his desk so it faced the office door. He hadn't felt this nervous since his mother found his Myspace account. Rudy had written some nasty things on his wall.

"Um, so how much of that did you hear?"

JenJen smiled evilly. "Enough."

Clever. Nick ran through the conversation again, and there was only one thing he thought might be remotely incriminating. "Penelope has moved in, but I didn't find out about it until after I left your apartment."

JenJen did not look impressed by this explanation. "So, you finished making out with me and sleeping over, then you went home in the wee hours of the morning to invite Penelope to live with you?"

"No. No, that is not it at all. I got home after... we did those things, to find she had already moved in."

"Break in, did she?"

"No, well, kind of. See, when I got home last night, there was a workman at my door. I thought he worked for the condo association, but he must have actually worked for Penelope's interior designer. I assume he let the others in." Nick paused.

"Yes. I'm listening."

Nick paused and thought about his situation. "You know what. I don't have to put up with this. I'm not in a monogamous relationship, and I haven't had sex with anyone. I have done nothing wrong."

She held up her hands in surrender. "Whatever. I'm going to go to lunch. See you at the meeting this afternoon." She turned and walked quickly from the room.

While Nick thought he'd brought up a very logical and reasonable point, JenJen still seemed upset. Was he supposed to go after her? Apologize? Buy her lunch? Oh well, if he knew what to say, she wouldn't be walking away.

For lunch, Nick grabbed a Mountain Dew and a bag of Doritos from the Edutacular break room. The only other person there was George, who ran their server farm with an iron fist.

"Hi George."

"Hello, Mr. Baker." This wasn't a great sign. George didn't call Nick "Mr. Baker" unless he was pissed off with management.

"Looking forward to the meeting this afternoon?"

"Oh yes, I love sitting around and smiling while some corporate wanker decides if he should lay me off. Actually, I scheduled server maintenance for this afternoon, so I won't be able to make it. I hope you weren't planning to do a live demo," George said as if he hadn't completely inconvenienced everyone just so he could skip a meeting.

"I guess I can pre-render some files for them."

"You better hurry, I'm taking everything down in an hour."

Nick decided George didn't feel like talking and took his lunch back to his office. He had video files to render anyway.

Once the video started rendering, there was nothing for Nick to do but drink his soda and eat his chips. He decided to do some web searches on Penelope Stafford Jennings.

A great deal of Internet chatter had gone on in reaction to Jason Scotmoore's (and his perfectly chiseled abs) recent proposal and Penelope's subsequent refusal. However, there were a series of other relationships outlined on the various forums and websites devoted to Penelope. In addition, there was a rumor that she had broken up the marriage of an Illinois Senator after he took her to a series of S&M sex clubs.

A member of the *Elderly Golfer* online forums reported Penelope had invited a pizza delivery boy into her hotel room in St. Andrews, Scotland and made him a pizza delivery *man*. The forum posters mostly agreed that it was justified as she was not an avid golfer. Nick found this especially shocking. Did Uncle Earl know she didn't golf?

There were several series of naked paparazzi shots...

"Checking out the goods?" asked Uncle Earl from behind him.

Nick closed his browser window, currently showing a topless PSJ in France, and turned to face Uncle Earl, who looked hung-over. "Just getting ready for the meeting."

"Great. I'm going to duck this afternoon, but I'm sure you can handle flying solo. Right, son?"

"Yeah, sure, I guess." Of course, Nick knew this meant Uncle Earl would be sleeping off the hangover in his office, but he appreciated being given a heads-up. He turned back to his computer and dropped the video files of the game renders onto a DVD. "I'm just burning the newest renders now."

"That a boy." Uncle Earl swatted Nick a little too hard on the back and left.

A half hour later, Nick sat at the head of the big conference table in the Baker Dental Distributing boardroom. Due to careful last minute scheduling from the other programmers, he and JenJen were the only team members in attendance.

Leopold started the meeting. "Good afternoon, Edutacular employees. I am Matt Johnson from the Stafford Corporation. Why don't we go around the table and you can tell me your names and what you do on this project?" The faun was wearing the white cowboy hat. Nick had been taught to take hats off indoors, but maybe that didn't include cowboy hats, or he was just covering up the horns.

Although it felt a little silly going around the table for two people, Nick started. "I'm Nick Baker. I write code for the mini-games within the Edutacular region packages."

"And I'm Jennifer Jenkins. I draw the concept art and digitize it for inclusion into the game."

Leopold nodded. "Okay, let's get started. According to the notes given to me by Earl Baker, Nick, you are also the Creative Director and the vice president in charge of this division."

"What?!" said JenJen.

Nick held up his hands. "No. No, that is a total mistake. Uncle Earl wanted me to take the job, but I refused the promotion."

JenJen glared across the table. "Well, thanks for telling me, Nick. What the hell?"

"Why are you so upset? I didn't ask for it."

"Why am I upset? You made me look like an idiot. I bet you two had a good laugh at me when I pranced into your uncle's office in my business semi-formals and handed him my resumé."

"JenJen, no, it wasn't like that."

"You know what, screw you and screw this place. I'm out of here." JenJen stood up so fast the chair rolled into the wall with a solid thunk. "If you would excuse me, Mr. Johnson, my gay boyfriend is coming home from baseball camp today, and I'm going to go home to the joys of my high maintenance non-relationship." She turned and walked out the door.

Nick stood up and called to her. "JenJen, I'm sorry." She never looked back. He collapsed into his chair and rested his forehead on the table hard enough to make a sound.

After a moment he said softly, "Leopold?"

"Yes, Nick?" The faun had been waiting silently for him to say something.

"I really think I'm just not your man. I mean, this whole church deal, I don't think I can stop it from happening."

"What would you like me to do, Nick?"

"Go to your boss, tell him everything that is going on, and see if you can get me off the hook."

"I'm sorry, I can't do that, Nick."

"Why not?"

Leopold didn't say anything for a second.

"Why not, Leopold?"

"Well, I was the one who picked you out as the right person to stop the church from being built."

Nick picked his head up off the table. "You mean it was not the 'Great God Pan' who has been putting me through this torment. It has been you."

"He delegates. Pan asked me to handle it, and I had to suggest somebody. Besides, I think you are the right person for the job. You are the Baker heir, after all."

Although his mother taught him never to point, Nick stood up and pointed at the faun. "It was you? You're the reason behind all the torment in my life. You are the reason my mother has run off with a well-hung mythological creature?"

"I'm not responsible for all the torment in your life. The whole JenJen-Penelope thing is all your doing."

"You ask me to double cross my mother, uncle, and pastor. You do unspeakable things to my courtyard. I had to look at my great grandfather naked, you know."

"Nick, let's be reasonable."

"Maybe I'm tired of being reasonable. Maybe it's time to get a little crazy." Nick jumped out of his oversized boardroom chair, picked it up, and threw it at Leopold.

14

THE DOG INFLATION INDEX

Even as the chair left Nick's hands, he knew it was a bad idea. Throwing a heavy office chair was much harder than he'd imagined. It wasn't the weight that was the problem, but the hydraulics and springs, which made it wobbly in the middle. As he'd hefted it, the center of gravity shifted, so the force he put into the throw only succeeded in dropping the chair awkwardly on the board table and rolling it in Leopold's general direction.

At first Leopold didn't seem to understand Nick's intention of doing him harm. He calmly watched the chair roll across the table. "I'm not sure... Umm... Do you want me to have this chair?"

Nick didn't answer, as he had totally lost his shit and was running around the table to throttle Leopold. He leapt at the faun, arms outstretched.

The faun, limber from many a woodland dance, easily sidestepped Nick, who only caught a corner of his cowboy hat as he hurtled into the conference room wall, embedding his head in the drywall.

"Ouch," said Leopold, reappropriating his cowboy hat and placing it atop his head. "At least you didn't hit a stud." He grinned. "And yes, by 'stud' I mean me," he said, tipping his hat. "Well, I'm going to consider this meeting over. Remember, it doesn't matter how mad you get at me, you're going to have to preserve our land if you want things to go well for your family." He started to leave.

Nick pulled himself out of the wall and turned to face Leopold. "You come back here, you, you, you little demon."

Leopold turned around. "What did you just call me?"

"Demon! Satan-spawn! What do you have to say about that?" Nick crossed his arms and straightened up, towering over Leopold.

"Sorry." Leopold punched Nick in the nuts. "I'm a little sensitive about that sort of thing. And just for your information, when I say your family will feel the consequences, I'm not just talking about your Uncle Earl and you. I mean anyone who works for this company will be out of business. I mean a dozen generations from now, your descendants will only be able to get the worst jobs possible, like space-dishwasher or something."

He turned his back on Nick and left the office. Leopold seemed to have a habit for beating Nick up, giving him advice, and leaving.

Nick staggered back a step and tried to sit in one of the boardroom chairs, but it swiveled out from under him. He landed on the floor. He decided to stay there for a while. "Ow."

After a few minutes, Nick got bored of lying on the floor and limped back to his office. Verifying Leopold was no longer in his courtyard, he answered a few emails, and looked over some code. His balls started to feel better.

A pair of hands grabbed him from behind. "Boo!"

"Ah!" Nick jumped about a foot out of his chair. He turned and went into his karate pose.

Delores was standing behind him. "Aren't we the nervous one today."

"Well," Nick said, "you did sneak up behind me."

"You know, you could turn your desk to look out the door. Just grab a couple guys from the warehouse and have them move it. I do it all the time."

"Yeah, I guess." Nick did not want to involve the warehouse guys. They always wanted to discuss the last Hawkeye game. Also, moving the desk would put his back to the courtyard. He decided to change the subject. "Shouldn't you be answering the phones or something?"

"It's on automatic attendant. I couldn't resist the chance to come back here and see your smiling little face." She pinched him on the cheek. "Plus, you have free snacks over here."

He batted away her pinching hand. "Hey, stop it."

"Okay, kid. Just so you know, your Uncle Earl wants to talk to you." She held up her hands in surrender and backed out of the door.

Nick closed his code and checked it back in. He looked through his email for any hint of what Uncle Earl wanted to talk to him about, but he didn't find anything. Finally, he stood up. He could only avoid Uncle Earl for so long.

As he walked through the building, he toyed with the idea of walking out the front door and not looking back. After all, he was part of the family. It wasn't like Uncle Earl was going to fire him. After a moment gazing wistfully at the parking lot, he walked into Uncle Earl's office and flopped down into one of his overstuffed, leather chairs.

Uncle Earl was sitting back in his big manager's chair. He didn't say anything for a long moment. Then he let out a long snore. He was asleep. Nick slowly stood up and started backing out of the office. This was a mistake.

In the course of his backward egress, Nick tiptoed backward onto a golf ball, lost his balance and fell, making sort of a *whoomph* sound.

A loud snore came from behind Uncle Earl's desk. "Hello? Who's there?"

"I'm down here, Uncle Earl."

Uncle Earl leaned over the desk to see Nick. "What are you doing down there, son? Get up. Bakers don't lie around when there's work to be done."

"I wasn't lying around," Nick protested. "I fell—"

"Never mind, stand up and have a seat. We have something important to discuss."

Nick stood up. Nick sat down.

Uncle Earl lit a cigar. "Now, I understand you assaulted this Johnson person."

"Who?"

Taking a puff off the cigar, Uncle Earl said, "That little fella with the big hat."

"Oh, yes. I kind of threw a chair at him."

"You tried to grab him too."

"Um, yeah. I guess I did."

"No problem, son. Beat up whoever you want. Just don't get the company sued. I once watched your grandfather, Earl Baker II, beat a man to within an inch of his life just for showing up late to a meeting. That's why he always carried a cane, the old bastard didn't need it for walking."

"Well, I apologize. Even if Grandfather Earl did, I don't think we should beat our employees."

"Employees? He was a buyer for Woolworth's. Lost us a contract. Your grandfather was a stickler for keeping appointments."

Nick silently wondered if there was anyone in his family who wasn't insane. He didn't really have room to complain, as lately he had been traveling to enchanted forests to cavort with nature spirits. Maybe he was lucky it had taken so long for his disorder to fully manifest. "So, did you just bring me in here to give me a charming family history lesson?"

"No. I think you know why I brought you here."

"I have absolutely no idea why I am here. None."

"Don't play coy with me, son. I've been playing this game longer than you have."

"What game?"

"Business, son. I know what you're trying to pull. Don't get me wrong, I'm glad you're finally taking an interest, but you've picked the wrong guy to cross."

"Who?"

"Me, son. Try to keep up. I know what you're trying to do. There's no use in denying it. You're trying to stop this deal with the church. I know you've been talking to Collins, about stopping construction or moving it to a different plot of land."

Nick tried to look innocent. "Well, I may have mentioned it was a shame to cut down all those old trees."

Uncle Earl made a face and said in his most disgusted voice, "You sound like a hippy." He wagged his finger, scolding Nick. "If you want to continue to walk this path, you know I will do whatever I can to stop you. But there is another option."

"And what would that be?" Nick asked.

"Help me make this deal go through, and I'll make sure there's a big bonus waiting for you when the deal is done. How does a quarter million sound?" The way Uncle Earl said "bonus" made Nick think it would not be entirely on the books. "However, I will expect you to take that VP spot as part of the deal. Consider it a signing bonus."

"Oh." Nick paused.

Uncle Earl held up a hand. "Now don't go worrying too much about the deal. I don't want to rush you or anything. Just think about it and tell me when you have a decision."

"I think I can do that."

Uncle Earl smiled. "Good, now how are things at home with your new fiancé?"

"Actually, I have been meaning to talk to you about that. I do not think it is going as well as it could be. I'm not sure we are all that compatible."

"Nonsense, I didn't know your Aunt Sonia before we were married either. I remember, at first, we used to fight all the time, but then, she was taken from us in that car accident and I inherited her trust fund. So you see, sometimes the things we don't want turn out for the best."

Nick had no idea how to respond. He just stared blankly at his uncle.

"Well of course that crash also took the life of your father, and I still miss him dearly." Uncle Earl's attention drifted off as if he were lost in a memory.

Nick so wanted this conversation to end. "So, um, is that all?"

His uncle started. "No, sorry. I also need you to do a favor for me. Go over to the house and pick up your mother's dog. I don't think she's coming back and the damn thing is a hassle."

Nick was confused. "Just wait a minute. You drag me in here and accuse me of trying to pull something, then you try to bribe me, and now you are asking me for favors?"

"You may be trying to put the screws to me, but you're still family. Besides, it's more a favor for your mother."

Nick nodded. "Sure, I guess I could swing by the house after work."

"Oh, don't worry about finishing your work. For the moment, your services are no longer required."

Nick stood up. "What?"

"There's no need to get hysterical. Like I said, this is business, and as far as Baker Dental is concerned, you have no more business here. Unless you accept my deal and show me you're on my side, I'm putting you out to pasture."

"What the hell? You are seriously going to fire me because of something that happened in that delusional little head of yours?"

Uncle Earl held up his hands in surrender. "Nick, why don't you take this a little easier? There's no reason to get upset."

"No reason to get upset? No reason to get upset?! My mother's gone. My fiancé—who I did not choose, thank you—has taken away all my furniture. Oh, and she gave away my car. My best friend is going nuts to bone the aforementioned fiancé. You are accusing me of plotting against you, and now you are firing me. Would you like to punch me in the crotch while you are at it? Oh wait, that already happened today too. Matt Fucking Johnson took care of that."

"I won't fire you. You're an owner and a member of this family. I am going to place you on indefinite leave." Earl sighed. "Son, if you ever want to get anywhere in business, you're going to have to learn to stop whining every time something doesn't go your way." He brought his finger down on his phone. "Security, I need you in here right now." Then to Nick, he said, "I'm sorry it had to be this way, but you were becoming irrational."

Two copiously large men in security guard uniforms walked into the room. One of them put his hand on Nick's shoulder. "If you would come with us Mr. Baker, we have your things waiting for you outside."

"How can you do this to me? I am your only living blood relative." The other big man took Nick's other shoulder and they started pulling him toward the door.

"You started this, Nick. We'll always be family. I'm even going to let you keep the Hummer for as long as you need. You'll need something bigger to drive now that you'll be taking care of that dog."

"But we don't even have security guards."

As the door closed, Nick heard Uncle Earl say, "They're temps."

Nick parked in front of Baker House around three o'clock. Just two hours ago, a diminutive nature spirit had proclaimed him a vice president of Baker Dental. Now, he was unemployed. Funny how fast things could change.

As he walked to the front door, he considered taking some time off. He could dip into his trust fund, take Penelope to somewhere tropical, and run naked with her on a beach for real. Then again, after seeing the finely muscled well-endowed body double in the mural on his condo wall, maybe that wasn't a good idea after all. Maybe he could get to know Penelope better sitting around his condo, playing *Global Fight!* and eating Doritos. That was more his speed.

Gladys, the family housekeeper, answered the door. "Mr. Baker, thank goodness you're here. I was going to call you when you got home from work." She took his hands in her own, which were wrinkled and leathery. "You have to do something about David, the poor little thing. Your uncle, well, what he's done is just plain abuse."

"Animal abuse?" Nick asked. He knew his uncle capable of many things when there was money on the line, but there was no profit in animal abuse. "What's wrong with David?"

She pulled Nick into the house. "You'd never believe me. You have to see for yourself."

Nick allowed himself to be pulled into the house, and Gladys led him upstairs to his mother's room, where David's basket sat in the corner. What he saw there left him speechless.

"You mother had him on a special diet. He has metabolism and hormone issues, and he's allergic to most dog food, but your uncle wouldn't listen. He said it was too expensive."

Nick shook his head. "How could that happen?"

"It's the allergies. I begged your uncle to get him some help. He kept telling me that David was too pampered, but he wasn't here to see what was going on. I would have taken him to the vet myself, but I didn't think I could pick him up."

"Good God," Nick said. The little corgi's body was swollen to over twice its size. "I didn't even know something like that was possible." How were they going to even get him to the vet? Should he call the fire department? They would get cats out of trees. But would they get dogs out of mansions? Maybe he could get a temp from the company that provided Uncle Earl's security guards.

Nick stood looking at the swollen dog and took a deep breath. He knelt down, wrapped his arms around the dog, and heaved. David whimpered under the crush of his own body weight, but Nick was able to hold him up off the floor. He got the dog all the way to the bottom of the steps before he had to set him down.

He deposited David on a settee and caught his breath for a moment. Gladys had followed him down the stairs, so he asked her, "How long has he been like this?"

"Yesterday, it started getting really bad. This morning, he wasn't able to walk himself anymore."

"Have you been cleaning up after him?"

"Yes. It wasn't any big thing. No different than taking care of a baby. I've only been giving him water today though, as I didn't want to give him any more of that food that hurt him."

"Good thinking, Gladys. I'm going to see you get a bonus for this. Thank you." He nodded to the front door and handed her the keys to the H2. "Could you get the door and open the back of the car?"

With a groan Nick picked up the dog. By the time he got him down the front steps, Gladys had the door open. With a final heave, he lifted David into the back of the H2. He was about to get in and drive to the vet when he realized Gladys was trying to ask him a question.

"Is there anything else, Gladys?"

"Um, yes, Mr. Baker. Now that your mother is... gone. What will become of the house, and I suppose, more specifically, will you still be wanting my services?"

Nick hadn't really thought about this. Gladys had worked for his mother for most of her life. He'd always assumed that she would retire at some point, but with his mother cavorting with Pan, did they need her to keep the house? Would his mother be coming back anytime soon? "I guess you should just keep working for now, Gladys. I'll let you know if the status changes. But don't worry. I'll always have a job for you."

Gladys grabbed his hands. "Oh, thank you so much, Mr. Baker."

So far, it had been a big day. Nick had pissed off JenJen, attacked a god, lost a job, and taken responsibility for both a housekeeper and a corgi. Did he have to be a programmer all his life? Maybe it was time to start fresh. He could become a private detective, and David could be his canine companion, going on adventures and solving mysteries. Maybe he could pitch the idea as a TV show: *Baker and Baker, Dog Detectives,* or *Nick and the Fat Dog.*

Sitting in a veterinary office waiting room felt a little anticlimactic. Even worse, it left Nick with nothing to do but think about how much he'd screwed up. He should have taken care of David himself rather than leave him to the mercies of Uncle Earl.

He also had time to think about Gladys. Even as he made her the offer, he wondered how, if worse came to worse, he was going to employ a housekeeper. In the short term, money wouldn't be a problem. He just didn't know if she'd have enough to do. His condo had been small when he was living alone, let alone the addition of Penelope. Maybe he would have to move into Baker House.

He could already see himself in five years: married to Penelope, living in the ancestral home, and surviving off his trust fund, giving into all the clichés of the idle rich. Maybe he would take up alcoholism to dampen the pain of his failure. He wouldn't have to mope around the house though, he could work on his golf game.

Nick shook his head. Enough rumination. He glanced at the clock on the lobby wall. Had David really been here an hour? He walked up to the receptionist desk. "Hi, could you tell me, is David all right?"

The woman refused to make eye contact with him. "Please sit down, Mr. Baker. I'll let you know as soon as I hear something."

Around ten minutes later, two uniformed police officers walked through the front door, and the receptionist pointed at Nick. Nick started to get the feeling that things had taken another turn for the worse.

One of the officers was tall and bald. The other was an average height Latino. The tall, bald one spoke first. "I'm Sergeant Price, and this is Officer Vega. We'd like to ask you a few questions. To start, could you state your full name for the record?"

"My name is Nicholas Randall Baker."

"And you brought in the dog, David?" asked Sergeant Price.

"Yes. He's my mother's dog. I stopped by to check on him, and when I saw the state he was in, I brought him here right away."

The sergeant took over again. "So, your mother was taking care of the dog?"

"Well, yes," Nick said, "but she disappeared last week. My Uncle Earl, Earl Prescott Baker, was supposed to be taking care of him."

"Ah," Officer Vega said, "you're one of those Bakers." Both detectives began writing in their notebooks.

Sergeant Price asked, "Is there anyone who can verify that you've just taken custody of this dog?"

Nick thought for a second and nodded. "My mother's housekeeper can tell you I was not taking care of this dog. Also, my fiancé, Penelope Stafford Jennings has been staying in my apartment over the past couple weeks."

Sergeant Price dropped his pencil. He and Officer Vega seemed temporarily frozen in time. Before Nick could determine what was happening, time restarted.

"Penelope Stafford Jennings?" Sergeant Price asked. He momentarily had some trouble writing in his notebook, until he realized he had dropped his pencil. As he was picking it up, he said, "Do you think it would be possible for us to visit your apartment?"

"I don't think—" Officer Vega started to say, but he was interrupted by Sergeant Price stomping on his foot.

"To look for dog-related evidence," Price said.

Nick shrugged. "Sure. I don't think Penelope's shy. Just give me some time to get David home and make sure she has some clothes on. She walks around naked half the time."

Sergeant Price looked at his watch. "Actually, we need to look at your apartment now, so we can verify the dog hasn't been there."

Nick shrugged. "Okay, whatever."

After they reiterated their intention to visit with Penelope, the two policemen left to speak to the veterinarian. A half hour later, the vet came to speak to Nick.

"Mr. Baker, I apologize for any inconvenience. However, we take any appearance of animal abuse very seriously. David's condition was caused by an allergy, but it was a known condition, and it could have been prevented with the diet I proscribed for him."

Nick nodded. "I'm aware of that, and I'll make sure to feed him properly from now on."

"It is questionable whether feeding him generic food could be considered neglect. However, the police tend to defer to the judgment of the veterinarian examining the animal. In addition, I could determine whether David should be removed and placed in a shelter."

"I promise. I'll make sure he gets the proper treatment." Nick did not look forward to taking care of the dog in his tiny condo. Then again, he was slightly horrified at the thought of what his mother would say about David in an animal shelter.

"I'm writing down exactly what to get. Now, if you'll come into the examination room, I need to show you some special exercises for David."

The veterinarian led Nick to one of the other examination rooms. "We gave David a shot of liquid Diphenhydramine, basically a huge dose of Benadryl. The swelling's gone down considerably and he will continue to get better, but he's going to experience discomfort throughout this process. You will need to help him do some special exercises to keep his joints pliable, and hopefully offset arthritis. I'm not going to kid you. This is going to be a major commitment.

If you want, we could kennel him here and take care of him, but honestly, I think he needs more affection than we can give him."

David chose that moment to look up and see Nick. *"Woof!"* He started wagging his tail.

Nick couldn't help but take pity on the poor little dog. "I'll take care of him." After all, his mother had considered them like brothers, even if Nick was the least favorite.

The veterinary workers had helped Nick load David into the H2, but when he got back to his building, he needed a way to transfer him into the condo. His arms were still tired from carrying the dog out of Baker House. The answer came to Nick when he saw the little shed where the association kept its lawn care equipment. The door was open.

In the shed, Don was sharpening a lawnmower blade with a long file. "Hey there, Nick. How's it going?"

"Not too bad. I was wondering if you could lend me a wheelbarrow for a couple of days. It is for a mission of mercy." There were three wheelbarrows in the shed, which were only used once or twice a year.

"Fine by me, just don't tell anyone I let you do it, and try not to let too many people see you. Otherwise somebody will complain."

"I will try my hardest not to be seen."

"What's with this mission of mercy?"

"Don, I have inherited an oversized dog with undersized legs. It would not have been my first choice of an animal, but when God drops these kind of things in your lap, you can hardly turn away from them."

"That's very enlightened of you, Nick."

"Is it? I suppose so. Well, I'd love to stand around all day and talk, but I must unload a dog. Have a nice day, Don."

"You too, Nick." Don went back to sharpening his blades.

Nick took the wheelbarrow down from where it was hanging and wheeled it out to the H2. After a little lifting, David seemed comfortable enough. "Are you comfortable, David?"

"Woof!"

He wheeled David inside to find Penelope nude and talking on a Bluetooth headset. "No, I still want you to drop the Apple shares. They're not overvalued, but they're running to the high side and too volatile. What's the difference between my buy-in on my Stafford options and the current selling price? Yes, but I'm not sure the Baker merger is going to go through. If you were here, you'd be less optimistic. Right now, the stock is running high because of the rumor mill. The merger isn't going to take it much higher. Let's go all in, but start quietly selling off some small chunks.... Oh, right... Park the remaining money in the blue-chip fund until I decide what I want to do with it, but put another hundred thousand in my checking account. I've run into a few extra expenses here. Okay, you have a good day too."

She hung up her call by tapping her headset. "O M G!" She walked over and squatted by the wheelbarrow. "What happened to little David?"

"Woof."

"Actually, he's looking quite a bit better. Uncle Earl was supposed to take care of him, except David..."

"Woof."

"...is allergic to almost everything, and Uncle Earl failed to give Da... him his special dog food."

Penelope scratched David behind the ears. "Oh, the poor baby. Someone should go and arrest that mean old Uncle Earl of yours."

"Well," Nick said, "that might happen anyway. Did two police officers just stop by?"

"Oh, was that why they were here? They just asked for an autograph and a couple pictures."

Someone knocked on Nick's patio door, and he slid it open. Rudy was standing outside. "Hi, Toxic. How's it going?"

Before Nick could say anything more, Rudy had walked into the condo. He saw Penelope and stopped in his tracks. "It's really her." He raised his hand to his face and examined it. "My entire body is tingling right now."

Penelope stood up from the dog and contemplated Rudy. "Is this a friend of yours, Nick?" She seemed more curious than frightened.

"Um, yeah," Nick said, trying not to sound embarrassed. "This is Rudy. He's a big fan of yours."

Rudy nodded. "I have seen every picture of you on the Internet. I have the *Maxim* with your photo-shoot. I know your statistics by heart."

Penelope seemed amused by this. "Do you know my net worth?"

"According to April's *Maxim*, you are worth fifty-seven million dollars."

Nick's head turned toward her so fast, he heard something crack. "You said you were on the last of your savings."

"I was Nick," she said. "I had to transfer money in from my stock portfolio."

"I thought you were destitute."

She gave him a pouty look. "It was a bad time to convert."

"Shut up, Nick," Rudy said. There was no emotion behind his voice. Nick was simply in his way. Then, as if he didn't even know he was saying it out loud, he said, "This is just how I imagined it. You're stunning." He walked up to her, and held out his hand like he was going to touch her breasts. "May I?"

Penelope regarded him for a moment. She seemed more curious than afraid. "Okay," she said with only the briefest hint of wariness.

Rudy ran his fingers up and down her body. Tracing around her breasts, her eyes, nose, cheekbones, and lips. This went on for what seemed like a long time. "You're... exquisite. You're Helen of Troy. You're Cleopatra. You're Aphrodite. Demeter. Venus." And then he broke into poetry.

O Venus, beauty of the skies,
To whom a thousand temples rise,
Gaily false in gentle smiles,
Full of love-perplexing wiles;
O goddess, from my heart remove
The wasting cares and pains of love.

Penelope smiled. "Thank you."

"Rudy, are you okay?" Nick asked. He'd never seen his friend act like this.

Rudy then did something that surprised Nick even more. He started to cry.

"There, there," Penelope said, pulling him into her arms and holding him. "It's all right."

Nick gave Penelope a look that said, "Does this happen often?"

She returned a look that said, "No, I'm as puzzled as you are."

Rudy hid his tear-streaked face in the crook of Penelope's neck. He also reached down and squeezed her ass.

While Rudy's behavior had caught Nick off-guard at first, as he watched his friend, crying, holding himself against Penelope's naked body, and squeezing her buttocks, Nick realized that, to Rudy, this was the equivalent to a painter seeing his first Van Gogh or the most devoted Christian seeing Jesus.

15

ELECTRIC CHICKEN

At first, Nick was merely shocked at Rudy clinging to his naked fiancé, but after a while he became annoyed. Then, he got bored. "I'm going to go buy David some dog food," he announced.

"Oh, wait just a minute," Penelope said. Still holding Rudy, she walked over to the Transformer/couch thing and gave it a few kicks until it turned into a sort of chaise lounge. She sat Rudy down and ran over to the table. Snatching something up, she threw it to Nick.

Nick looked down to find he was holding an electronic car key, a little black box with lock and unlock buttons on it. It was attached to a keyring with the Toyota logo on it.

"I knew you hated that Hummer thing. And since I gave away your old car, I decided to buy you a new one," Penelope said in way of explanation.

"You bought me a car?"

"Consider it an apology for the car and the furniture. You're right. I should have asked you first. It was presumptuous."

"Um, cool," Nick said. He felt like this was a big thing. He was pretty sure Penelope Stafford Jennings wasn't into making apologies. "Thanks." He lowered his voice to a whisper. "Are you going to be okay with him?"

"Oh, I think he's harmless enough," Penelope said. "Actually this reminds me of the time I went swimming with dolphins."

"Was it like a spiritual experience?" Nick asked.

"Not really. One of the dolphins vigorously humped me. They don't tell you about that in the brochures. Compared to them, Rudy is well-behaved." She put something in Nick's hands. "Consider this my engagement present to you."

When Nick got out to the patio, he hit the door unlock button a couple times, until he got a polite honk from a red Camry sitting beside the H2. The license plate read, "PENYSBOY." It took him a moment to realize it was meant to read "Penny's Boy" and not "Penis Boy."

When he opened the door, there was a note on the front seat.

Mr. Baker,

I hope you enjoy this Camry Hybrid. I thought it would be a good match for you considering your love of your old Corolla, your affinity for technology, and your desire for a practical, energy efficient vehicle.

I hope you enjoy the car.

Darien Mueller

Penelope's Personal Shopper

"Good choice, Darien," Nick said out loud. "Except for the license plate." How did he even manage to get a personalized plate that fast? Nick thought they took weeks to get and eventually came in the mail. Was there a special DMV for rich people? Maybe Penny's personal shopper knew the governor's personal shopper.

Nick went to three stores trying to find David's food before he finally surrendered to the fact that he already knew one store that carried it.

Nick pulled his new Camry into the church parking lot. As he was getting out of the car, a group of teenagers drove by. One of them stuck his head out the window and yelled, "Hey, Penis Boy!"

He had been hoping to avoid Reverend Collins, who had obviously talked to Uncle Earl about Nick's suggestion to move the church building.

He went to the garden center first, to obtain the optimum wheelbarrow for an immobile dog, intending to return the condo association's property as soon as possible. Wheelbarrow obtained, he went to the dog food aisle, where he was soon joined by Reverend Collins.

"Nick!" The reverend wore a gold tracksuit with a black cross across the front, the perfect outfit for the Hawkeye-supporting fundamentalist. "I see you are picking up some of David's..." Despite the dog's absence, he automatically paused just long enough for a bark. "...food."

"Nice to see you, Reverend," Nick said. "I didn't expect to run into you. I was just going to be in and out."

"I was up in my office, but praise Jesus, I saw you in the security monitor. There's not an inch of this store I can't see." For some reason, Nick couldn't help but wonder if that included the bathrooms. "I was wondering if you might come back to my study for a little while."

"I really have to get back to David." And despite Penelope's assurances, he was kind of freaked out leaving Rudy alone with her.

"Oh, and how is that little fellow?"

"He's been better. Uncle Earl was giving him the wrong food." Nick patted the dog food bag in front of him. "No worries though, the vet gave him a shot of liquid Benadryl, and the little guy should be back to normal in no time."

"Good to hear it. Are you sure you can't join me for just a second?"

Nick tried desperately to come up with an excuse not to join the elderly cleric, and came up blank. "Well, I guess so, but not too long."

"Oh, this won't take long at all." The reverend smiled in a way that made Nick suspect something was up.

Nick put another fifty-pound bag of dog food into the wheelbarrow and followed Reverend Collins back to his study, a quiet room with plush carpet, simple furniture, and a large monitor displaying every activity in the church.

After Collins made sure Nick was comfortable and offered him a beverage, he sat down behind his desk and said, "I spoke with your Uncle Earl today, and he's a little upset. I told him about your idea of relocation, and he thinks you are trying to stop the church from being built. I just wanted to give you a heads-up."

Nick sighed. "My uncle is paranoid. I would like you to build the church somewhere else, but I believe in the importance of big savings for the saved. I'm shopping here right now."

The reverend bit his lip and was lost in thought for a moment. He nodded to himself as if coming to a decision. "You see, Nick, it is not that simple. All the surveying and planning is done. We have permission from the county. We would have to spend tens of thousands of dollars to move the church site now. And I know your family is providing the bulk of the funds, but the budget is cut to the quick. When you factor in the workout center, we are going into debt by two million. Even if we wanted to move and we could spare the money, between permits and land acquisition, we would be putting the project back months if not years."

"But it could still be done?"

The reverend leaned forward and lowered his voice. "I don't have that kind of time. I'm dying, Nick. Jesus is calling me home."

"What?"

"I have a bad heart. If we put off this project, I might never live to see my life's work accomplished." Then Collins dealt the low blow. "Do you really want to deny an old man his dying wish?"

"No, I guess not." The old man had won. Nick was going to have to risk the wrath of Pan.

Reverend Collins got up slowly and walked over to Nick. He held out his hand for Nick to shake. "I was hoping you'd say that, Nick. It is good to have you back on board. While you're here, I want to show you something. Please, follow me."

The reverend led Nick to the back door in his office, which opened into the grocery storeroom. A seven-foot tall, Technicolor statue of Jesus stood in the center of the storeroom. The savior had a big grin on his face. He held two shopping bags in one hand and a large fan of money in the other. He stood upon a stone into which was carved, "The Son of Man is come to seek and to save."

"What do you think, Nick?"

"I am stunned."

"I'm dedicating it to your family. Until the church is finished, it will sit in the lobby of the Baker Dental offices. We call it Consumer Jesus."

"Wow. That is great." So there was already one advantage to being fired, he wouldn't have to look at Consumer Jesus every day. "Well, I have to be going now. I have to get this stuff through the checkout and get it back to David."

"Don't worry about the checkout. As long as those things are for David, you just take them." He paused. "But if you don't mind me asking, why does little David need a wheelbarrow?"

"It is kind of a long story. I would not want to bore you with it." Despite his current dislike for Uncle Earl, Nick was reluctant to reveal how bad his uncle's neglect had hurt the dog. It was one thing to answer police questions truthfully, but it was another to badmouth a relative in front of someone who travelled in the same social circles.

Nick wheeled his dog food out to the Camry and had a fun time trying to figure out how to stow the wheelbarrow and the dog food in the car. Finally, he wedged the wheelbarrow sideways in the trunk, and put the dog food in the back seat.

On the way home, Nick thought about Pan and the church. On one hand, the church was Reverend Collins' dying wish, but on the other hand, Pan might smite him. Nick wasn't sure how Pan would smite him, but being he was the god of lust, it could be something pretty horrible.

Nick took Highway 965 home, enjoying the feel of his new Camry on the twisty road. He still missed his Corolla, but even he had to admit it had been getting old. His route took him past both the Baker Administrative Complex and the proposed church site, which was now just a field full of baked hornets. He wondered if Pan had called back his winged minions now that he had given Nick his directive, or if the National Guard had succeeded at clearing them away with their flamethrower strategy.

On the way into town, he thought about being fired. The thing that bothered him the most about it was he wouldn't see JenJen every day. This made him think of his mother, who he would not be seeing either, as she was in thrall of the well-hung god. Shouldn't he be more concerned about his mother's repeated penetration by Pan's hallowed wiener?

Driving into Downcastle, Nick slowed and then stopped. Someone had stopped their car right in the middle of Main Street. He looked again. Someone had stopped *his* car in the middle of Main Street. Officer Kevin was driving his Corolla. The suspended policeman revved the engine and let out the clutch just enough to let it jump forward a couple feet.

"So this is how it's going to be. You want to play chicken," Nick yelled, though he doubted Kevin would be able to hear him over the Corolla's revving engine. Nick popped the Camry into neutral and pushed down on the accelerator to rev the engine. Nothing happened. "Stupid electric car."

Kevin put the car in gear and floored it.

In college, Nick had studied the mathematics behind strategic decision-making. He happened to know there was no way to win a game of chicken if the other party was committed to strike, so he decided not to play the game. He put the car in reverse and floored the accelerator.

While Nick did not regret his attempt at nonviolent escape, there was a problem with this methodology. Nick was not that good at reversing. He made it to the first intersection before he started to turn, and crashed the back of the car into one of Downcastle's historic street lamps.

"Oh, fudge," Nick said, as Kevin accelerated into him. He would never remember the crash itself, only the airbag slapping him hard enough to make his ears ring and the horrible sound of metal colliding.

He sat there for a moment stunned until Kevin yanked open his car door. It took him a couple of tries.

"I got you back, you bastard. I wrecked both your cars."

Nick stumbled out of the car and tried to think of some kind of comeback, but instead, he just had to say the first thing that came to mind. "How does that even make any sense, you idiot? Seriously, what is wrong with you?"

"I bought your old car off the town mechanic."

"So you smashed your car to get back at me?"

"Well, yeah, kind of."

"What are you, some kind of moron?"

"What did you call me? I'm going to kick your ass."

Normally, Nick might be put off by the prospect of an ass-kicking. However, it had been a long week. "You want to kick my ass? Try me."

"Oh, yeah I'm going to." The policeman circled him like a boxer looking for his opening.

"You are going to kick my ass in public."

"Yes."

"In front of everyone. In the town where you are supposed to keep the peace?"

"Who cares? I'm on suspension anyway."

"I'll tell your mother."

Kevin was losing his resolve. "You would really do that?" He lowered his fists and stopped circling.

"Oh, yes." Nick nodded. "I'm sure you could beat me up, but what's the mayor going to think? Maybe this isn't the best idea if you want your badge back." Nick doubted he was going to get his badge anyway, especially after the crash, but maybe Kevin was an optimist.

"I guess so." Kevin *was* an optimist.

"No matter what happens though, I want you to do one thing."

Kevin scratched his head. "What's that?"

"Take an anger management course."

16

FASHION TIPS

The sheriff seemed irritated with Officer Kevin. He gave the police-man quite a stern talking to and then made him sit in the back of his patrol car while Deputy Randall questioned Nick.

Randall had his notebook out and he made Nick wait while he slowly reviewed his notes. Finally, he spoke. "Did Officer Kevin ever meet your mother?"

"He might have seen her when she donated some computers to the Downcastle library, but when he tried to taze me the other day, he didn't seem to know who she was."

"Just seems interesting how often I'm running into you these days, Mister Baker." Officer Randall wrote something in his note-book. "Did your mother ever coerce you into committing a crime?"

"No. And I don't know what this has to do with being run down on Main Street." Randall seemed to be grasping at straws, like he knew there was something funny going on, but he couldn't wrap his head around it.

Once Deputy Randall seemed satisfied, and Kevin was taken away for evaluation, Nick was left waiting for Jim, Downcastle's only mechanic, to assess the damage. Jim started by winching the old Corolla away from the new Camry. This resulted in a great crunching and scraping of metal, but little movement, other than Jim shaking his head.

Nick felt like he should say something. "I'm sorry my fiancé turned down the Corolla after you put so much work into it. She misunderstood. I really wanted to keep it."

"I hold no grudge. It was money in my pocket both ways." Jim walked over to the intertwined engine compartments and started beating on something with a five-pound hammer. *Thunk. Thunk. Thunk.*

"Should you be doing that with a hybrid car?"

Thunk. "What do you mean?" *Thunk. Thunk.*

"Well, the batteries—"

Thunk. CRACK!

For an instant, Nick felt he knew what it was like to watch Thor wield the mighty hammer Mjolnir, for there was a mighty sound, a light brighter than the sun, and a wave of heat. When Nick regained his senses, Jim was lying on the ground, ten feet away. Unlike the great Mjolnir, his hammer had melted to the Camry.

Nick walked over to Jim. "Are you all right?"

Despite the inanity of the question, Jim sat up, smoke rolling off him, and said, "I think I am."

"Can I do anything for you? Call an ambulance maybe? I don't have a cell phone right now. I've been meaning to replace it. But I could probably go into one of the stores—"

"Could you stop jabbering at me?" Electrocution seemed to bring out Jim's anti-social side.

"Oh, okay. Do you mind if I take my wheelbarrow? It is in the back of the Camry."

"Do whatever you want, Penis Boy."

Nick felt like he should say something, partially because it was his car that had just electrocuted the mechanic, but also because Jim was supposed to be his ride home. He started to open his mouth.

Jim shook his head. "Just go."

The lamppost had done a lot of damage to the back of the Camry, but neither dog food nor wheelbarrow had been damaged. He loaded up the wheelbarrow and started to push it home. It got heavy after a few blocks, and by the time he got back to the condo, he was in a bad mood.

Nick parked the wheelbarrow on the patio. Someone had locked the patio door, so he had to walk up the stairs to the front entrance and down the inside stairs to his condo. Usually, he didn't mind doing this, but he'd just pushed dog food halfway across town and he had been in a car accident earlier.

In the living room, Penelope had somehow reconfigured the sitting thing into a reclining chair and ottoman. She was reading a magazine called, *Passion Rag.* David looked on from his wheelbarrow, as if he wanted the magazine when she was done.

"You read fashion magazines?" Nick asked.

"Yes, and I write for them as well." She flipped through the magazine and showed him a page titled "Penelope's Poise" with her picture on it.

"But you barely ever wear clothes."

"When I do, everyone wants to know about it. I have a regular column."

"Wow. You write a column. You play the stock market like a broker. Rich men and movie stars trip over each other to propose marriage to you. You really are an amazing woman, Penelope Stafford Jennings."

Penelope smiled. "Really? Then why aren't you lining up to marry me, Nick Baker?"

"Well... Um..." Nick had been caught off guard by the question.

"Are you scared by my femininity? Or maybe you're in love with someone else? That's it, isn't it?" She adopted a sarcastic tone. "You've been cheating on me, you cad."

"I um..."

Penelope grinned at him. "I'm just kidding. Why don't you take your new car over to see her?"

Nick shook his head. "I can't. She's mad at me, and I just wrecked the car."

Penelope looked concerned. "Oh my God, what happened?"

"I was run down playing chicken on Main Street."

"Don't you think that's a little inconsiderate? I just gave you that car, and you've broken it already. I think a lot of people would have liked to get a present like that."

"Hey, I didn't initiate the chicken. It was Officer Kevin, the local policeman. He hates me for some reason. It was not my fault."

"Not your fault? You were the one driving the new car, correct? It was your grudge with this policeman that caused the accident."

"Sure, it was my fault. Everything is my fault. My mother attacked by hornets? My fault. My crazy uncle fires me? My fault. My best friend wants to have sex with my fiancé? My fault. I can go on like this for hours. Would you like to hear other things that are my fault?" At some point, he had started yelling and waving his arms around like a crazy person.

"No, Nick, I don't. I'm not interested in your pity party. If you want to feel sorry for yourself, you can go do it somewhere else."

"And that's another thing. A week ago, this was my condo. What gives you the right to move in and take away all my things and replace them with this bourgeoisie crap? I should be the one throwing you out of my place."

"Oh, get off it, Nick. You're hardly the downtrodden proletariat. Besides, I don't think you have the balls to throw me out. Even if you did, I know you don't have the ability."

"What do you mean, I don't have the ability? You weigh eighty pounds."

"I weigh over a hundred pounds, and I got this skinny by doing aerobic kickboxing five days a week for years. You sit behind a computer all day and eat Doritos, don't even try to intimidate me." She dropped into a fighting stance that was much more convincing than Officer Kevin's.

As pissed off as Nick was, he would not, under any circumstances, hit a girl. Also, Penelope did not seem to be bluffing about the kickboxing. "Fine, I will go, but consider it under protest."

Nick stormed out of the living room. He came back and wheeled David out. As he was struggling to get the dog into the truck, he nearly pulled something in his back. Then, he went back to get

David's food and as long as he was there, he grabbed an overnight bag. Then he stormed out again.

It had been so much easier to storm out before he had a dog.

Despite his argument with Penelope, Nick decided to follow her advice and go to JenJen. Perhaps David could sense his tension, because the dog rode in silence.

When he arrived at JenJen's apartment building, her lights were on. He got out of the H2 and walked up the steps to knock on her door.

After a few minutes, JenJen opened the door, but she blocked him from entering with her body. "What do you want?"

"Do you mind if I stay here for a day or two?"

JenJen raised an eyebrow. She started to take a step back, like she was going to invite him in, but then she stepped out onto her welcome mat and closed the door. "Did your skinny girlfriend kick you out?"

"Well, we... I decided it would be best to spend some time apart."

"For the good of your relationship?"

"Yes."

"So you decided to spend the night at my house."

"Yes," Nick said before realizing the inflection JenJen had put on 'spend the night.' "Wait, no. You know I am not like that."

"Yes. I am painfully aware that you are not like that." JenJen sighed. "Well, come in."

Nick walked into the living room. There was something different. A few pieces of furniture were missing, leaving only their footprints in the carpet. And any object which was obviously Steve's had gone. "Did Steve move out?"

"He moved in with his catcher. I hope they are very happy together."

"It's probably the right move for both of you."

"I'm glad you approve."

Nick blushed. "It's just one of those things you say, like 'God has a plan' or 'things will work out for the best.' Really, as far as I know, you could have been happy as Steve's—beard, I think they say—for many years."

JenJen's cell phone rang. "Speak of the devil." She answered it. "Hello? No, Steve. I'm busy... Nick's here... That's none of your business, Steve. You lost the right to be jealous when you stopped treating me like a girlfriend... Okay, I guess I could do that. Yes, I'll be right over." She hung up.

"What was that about?"

"Steve wants me to bring over some of his things. Look, why don't you relax here, and maybe later we could play some *Global Fight!*"

"That would be great, but there is one problem with that. My console is back at the condo with Penelope." Then again, he wasn't far from Fang Dong's warehouse. "Scratch that, I think I know where I can get one. Why don't you run your errands, I'll go pick up a console, and we can meet back here in an hour or two?" So she could help him carry his dog up the stairs. "Oh, I almost forgot. Does your apartment allow pets?"

"Not really, no."

"Did I mention that I have my mother's dog with me?"

JenJen took a deep breath. "If I lose my cleaning deposit, you're going to pay for it."

"Fair enough."

"He's not going to jump on the counter or anything like that, is he?"

"Trust me. You have nothing to worry about."

"Okay, then. See you later. If you get back before me, here's a key." JenJen stepped off the welcome mat and retrieved a spare key from underneath it. As she handed it to Nick, she leaned over and gave him a little kiss on the cheek, and then she closed the door in his face.

After a visit to the cash machine, Nick drove the H2 down the tiny alley to Fang Dong's electronics store and beef warehouse. He knocked on the steel door and waited. He had to wait a bit, but the door was answered by the man with the spider web tattoo on his neck.

"Hi," Nick said. "Is Fang Dong in?"

The man with the spider-web tattoo stared blankly at him.

Nick began to realize that he may have made a mistake. Making the safe assumption that Fang Dong was well-placed in some kind of organized crime, perhaps dropping in on him late at night wasn't the best idea. At this point, he started babbling. "I was here the other night with Larry and Carrey Baker. I'm their cousin Nick. Fang Dong and I really hit it off, and I needed to buy another *Global Fight!* console, so I figured I'd stop by and see what he had in stock."

The man with the spider-web tattoo didn't move.

Nick showed him the money he had taken from the ATM. "Buy. Fang Dong."

The man with the spider-web tattoo nodded. He bowed, stepped aside and motioned Nick into the building. Nick put on one of the white coats and walked down the long beef hallway. When he arrived at the door to Fang Dong's office, Nick knocked.

The door was opened by Fang Dong's mother. Nick instinctively shrunk back from her, but the old woman snagged the arm of his white coat, said something in Chinese, and pulled him inside. Her little fingers were like pliers. She pulled him right through the office to a backdoor and a short hallway. At the end of the hall, he followed her into a large room filled with Chinese men and women in ragged clothing, hunching over black electronic boxes with soldering irons.

A man wearing business casual walked around the room with a yardstick, occasionally hitting one of the workers. He picked up one of the black boxes, a video player still missing its cover, and carried it to Fang Dong who stood silently in the corner. Fang Dong inspected the box and nodded. After a moment of not being noticed, Mrs. Fang pulled at Nick's arm again, dragging him over to her son.

"Um, hello, Fang Dong. What do you do in here?"

Fang Dong raised an eyebrow. "You interest me, Nick Baker. Your cousins would not have asked such a question. I do not know if this means you are foolhardy or brave. To satisfy your curiosity, my workers solder region-free decoders into video players. I mark them up thirty percent, the only item I sell over retail price."

"I have a friend who would love one of those." Rudy had been looking for something to play his large collection of tentacle-centric Japanese pornography.

"Then you shall have one."

"Um, thanks." This worried Nick a little. He had only brought one hundred dollars, and he needed the *Global Fight!* console to play with JenJen.

"Now, what can I do for you, Nick Baker?"

"I'm looking for a *Global Fight!* console, like the one you sold my friend the other day."

"You have problem with yours?"

"Not at all. I just need a spare."

"Very well. I am sure I can accommodate your needs."

Mrs. Fang grabbed Fang Dong's arm and started speaking at him with purpose. He listened to her and then waved in a dismissive way. She made her case with even more fervor, and he finally nodded to her. "My mother wants me to translate something to you."

She spoke and he listened. "The translation to English is problematic, but I will do my best. The creatures of nature are attracted to you. They are like the fox. They have a strong sense of smell. You must disguise your scent to hide, and they will not find you." When he was done, Fang Dong shrugged. "That is all she said. Gibberish I suppose."

"Oh, no. That's just fine." That information might actually be valuable to him. Nick leaned over and spoke loud and slow. "Thank you, very much." The old woman took his hand and patted it.

Fang Dong took Nick into an even colder section of his warehouse and found a worker. "Bring Mr. Baker a *Global Fight!* console and a headset controller." Then he yelled something in Chinese and clapped his hands. The worker ran.

The worker returned a few minutes later with a box. Fang took it from him and gave him more instructions in Chinese. He ran away again.

"Here you go. Full console system with all updates, *Global Fight!* Gold Edition with premium headset. For you, fifty dollars cash."

Nick took fifty out of his pocket and handed it to Fang Dong. "Thank you for your custom." Just then, the warehouse worker returned with another box. "And, as a gift to you, I present you with a region-free, multi-format video system. It will play any movie file from any region, and do slideshows from presentation programs or image files."

"Oh. Thanks."

Fang Dong took hold of Nick's hands. "Nick, let me reiterate. I do not forget my friends. I held your father in the highest regard. If you ever need anything, you just have to ask."

Nick nodded. "Um. Thank you for your generous offer." He felt like he should say something more profound.

Nick carried the game console and video player out to the H2 and put them in the back with David. Then he played with the dog a bit. He felt a little guilty leaving David in the H2, but it was a cool spring evening, and the temperature in the Hummer hadn't even warmed. "Who is a good dog then? Who is a good David?"

"*Woof!*"

Nick drove back to JenJen's looking forward to a night of *Global Fight!* It had been too long since he had entered the slightly more heavily-armed analog of real life, and he was afraid his rank might be suffering. He even managed to get a parking space close to the stairs, the better to facilitate the unloading of his gray-market electronics and injured dog. He ran up the steps and knocked, to see if JenJen had made it home before him. No one answered the door, so he took the key from under the mat and unlocked the door.

It took over a half hour to get David up the steps and in reach of his special food and a water dish, but once the swollen dog was as comfortable as possible, Nick applied himself to the job of linking his *Global Fight!* console to JenJen's console, so they could play together. He turned on the TV. The local news was on.

Two police officers, one black and one bald, escorted Uncle Earl from Baker Dental Distributing in handcuffs. Over the footage, a happy, shiny news anchor spoke. "Local businessman Earl Baker III was arrested today at his place of business. Mr. Baker has been charged with animal cruelty after allegedly mistreating a family pet. Mr. Baker recently suffered the loss of his sister-in-law, philanthropist Esther Baker." A picture of Nick's mother briefly flashed up on the screen. "Police may have given up the search, but a source close to the family believes Mrs. Baker may be staying alive by eating squirrels."

"Fucking Rudy!" Nick yelled at the TV.

Rather than trying to cover his head like some people did when the police escorted them, Uncle Earl faced the camera. The anchor's voice went away, and Uncle Earl spoke at Nick through the television. "I would like to assure the members of the public that these charges against me are totally spurious. I have been targeted for a vendetta from a person whom I once considered an ally, a friend, a person I treated like my own son. Well if that person is listening right now, I want him to know I am not going to take this treatment lying down. As of this moment, the gloves are off."

The television cut back to the news anchors. "Wow, strong words from Earl Baker. I don't know who he was addressing just then, but I know if I were that person, I would not be sleeping easy tonight."

"Nor would I, Bill. It has been a tough week for the Baker family. Next up, sports."

"Shit!" Nick sat up and fought the impulse to flee. Why should he panic, though? Uncle Earl was going to be in jail for at least the rest of the night. Even if he was free, he had no idea where Nick was. JenJen's apartment should be perfectly safe.

Behind him the front door opened. "I see you're making yourself at home," said a voice behind Nick.

Nick turned around to see Steve standing in the doorway, holding a baseball bat. "Shit."

17

BATTING PRACTICE

Nick was sure the look on his face was that of a guilty schoolchild. He knew this didn't make any sense—JenJen and Steve had broken up, and he was here by invitation. "Hi, Steve. What are you doing here?" *Don't mention the bat. Don't mention the bat. Don't mention the bat. Don't mention the bat.* "With a baseball bat." *Shit.*

Steve raised the bat. "I'm on my way to the batting cage. I just thought I'd stop by and have a word with you."

"You know JenJen is over at your new place. She said you'd be there."

"I know. Tony, my... friend is talking with her. He's keeping her busy so I can have some time with you."

Nick took a step back and ran into the TV cabinet. Remembering how unstable it was, he forced himself not to lean back against it. "So, what do you want to talk about?"

"I'd like to talk about why you're here. Why do you keep hanging around Jennifer?"

"Well, if you must know, I am here right now because my fiancé threw me out. However, the reason I 'keep hanging around' is because JenJen and I are friends and co-workers. What I cannot understand is how it is any of your business."

Steve pointed the bat at Nick like he was about to hit him out of the park. "You sound just like her. I didn't stay with Jennifer for so long because I was trying hide who I was. I stayed with her because I love her. I just love her more like a little sister."

"Generally, I have a policy about arguing with the guy holding the club, but seriously, do you realize how screwed up that sounds? I mean, you've been having sex."

"I know. I suck at this whole relationship thing." Steve walked to a chair and sat down heavily. Holding the bat between his knees, he buried his face in his hands.

"Yeah," said Nick in a surprise moment of camaraderie. "Relationships are hard." The two men sat momentarily in the silence of mutual sympathy.

"Relationships aren't so hard with guys though," Steve offered.

"Really?"

Steve thought about it for a minute. "They're easier to talk to, especially about baseball, but they're not as much into the commitment thing. Before I met Tony, I didn't think I'd ever find a guy interested in commitment. That's why I stayed so long with Jennifer. I'm fond of her, and she seemed more open to a committed relationship."

They shared another silence.

Steve broke the silence again. "What's up with your dog?"

"Severe allergic reaction."

"That's a bummer." Steve stood up. "Well, this conversation went differently than I had imagined it."

"Yeah, for me too." Of course, Nick had expected to have a baseball bat buried in his head by this point.

"I guess I'll just go home now." He stood up, using the bat as a cane to push himself up. "Oh, yeah, if you hurt her, I will kill you."

Nick nodded. "Yeah, big guy. I know."

It is often said that small decisions can nudge events one way or another, setting off a chain of reactions that ends in a spectacular result. A butterfly flaps its wings in China, and suddenly there's a hole in the moon, or the Universe explodes. Some people call this the Butterfly Effect. Some people don't.

This phenomena is important to note because Nick was standing at the crux of one of these points in his own life. He was about to do something very small which would alter the entire course of his life for good or for bad.

As Nick watched Steve walk down the steps, he wondered if he shouldn't call him back. Weighing his options, having his brains bashed in might actually be his best move. Still, not having to worry about Steve was a good result. Now, he just had to worry about the demands of the goat god, his betrothal, and his uncle's plan for vengeance. He sat down on the carpet next to David, and scratched the dog's ears while he waited for JenJen. This caused David's tail to make a constant *thump, thump, thump* noise against the carpet.

Mrs. Fang had told him to disguise his scent. There were plenty of hunters in Iowa, even in the tech community, and he'd heard people talking about this concept before. It usually involved smearing oneself with concentrated animal urine.

Nick wandered into the kitchen. He needed room to work, so he picked up and did the dishes. When he was putting the dishes away, he found an electric mixer and a mixing bowl.

He looked in the cupboard and the fridge. After crafting the impromptu vintage yesterday, it became clear that JenJen and Steve hadn't been into organizing. He was sure they had never cleaned their refrigerator, and he felt he could mix anything from the contents therein. He grabbed some rotten minced garlic, moldy German mustard, a half-full beer, and some briny blue objects that he presumed were olives. To this he added some ancient mayonnaise and a bottle of omega-3 fish oil. He poured all of it into the mixing bowl. Before he even picked up the hand blender, tears streamed down his face.

He poured the entire mixture into a saucepan and turned a burner on low. He almost set the mixture down on the heating coil. Then he looked around. He was in JenJen's apartment, and she might not appreciate him creating the stinkiest synthetic urine concentrate ever conceived by man. He would have to find another way to deal with the Pan situation. He ran the concoction down the garbage disposal, saving himself from swift and brutal annihilation.

He was sitting on the couch when JenJen came through the apartment door. "That was a waste of time," she said. "Steve wasn't even there."

"I know," Nick said. "He was here."

"O M G! He didn't threaten you, did he?" She came over to the couch and sat down beside him. Their knees were touching.

"Mmm... There was an implicit threat, I think. He was holding a bat."

She took one of his hands in hers. "I'm sorry. I didn't know he would try something like that."

Nick shrugged. "You know what? It's no big deal. Compared to the rest of my week, Steve's threats aren't that bad."

"Really?" JenJen asked. "Do you want to talk about it?"

He nodded. "Actually, yes. I do." So Nick explained to JenJen all the problems of his past week. He wanted to tell her about everything, Greek gods, woodland spirits, oversexed mothers, naked fiancés, allergic dogs, Chinese gangsters, and irate uncles. He told her all of the problems, except for the ones she had caused.

JenJen listened to Nick's carefully, nodding here and there, and when he finished, he waited for her reaction. He had told her everything, even about Pan. Was she going to think he was nuts? Was she going to throw him out? Call the police?

She seemed lost in thought for a moment. Then she pulled a strand of hair out of her face. "This is why you suck at *Global Fight!*"

"What?" Nick couldn't believe what he was hearing. "I'm ranked third in the Midwest region."

"Yes. And I'm ranked first."

Nick's jaw dropped. He pulled his hand away. "That means you're... you're... you're..."

"DeathChick82, first in the Midwest region and sixth in the world."

Nick found himself backing away from her. "You're my nemesis."

JenJen raised an eyebrow. "I thought you knew. I took vacation during Headshot Con last year. I was a featured guest."

"I've been trying to take you down for years," Nick said. Maybe not the best thing to say to your dream girl.

"Yes, and you've failed because you're a good tactician, but you fail when it comes to strategy. You can improvise, but you can't plan."

"I can plan," Nick protested.

"Really, yesterday, you came down to the Ped Mall, and I blew you up. What was your plan then?"

Nick made a face. "Go to the Ped Mall. Kill people."

JenJen sighed and nodded. "You see, no strategy."

Nick crossed his arms. "So, what would have been a good plan?"

"Think about how I was positioned that day. Not only was I ringed with multiple levels of defense and plenty of early warning, but I also had full view of the Ped Mall for sniping purposes. I knocked out fifty kills that day. How did you do?"

"Not as well. I took down a helicopter gunship though." Nick could feel his cheeks heating. "Um, about the whole Pan thing. Do you think I'm..." He tried to think of a softer word than insane. "Do you think I'm weird?"

JenJen shook her head. "No, Nick. I know you're weird. You're an okay kind of weird though. Normally, I'd be put off by someone telling me their great-grandfather summoned a god, but I've met your family. The big question is how you're going to deal with it."

"I actually had an idea about that. Fang Dong's mother said, since I'm being bothered by nature spirits, I should disguise my scent. I was going to mix up some synthetic urine concentrate, like hunters wear, but then I thought it might annoy you, so I poured it out."

JenJen looked slightly annoyed that he'd even considered it. "You were going to try to do that in my apartment?"

Nick quickly shook his head. "No. Well, I might have started to, but then I realized you wouldn't like it, and I poured the whole mess down the sink," he said, repeating that he'd poured it out for emphasis. Realizing she didn't look too happy, he added, "And I did the dishes."

"That was very smart," JenJen said. "If you had not poured that concoction down the sink, I would have also been on your list of enemies, and you are no match for me."

"I'm not, huh?" Nick crossed his arms in defiance.

JenJen sighed and shook her head. "No. You're not. Because I already know what you need to do to get yourself out of this situation."

"You do?" How was that possible? She'd only heard about it ten minutes ago.

JenJen nodded, and then her face twisted into the most evil little smile Nick had ever seen. "Oh yes. There's only one way to solve all your problems, and with the resources available to you, it won't even be hard. You have to destroy your Uncle Earl."

18

JenJen is an Evil Genius

Their conversation was making Nick anxious. He stood up and started to pace back and forth across JenJen's living room. "What do you mean, *destroy* Uncle Earl? Uncle Earl is... Well, he's my uncle, the family patriarch."

"Look, I can make you a flowchart, but in the scenario you've described all roads lead to Earl. Earl is the one who queered the deal with Pan. Now that your mother is gone, Earl is the one giving away all the family money. Earl is the one who wants to destroy you for getting him put in jail—"

"I didn't do that."

"Don't interrupt. Earl is the one who arranged your betrothal and the merger with Stafford Corporation. Remove Earl and you clear away all your problems."

"You keep tossing out these terms 'destroy' and 'remove.'" Nick lowered his voice. "Do you mean we should have him killed?"

JenJen rolled her eyes. "No, I don't want to kill anyone, outside of *Global Fight!* that is. We just need to take him out of the picture. It's too bad this animal cruelty charge isn't going to stick, but I doubt it will. David can already roll over by himself."

"*Woof.*"

This was not the JenJen he knew, the shy, competent graphic designer. "You're some kind of evil genius."

JenJen shook her head. "No, Nick. I'm just really pissed off at your uncle." She stood up and crossed the room to him. "And honestly, I'm feeling quite protective of you."

Nick took a step back and ran into the wall. JenJen closed in and kissed him. Her lips were luscious and comfortable, still new enough to be exciting, but familiar at the same time. Remarkably conscious of the heat of her body, and her breasts pressing against him, he wrapped his arms around her and gave into her embrace.

"Now," she said, "let's go to bed."

"Okay," Nick said, "but I think I should sleep on the couch. You know, I'm still engaged to Penelope." Which was true. Also, after their conversation, he was just a little scared of JenJen.

She shook her head. "No. You're coming to bed with me. No arguments."

"Yes, ma'am."

The next morning, Nick woke up early. Feeling energized, he decided to run errands. When he returned, JenJen had been sitting on the living room carpet, petting David with one hand and paging through the Baker Dental annual report with the other. She looked up when the door opened. "I actually consider myself pretty good at math, but this does not make any sense to me. Did you get your new phone?"

Nick held up his premium smartphone. "Yes. I have rejoined the modern world. No luck with the report then?"

She shook her head. "No. I don't know if they're trying to purposefully hide something, but I can't even make the numbers add up. I know how to add. It looks like there's something funny going on, but I don't know enough about business and accounting to tell you what it is."

"Is David helping?"

"*Woof.*" David confirmed he was helping by thumping his tail on the carpet. He was looking at lot better, almost back to his old self.

JenJen had come up with the plan this morning in bed, while Nick held her warm body against his. It read like the plot from an intrigue film. The first step was to search the annual report for signs of malfeasance. With the amount of money Reverend Collins claimed the Bakers had given, Nick was sure they would find something fishy.

The second part of the plan was more dangerous. Nick would have to go to the board meeting and accuse Uncle Earl of stealing from the company. If the family attorney agreed with Nick, Uncle Earl would be automatically suspended from the board until they could investigate further, allowing Nick to make decisions despite owning only ten percent of the stock.

Nick sighed. "Well, I can hardly blame you for not being able to figure it out. He is trying to hide what he's doing. It's probably not anything obvious." Nick hesitated for a moment. "I know a couple of people who can help, but you're not going to like it."

"Who?" JenJen asked with only a tinge of coolness to her voice.

"Rudy and Penelope."

"The pervert and the ho?"

"Well, the pervert has a master's degree in mathematics, and the ho has more stock market and business experience than... well, the two of us for a start. And can we not call Penelope a ho? Technically, I'm the one cheating on her."

"Whatever."

Nick dialed the office on his new phone. "Hi, Delores."

"Hey kid. What can I do for you?"

"Do you have the cell number for Penelope? I know I don't technically work for the company anymore..."

"Who told you that?" Delores asked.

"Uncle Earl did."

There was a moment of silence on the other side of the phone. "Actually, Nick, your Uncle Earl is in jail right now, and since he didn't actually tell anyone you were fired, my instructions say to take my orders from you. Right now, as the only board member not missing or incarcerated, you're acting president of Baker Dental."

"Oh. Well, um... if anything important comes up, you can contact me on my cell phone. Otherwise, just carry on as usual, and I'll call you if I need anything."

"Do you still want that phone number?"

"Oh, yeah. Actually, there are a few numbers I could use from Uncle Earl's Rolodex." That wasn't a metaphor, Uncle Earl still had a spinning Rolodex system like an executive from an 80's movie.

"Sure thing, kid. You know, if you are working on something important, you could ask for my help. I'm really good with filing things. I even used to file things for your mother."

"Yeah. I know that. For now, I just need the numbers."

Nick got the numbers and then told JenJen the story. "Here's the funny thing. Right now, according to Delores, everyone thinks I'm in charge."

"That means you're my supervisor." JenJen grinned. "I'm taking a vacation day."

A half hour later someone knocked at the door, and JenJen went to answer it. She opened it to find Penelope outside. The two women, the two women in Nick's life if you didn't count his mother, spent a moment staring at each other. Finally, JenJen said, "Penelope, come in. I'm Nick's friend, Jennifer. You can call me JenJen."

For the first time, Nick looked at both women together. Penelope looked perfect, like some kind of prototype for the next stage in human evolution. Almost any woman standing next to her would have been invisible to most men, despite being physically larger in size. This didn't matter to Nick, though. JenJen had always been and would always be his dream girl, and now that he knew she could kick his ass in *Global Fight!* it just made her that much hotter.

Penelope looked around the apartment. "So, Nick, this is where you spent the night?" She said it in her snooty voice, the one that said she was too good for her current surroundings. Nick knew this meant she was just annoyed.

"Yeah," Nick said. "Look, Penelope, I know you have an inheritance at stake and everything, but I just don't see us working out. JenJen and I, well, we're together now. I'm sorry if that messes up your plans, but that's just how it is."

Penelope nodded. "That's all right. I didn't really want to marry you either. Face it, Nick, your family is a bunch of kooks. I mean every old family is supposed to have a few eccentrics, but you seem to be the only sane one of the bunch."

This made Nick smile. "Thank you!"

JenJen seemed to remember her hosting duties. "Penelope, please have a seat on the futon, and let me bring you a beverage." Nick's mother would have approved.

While JenJen was fetching iced tea from the kitchen, another knock sounded at the door, and Nick answered it. Rudy was waiting outside, so Nick invited him in.

"Hey, Toxic, what do you need from me on a Thursday morning? You know I don't like to get up before noon, and... Oh. My. God. She's here," he said, spotting Penelope on the futon.

Penelope gave Rudy a little wave. "Good morning, Rudy. How are you today?"

Rudy smiled. "Much better now."

"Why don't you come sit beside me?" She patted the futon seat next to her.

"And how!" Rudy nearly tripped over the coffee table, but he made it to the futon without major incident.

Once Penelope and Rudy were settled in with drinks, Nick gave them a rundown of what he was looking for. While he explained what he was doing, Penelope paged through the annual report. When he finished telling them the plan, she set the papers down.

"Well," Penelope said, "I can tell you why you couldn't figure out anything from this report. It isn't complete. Don't get me wrong, there's enough information to satisfy the minimum requirements of law, but it's not enough to really know what's going on. We simply need more information. As a stockholder, you could probably get a judge to subpoena what we need, but that would take forever."

"Actually," Nick said, "due to a strange turn of events, I'm temporarily the boss." He took out his cell phone and dialed the office. "Hello, Delores. I need to exercise my executive initiative."

"That may be a little difficult." Delores didn't sound happy. "Your uncle just came in. He's out of jail, and he's really mad at you. He told me that if you called, I should hang up on you."

"All I wanted was a few documents that weren't in the annual report."

"I'm sorry, Nick. I really shouldn't even be talking to you."

"Okay, Delores."

Nick hung up the phone. "Well, my uncle's back in the building, and apparently my access has been revoked."

JenJen held out her hand. "Hand me the phone." She took the phone away from Nick and started hitting buttons. "Let me show you a little trick. If you use a DID into the PBX and connect to the voicemail computer, you can have it dial an inside line and make it look like you're calling from inside the building."

This left Nick so impressed he had to say something. "Damn, you're sexy when you use three letter acronyms."

She waved for him to be quiet. "Hello, Delores. This is Jennifer down in IT. Do you have the inventory control system running? Could you do me a favor and start it for me? Great, can you tell me what the refresh rate is on the data stream? You don't know how to do that? Okay, let me shadow your session. What's your password?" JenJen carefully wrote down the password. "Thanks Delores. This will help us out a lot."

She held out the paper to Nick, but Penelope snatched it away from him. "JenJen, show me to your computer."

After they left the room, Nick sat down next to Rudy. "You're never going to believe this. JenJen is DeathChick82." He waited for this revelation to sink in.

"Hell," Rudy said, "everybody knows that. She was a featured guest at Headshot Con."

19

THE BOARD MEETING

At 11:45 AM Saturday morning, thirty minutes before the Baker Dental Distributing board meeting, a red H2 drove across the clearing where a church groundbreaking had taken place. Afraid Uncle Earl would have some kind of plan to keep him out of the board meeting, like a new security force, Nick had come here. He parked the truck and stepped out, being careful to keep his dress shoes as clean as possible. The first thing he did was open the tailgate to let David out. Feeling better again, the dog jumped down and started running around.

Rudy helped Penelope out of the H2. They were also dressed in formal business attire. The two had formed a strange bond while working on the Baker Dental paperwork, and they were spending quite a bit of time together lately. Nick supposed this meant the engagement was finally and truly off, which was okay with him. They would be attending the meeting as his business advisors.

Everyone stood for a moment, watching David run around the field. Then Nick whistled and called out, "Here, David," and the dog came running. "This way, everyone," Nick said, leading his entourage toward the tree line. It felt weird, dressing up and walking into the woods like this.

When Nick reached the edge of the field, he called out, "Leopold?"

After a few moments, Nick heard flute music. He peered into the woods and saw Leopold walking toward them, playing pipes. He wasn't wearing pants, typical.

David ran up and peed on him.

JenJen looked at the little man and started. "Shit!" She grabbed Nick's arm and held him close. "I know you told me about him, but I just wasn't ready... Wait, isn't that Matt Johnson from Stafford Corp?"

"Um, yeah," Nick said. "I guess I forgot to tell you that part."

JenJen glanced down. "He isn't wearing pants."

Rudy pointed at Leopold. "Check it out. It's a faun. I guess that Narnia movie wasn't that far off."

"Except for the huge wang," Penelope pointed out.

Nick walked over to Leopold and knelt down so he could speak softly. "I need to take all these people to my office," he whispered. "Will you help me?"

"With a walk in the woods? Sure." He winked at Penelope. "How you doing, Penny?"

"Um, do I know you? Oh, you're the little guy from the club."

"Yes," Nick said hurriedly. "That's the only way you know him." He didn't know if her hidden memories could be somehow triggered like they sometimes were on television or not, but he'd rather not have her remember what had gone on, what was probably still going on, between the goat god and his mother.

Leopold led them though the forest, in the seemingly random, twisty way he had done before. When they arrived at the clearing, he pointed out the right path to follow to Nick's courtyard, and a few minutes later, they walked through the sliding glass door into Nick's office.

"So, this is where you work?" Rudy asked, walking over and giving his desk a couple shoves as if to test the stability. "Have you taken JenJen roughly across this desk yet?"

Nick sighed and shook his head. "Rudy, how would I even do that? I'd have to move the computer first."

"Yeah," said Penelope, who had opened the door to Nick's bathroom. "If you wanted to bang someone, you'd want to come in here. There's a walk-in shower."

Rudy paused as if lost in thought. He glanced at his watch and then seemed to mentally calculate something. Nodding to himself, he put his arm around Nick and walked him to the office door. "Why don't you go ahead, buddy? We'll catch up."

Nick made a face. "Really? Now?"

Rudy glanced at his watch again. "Plenty of time."

When Nick walked into the board room, he was surprised by how many people were already there. As the chairman, Uncle Earl was present, of course, and he had brought Larry and Carrey. Delores was there, sitting behind both a computer and a stack of binders and envelopes. Charlie Stevens, the company attorney, had come in from Des Moines.

Uncle Earl looked up when Nick entered the room and made a face. "Nick, you made it," he said with no joy in his voice.

"Since I forgot to fill out my proxy documents, I figured I'd just come in and vote in person." Nick sat down at the boardroom table. David hopped up into the chair next to him.

"That's not necessary, you know." Earl's face was turning crimson. "I've never needed your help running this company before."

"Actually, Earl, that's not entirely true," Stevens said. "Some board decisions only require a majority of the shareholders present. However, some actions such as a merger or massive reorganization specify a majority of the voting stock, regardless of who is actually in attendance at the meeting. That included Esther's shares, and it means we need Nick for our majority. Plus, there is the matter of what constitutes quorum."

This information made Earl even less happy. He adopted the expression he sometimes wore after eating too much at Sunday dinner.

The door opened, and Nick looked up to see JenJen.

Nick stood as she entered. "What are you doing here?"

JenJen smiled. "Well, I am an employee, and technically, this meeting is open to all employees. Besides, that vice president job is open again, so I thought I'd show my eagerness for being more involved in the company."

Uncle Earl smiled, and Nick just barely heard him say under his breath. "You can show me your eagerness anytime."

Nick ground his teeth. He could feel his face starting to redden, so he hid it behind the folder he had brought, pretending to look through documents. This was not the time or place to start a confrontation, or it wouldn't be for another ten minutes, at least.

"What do you have there?" Earl demanded.

Nick looked up and said, "Papers," knowing this would annoy his uncle.

Just before the meeting was supposed to start, Penelope and Rudy came in, looking very clean if still a little wet. Great, now he could never use that shower again.

"Well," Earl said, "it's noon, so I'm going to go ahead and officially start this meeting. We'll begin with the approval of the previous meeting's minutes. I was expecting a visit from Reverend Collins, who has a gift for us, but we'll just have to work him in when he gets here."

"Actually, Uncle," Nick said, "I have something that takes precedent over that." He took a document and handed it to Charlie Stevens. "This is a list of payments made to The Church of Great Savings. While this company has pledged millions of dollars toward the construction of a new church, as well as land on which to build it, no payments have been authorized by this board. This constitutes a misappropriation of funds, and I would like an investigation into the missing funds as well as the removal of Earl Baker as Chairman of the Board and President of Baker Dental."

Earl shook his head. "Nick, those were just a few pre-payments to smooth the way. We used it to get the surveying work done and ground samples and such. I don't know why you insist on digging your own grave, but if you think you can throw me out of the big chair, you've got another think coming."

Nick opened his mouth to rebut, but he realized he had no idea what to say. He glanced from Rudy to JenJen to Penelope, but none of them seemed ready to speak up. Was this it? Was he going to fail his friends and employees?

Charlie Stevens cleared his throat. "Actually, Earl, we need to take this very seriously. Nicholas is well within his rights to request both an investigation and your temporary suspension. Just give me a minute to look at this document." After a quick scan of the numbers and conclusions supplied by Rudy and Penelope, he nodded. "Yes, I do think there are grounds to start an investigation."

For a moment, Nick felt his fear shift to anticipation. He was actually going to do this. He was actually going to take over the company based on this small technicality. He had been right to trust Penelope and Rudy.

"However," Stevens said, "to remove Earl from the chair, even during this investigation, still requires a majority vote of stock. Earl's forty-five percent won't be included in that tally, but Esther Baker's shares will be. Unfortunately, that prevents you from being able to remove Earl."

Earl smirked. "Good. Well, I'm glad we got that all sorted out. Now, let's get on with the meeting—"

Delores raised a finger and said, "Um, could you all hold on a minute. I have a document that Mr. Stevens needs to read. She opened an interoffice envelope, removed a document, and passed it to Stevens. "I hate to do this, Earl. It will probably mean some legal battles and bad press for the company, but Mrs. Baker wanted the contents of this envelope read if she was ever incapacitated or missing for a long period of time."

Charlie Stevens took a long time reading the document. After a moment, he nodded. "Yes, that's all in order." He seemed to be trying to hold back a chuckle. "It took me a moment to figure out if this was a valid document, as it did not go through my office." He held it up and addressed the room. "In the event of the disappearance of Esther Baker, this document gives proxy voting ability to whomever is taking care of David Baker."

"*Woof!*" David said.

"Let me see that," Earl said, practically jumping across the table to grab the document from Steven's hand. Without reading it, he said, "I believe this document is a fake, and I'm going to rip it up."

Nick was so shocked at his uncle's behavior that he didn't even think to try to stop him. Fortunately, JenJen was not so slow. She plucked the document out of Earl's hands.

"You little bitch," Earl said, pulling his arm back to slap her.

Nick ran forward, grabbed his uncle's arm and twisted it behind his back. "Don't you dare hit her."

Earl struggled for a few minutes. "Larry, Carrey, help me."

Carrey looked conflicted for a moment, but Larry held out his hand and stopped his brother from moving. "Am sorry, Papa, but Nick seems to be in the right here."

Finally, Delores yelled, "Jesus, Earl, calm down. I have notarized copies."

Earl relaxed against Nick's grip. "Okay, I can see when I'm beaten, just let me take my dignity and go."

Nick let go, and his uncle, head down, sighed and walked toward the board room door.

Before he got halfway there, the door opened and Consumer Jesus was pushed into the room on a two-wheeler by Reverend Collins. "All hail, Bakers. I have brought you this wonderful statue."

Earl immediately headed for the door. "Reverend, this isn't the time. Let's wheel that guy back out to the lobby."

"Nonsense. This is the reason I've come here today. To deliver this beautiful work of art."

When Nick had seen the statue before, he had hated it. But in the bright lights of the boardroom, it looked truly horrible. He shook his head. There was no accounting for taste.

"Is that ceramic?" Larry asked.

"Yes," Carrey answered. "Like a giant cookie jar."

Larry nodded. "I wonder if the head comes off."

"The head doesn't come off. That would be silly," Carrey scoffed.

Earl grabbed a handle of the two-wheeler, and attempted to turn it around. "No, Reverend, we have to get out of here now."

Sensing the tension between the men, David jumped down from the chair, ran across the floor, and started barking at them.

Collins seemed more confused than anything else. He tried to tug the two-wheeler out of Earl's hand, took a step back and trod on David's tail.

David let out a yelp and nipped at Collins' track pants.

Collins, realizing he'd stepped on David, let go of the two-wheeler and raised his hands in prayer. "Oh, Lord, forgive me."

Earl gave the two-wheeler, unencumbered by Collins, an extra hard tug, and the whole thing tipped over. The head popped off, and stacks of money fell out of the neck.

The head continued rolling and came to a rest at Larry and Carrey's feet.

Larry shrugged. "I stand corrected."

"You idiot!" Earl yelled at Collins, "you've ruined everything." He reached down the neck of Consumer Jesus and pulled out a handful of money. It looked to Nick like about fifty thousand dollars. Then he turned and ran out the door.

After a moment of silence, Rudy said, "This is my first board meeting. Are they all this exciting?"

20

WALKIES

The noon sun was warm, the wild flowers were in bloom, and Nick didn't see any reason to hurry. David ran around the clearing, chasing a butterfly under the sign reading, "Esther Baker Park."

"David!" called a familiar voice, and the dog barked and ran toward the edge of the woods, where Nick's mother appeared. Thankfully, she was dressed. There was something very different about her, and it took Nick a moment to figure out what it was. She looked healthy and happy.

Nick stood up and jogged after David. By the time he caught up, his mother was sitting on the ground holding the little dog in her lap. "Hello, Nick," she said. "How's it hanging?"

"Ah..." Nick had never felt comfortable answering that particular question when Rudy asked it. He had no idea how to respond to his mother.

"Just kidding. Come down here and give your mother a hug." This was another alien thing. His mother had never been a hugger.

Nick crouched down and gingerly embraced his mother. "Are you ever coming back for good? It would be nice to know. Charlie Stevens is putting through paperwork to have you declared legally dead, but I could tell him to stop."

His mother shrugged. "Let him. I'm no longer attached to the mortal plane. Actually, you know what I was thinking? I've been living on this earth for over fifty years. Maybe I'll come back in another fifty to see what things are like. Maybe I'll see those flying cars they're always talking about."

Nick shook his head. "Mother, I've told you before, that would never happen. They'd never be able to handle the air traffic control."

"Whatever. Now before I go, I have a message from Pan. Leopold has been keeping him apprised of the situation here. He says he's quite pleased with how you took care of his little problem with your Uncle Earl, and he's reinstating the boon to our family."

"Um, that's nice."

"I wonder why you didn't try to prosecute Reverend Collins."

"Charlie Stevens persuaded us not to. He said it would be better for public perception if we covered up the whole business. And he suggested that if we needed anything from Collins, we would have leverage on him. Also, Collins and Uncle Earl had hidden millions of dollars of the company's money in their statue, a good portion of what they'd embezzled. If we prosecuted Collins, that money would have become evidence. We needed it to make the payroll. It was a choice between taking care of our employees, or putting one greedy old man in prison."

"I never should have let Earl run everything, but he was my brother-in-law, and I did love him once." His mother looked momentarily uncomfortable. "Just think. Soon, you and Penelope will move into Baker House and start having babies. You'll be putting away your video games and taking over as CEO of the company, just like your father was."

"Yeah, sure." There was no reason to tell her that none of those things were going to happen. She'd find out in fifty years. Nick was going to take the chairman's seat, but Penelope was taking over as CEO. She had already poached two of her grandfather's top executives and appointed Rudy the head of research and development. Also, under the condition that no one would be fired in the Iowa factory, she had started to expand into the Chinese market, a joint venture with Fang Dong Industries.

After they had taken pictures on Nick's phone, his mother asked, "Why do you keep looking at me like that?"

"I'm trying to remember what you look like. You've been with me all my life. Now you're talking about not coming back for fifty years. I may be dead by then."

"Oh, Nick. I'm sorry. I do plan to stop by from time to time. I think I'm going to have a soft spot once you start giving me grandchildren."

Nick shifted uncomfortably. He hadn't discussed children with JenJen yet. They hadn't even been on a proper date.

His mother hugged him again. "Take care, Nick, my beautiful boy. I'll be back in a year or so. Pan likes May first. Maybe we'll aim for then."

Nick nodded. "Okay. Love you too... Mom." As he watched his mother disappear into the woods, he remembered what Leopold had done on May first, and he yelled after her, "Easter is good too. We'll bake a ham."

21

The Escape

Earl Baker accelerated his second-hand Porsche 911 onto the exit for Vaduz, Liechtenstein, cutting off a semi—he should start thinking of them as lorries. The Porsche was a little showy for his taste, but the price had been within his budget, the last of the sixty thousand dollars he'd managed to snatch from the boardroom floor. Tomorrow, he would cross the border into Switzerland and transfer his secret account into less traceable assets by starting a series of shell corporations in Liechtenstein.

Before he could do that, however, he had to find his hotel, and he had not yet figured out how to make the 911's navigation system stop speaking German. He kept taking the same wrong turn and ending up back in Switzerland. And being lost here was no fun. He had expected to see majestic European architecture, but other than the occasional cathedral and the big castle up on the hill, it pretty much looked like Iowa City, a happy little community with cute two and three-story shops, not exactly what he'd expected from the richest-per-capita country in the world. After the third time round, it was getting pretty dull.

Finally, Earl stopped the 911 and rolled down the window, addressing a little man with a brick-red goatee. *"Sprechen Sie Englisch?"*

The little man smiled broadly and walked over. "Hey, buddy. A fellow American. What can I do you for?"

"Actually, I'm British," said Earl, putting on his best accent. He had been British since he'd landed in Stuttguart and shown a very expensive fake passport identifying him as Edmund Curtis from Hull. "Could you possibly direct me to the Hotel Birkenhof?"

"No problem, buddy. I walked past it not too long ago. Just take a left here and then a right when you get to the big cathedral. It's a pretty swank place. You must be loaded."

"Yes, I am," Earl confirmed a moment before punching the accelerator and shooting away from the little man.

He followed the instructions and arrived at the hotel a mere ten minutes later. Leaving the car and his bags with the valet and bellhop, he made his way to the front desk and presented his passport. "Edmund Curtis. I made a reservation this morning." When he didn't get an immediate response, he added, "*Sprechen Sie Englisch?*"

"Good afternoon, Mister Curtis," the desk clerk said in heavily accented but painfully accurate English. "If you wait a moment, I will have your key. You are in 401, a suite of rooms balconied with a view of the mountains. Your assistant already checked you in earlier today, and took some of your luggage to your room."

"Assistant?"

"*Ja.* A little man... with a disturbing... *spitzbartz.*"

"Whatever," Earl said, taking his key. No doubt some idiot assistant had put his boss's things in his room. They could sort it out later. It had been a long day.

He rode the ancient, rickety elevator to the fourth floor, and walked down a hallway which had seen better days. That was the problem with Europe, so much of it was old. He found 401 and opened the door. The first room was a sitting room. The furniture was grouped in a way to make conversation easy, but also to give view of a large cabinet, which no doubt held a television. While Earl was pleased with this sign of civilization, something was wrong with the picture.

Someone had put an easel in front of the TV cabinet. A large canvas sat on it, draped with a simple, white cloth. Why had someone left that in the room? Was this the mysterious, misdelivered luggage?

Earl walked over and pulled the cloth away. There was a painting underneath, but for some reason, he eyes refused to focus on it. He squinted and stared at it, but he still couldn't make sense of it. Then out of the corner of his eye, a tree branch caught in a clump of leaves. It was a nature painting, a landscape. He shifted his gaze inwards, following the leaves and branches of the trees back toward the focus of the painting, a clearing in the woods. In that clearing was the subject of the composition, but he still couldn't comprehend it. He squinted hard, and suddenly he knew what he was seeing.

Earl screamed.

ABOUT SHANNON

Shannon Ryan writes books about loser vampires, Greek gods, and Satanic telemarketers. Living in Iowa with his wife Stephanie, Shannon enjoys lying on surveys and relocating sofas for no specific reason. He has studied paranormal investigation and conspiracy theory. Shannon is often found in the company of psychics and computer programmers. His work has been read by Art Bell on the *Coast To Coast* radio program.

He can be found at http://weirdauthor.com/.

ALSO BY SHANNON

David Graves is having a bad life. A bill collector is threatening grievous bodily harm. His girlfriend thinks he's an incompetent loser. His human resources manager, a creature of nightmare, is sexually harassing him. His Satanist bosses have tricked him into signing a contract that dooms him to an eternity of telemarketing. And, when he finally meets a girl he likes, she's more interested in rebuilding transmissions and random acts of violence.

Can David escape his evil bosses, win the heart of a wrench-wielding psychopath, and—just maybe—save his soul?

Not everyone who gets turned into a vampire becomes a sexy rock star.

At twenty-seven, Vincent Lester still looks seventeen, acne and all. He lives in his parents' basement, playing PlayStation and barely surviving by licking the blood off raw hamburger trays. His parents nag him to find a day job, but he's afraid the sun will make him burst into flame.

One night at the bar, Vinny picks up a drunk girl, literally, and gets his first taste of fresh, human blood. Then things get really weird.